The First Gift

RUTH LOGAN HERNE

Franciscan
MEDIA
Cincinnati, Ohio

Cover design by Candle Light Studios
Book design by Mark Sullivan

LIBRARY OF CONGRESS CATALOGING-IN-PUBLICATION DATA
Names: Herne, Ruth Logan, author.
Title: The first gift / Ruth Logan Herne.
Description: Cincinnati, Ohio : Franciscan Media, 2016.
Identifiers: LCCN 2016022195 | ISBN 9781616369576 (softcover : acid-free paper)
Subjects: LCSH: Interpersonal relations—Fiction. | City and town life—Fiction. | Mentoring—Fiction. | BISAC: FICTION / Christian /Romance. | GSAFD: Christian fiction. | Love stories.
Classification: LCC PS3608.E76875 F57 2016 | DDC 813/.6—dc23
LC record available at https://lccn.loc.gov/2016022195

ISBN 978-1-61636-957-6

Published by Franciscan Media
28 W. Liberty St.
Cincinnati, OH 45202
www.FranciscanMedia.org

Printed in the United States of America.
Printed on acid-free paper.
16 17 18 19 20 5 4 3 2 1

Beth... this one's for you.
Thank you for always believing and loving.
The cute grandkids are pure bonus.

acknowledgments

A long time ago I read "Christy" by Catherine Marshal. I loved it. I loved the story, I loved Christy's devotion to others, and her struggle to choose between two good men seemed far more real than most love triangle stories I've read or seen since… but mostly I loved seeing her effect on a troubled populace, a populace that in many ways reflected the childhood I experienced.

And so began this retelling, by a woman who not only experienced a Cassie-like existence, but a woman who refused to let the past govern the future. I inflected that into both Kerry's and Cassie's characters. Struggle can build character or wrestle it down a dark and dingy road, but I believe that faith and the warmth of good people around us…and good choice…strengthen the person within, the one God designed, the person he wants us to be.

Huge thanks to my friends at Franciscan Media for the chance to share this story. Katie Carroll, Ericka McIntyre, Ray Taylor, Mark Lombard and all the others who make working with them an absolute pleasure. The perfect cover by Candle Light Studios captured the nuance of the story I longed to tell, and I couldn't be happier with it. Bless you for seeing (and looking…) beyond the obvious.

And to my beloved agent Natasha Kern, who is always working, always advising, and cheering from the sidelines. She's amazing and I'm so blessed to be with her!

God bless Julie Lessman for her advice and encouragement from beginning to end. Her words were invaluable, and her prayer for me and this story was constant. I honestly couldn't have done this without her.

To the staff at Golisano Children's Hospital in Rochester, the doctors, nurses, techs and social workers who have worked with our family and others in times of need. We are fortunate to have this amazing facility here, and their expert advice has guided me in this story and several others.

To Alice McCarthy, my childhood Girl Scout leader, a woman who slipped my dues into the can out of her own pocket, who sat by my side at father/daughter or mother/daughter affairs, who encouraged me to try new things. Alice, you affected a child's life in ways you couldn't begin to know, and every kindness I pass on to others began with you.

Huge thanks to Aunt Isabelle and Gram, who believed from the beginning, who offered me a place to sleep during times of trouble. You might not have been churchgoers, but you set the example of simple Christian love, an example I want to follow forever.

And to the teachers and staff at Sacred Heart School and Nazareth Academy, who never made me feel like an oddity. Your encouragement helped brighten dark days and offered a light at the end of a very long tunnel. And it worked!

Also a big nod of appreciation to the folks from the Hilton Volunteer Fire Department, especially Ron Bourret and Michelle Kellaway for their advice on rescue efforts and treating hypothermia. I'm so grateful for your expert advice and time!

Every one of you helped make this beautiful story shine. I thank you.

—*Ruthy*

Let the children come to me; do not prevent them, for the
Kingdom of God belongs to such as these.
Amen, I say to you, whoever does not accept the
Kingdom of God like a child will not enter it."
Then he embraced the children and blessed them,
placing his hands on them.
—Mark 10:13-16

chapter one

"Brady, make sure that extra apple finds its way to the Carrutherses' mailbox this afternoon," Amanda Stanton instructed in a voice that meant business.

"I will," promised the eight-year-old as he stuffed a superhero folder into his book bag. "I'll stop by their place when the bus brings me back. And I'm so quick, no one will even hardly notice me. Except Cassie."

His mother nodded as she crossed the yard, heading for the smaller farm tractor. Jed Carruthers didn't want her coming around anymore, he'd made that clear, but if they could find other ways of doing acts of kindness for his preschool daughter, Amanda was determined to do it. "I appreciate it, Brady."

* * *

Cassie wasn't really watching. Could she help it if her eyes strayed to the window once she heard the bus lumber past that afternoon, wondering if Mrs. Stanton would send her something? When she heard the telltale squeak of the rusty mailbox hinge a few minutes later, a tremble of excitement tickled her spine.

What would it be today? A piece of fruit? A little cake? Or cookies, those soft, chewy ones Mrs. Stanton sometimes made? Still as a rabbit perched for flight, she watched the boy trudge back up the road, then slipped out, hurrying to the mailbox, alive in anticipation.

A big apple. Kinda' red and pink all at once. She scurried to an old stump just inside the tree line, then sat and chewed, licking every last drop of that good juice.

Crisp. Sweet. Biting into something as wonderful as this, she knew the true meaning of those terms, no longer abstracts on a TV lesson. "The apple is crisp," she murmured, practicing the words that were used so seldom in her house. "The apple is sweet."

She smiled at her efforts. She sounded like those kids on TV. The ones who said things like, "And *Sesame Street* is brought to you today by the letter *G* and the number *5*."

She wanted to sound like them. Look like them. In reality, scruffy legs dangled below the hem of a too-short skirt. Bare, dusty feet hung halfway down the stump. Maybe a little farther now that spring had come. She thought she was bigger. She felt bigger. And her pants showed bare ankle now when she wore them.

Licking the last bits of apple from her fingers, she went on with her practice. "The girl is big. The tree is bigger. The sky is blue. The leaves are green. Cookie Monster is blue. Elmo talks funny." Sliding from the stump, she peered into the dirt where a trail of ants marched rhythmically into a small mound. "One," she intoned in a voice imitating one of her favorite characters. "One little ant. Two, two little ants. Now three, three little—"

"Girl!" The harsh voice splintered her make-believe world like a hunter's shot. Cassie stood from her crouched position, heart racing.

"Where are you? Don't make me come lookin' for you. Not with my bad back an' all. Get yourself in here and sweep up this mess. Dang fool kid, leavin' stuff like that for a body to step in."

She walked in silence to the house and stepped past the man in the doorway. It took a long moment for her eyes to adjust, the bright outdoors a contrast to the darkness within. He gave her a shove. "Get goin'. It's near your bedtime."

She didn't look with longing at the vivid yard, the sun high in the sky. She didn't dare. Grabbing the broom into four-year-old hands, she plied it with care, sweeping the offending cereal and some stray ants onto a thin piece of cardboard.

She didn't count ants here. No, sir. In here she was quiet, moving from room to room on silent feet. Eyes wide, she watched as the man tipped a clear bottle back, taking a long swallow of the gold liquid within.

She'd tried it once. She tried lots of things while he slept, his snore telling her it was OK to do things she couldn't when he was awake.

It tasted nasty. Smelled bad, too. That's when she realized he smelled like that bottle. Nasty and strong. Her nose wrinkled in remembrance.

Once the sweeping was done, she went to the back room. The TV in the front blared a sports station. The man always turned it up. Way up. Shutting the door cloaked her room in almost total darkness, but leaving it open let the shrill voices invade her thoughts, making it hard to pretend.

She shut it, blocking some of the noise, and crawled onto the mattress, tangled with dirty sheets.

The bed smelled. Sniffing, her nose twitched again.

Everything seemed fresh outside, good and clean.

In here, her nose often wrinkled. In the kitchen, where food was left out to sour. In the living room, where the stench of her father filled the room. And here, in her bedroom, where the often-soaked sheets clung to the dark smell of pee. She waved a little hand across the flat of the bed. Well, at least they were dry again.

*　*　*

"Aunt Susan, are you sure you don't want me to tag along to the Carrutherses' place?" Deputy Sheriff Jake Slattery folded his arms and braced his legs the way cops do when they're making a point, and looked mighty good doing it, but his aunt couldn't risk messing up this mission. She'd dealt with high-risk families before, and she'd do it again, but she couldn't deny a heightened concern about Jared "Jed" Carruthers. She'd never heard one nice thing about the man, and that didn't bode well for the small child in his care. "You'll make him nervous, and then I'll never get that child to school. I'll be fine, Jake." She patted his arm to show appreciation. "Like you, it's not my first rodeo."

"How old did you say the girl is?"

"Four, near as we can tell. Home birth, and they weren't much on keeping records. A private sort."

Jake's snort said he knew why Jed Carruthers was private and so did half the town. Drug use and drug sales had mushroomed in the quaint hills of northern Appalachia, but Sue had only one priority: to connect with the child. The child's neighbor had shared concerns, and if nothing else, maybe they could get the little girl some kind of preschool help. That was the goal, anyway. "I'll call you when I'm on my way back to town. It will be fine, I promise."

"A coincidental drive-by might occur. Just so you know."

She laughed because she knew he meant it, and that was the blessing of small towns and a deputy sheriff in the family. In Phillipsburg, New York, folks looked out for one another. Knowing Jake had her back wasn't a bad thing.

She pulled up to the Carrutherses' shack a quarter hour later and climbed out of her car. On the rural roads of New York's Southern Tier, there were still some who'd just as soon pull a gun to discourage folks coming around their backwoods homes, but Jed hadn't had trouble with the law that way since moving here. Not that she was aware of, in any case. She spotted him along the back walk, climbed out, drew a deep breath, and moved that way.

* * *

The pretty lady came back!

Cassie stared from just inside the tree line as the woman walked from her clean, white car up their broken walk and faced the man. "Mr. Carruthers?"

He'd watched her come his way with a mean look and then dropped his gaze when she drew near. "You again."

"Yes, Susan McCabe from Becket County BOCES, remember?" The woman handed him a little white card. "We contacted you about a preschool placement for Cassandra."

The man looked up, suspicious and confused. "You did?"

"Yes, sir. Nearly two weeks ago."

"Don't remember nothin' 'bout school, just remember folks bein' a bother. She's too young for school, ain't she? You maybe got the wrong place."

"We have a preschool program for kids exactly Cassandra's age," the woman said, and Cassie's heart began thumping in her chest so loud she was afraid they might hear it. "I wanted to stop by and tell you the bus will pick her up each day at eight forty. It will bring her back about three hours later, just before noon." The woman's jacket was like the sweet and clean blue of the sky before the weather got too hot. So perfect. Cassie watched from her special place, feeling a spark of animation.

A school bus? For me?

Excitement buzzed straight to her fingertips.

A school bus. The same thing that rolled by with Brady and Addie Stanton. Other kids, too. She clapped her hands in silent glee. A school bus. Just for her.

"Is Cassie here?"

The man looked around as if wondering the same thing. "Somewheres."

"May I talk to her?"

He shrugged and picked up a faded, crumpled newspaper. "Suit yourself. Girl!" He barked the last, his voice coarse.

Cassie sidled out of the bushes and came around the edge of the house. Sparkly eyes regarded her as the golden-skinned woman bent to her level. "Hello, Cassie. I'm Mrs. McCabe. Remember me? I stopped by a couple of weeks ago. We talked about school. Would you like to go to school, honey?"

For the life of her, Cassie couldn't produce a word. She stared, amazed at the tawny prettiness of the woman. She drank her in, from the swirly-printed dress and light blue jacket to the wavy, black hair and kind, shiny golden-gray eyes. Without thinking, she reached out to touch the clothes, to see if they were as soft and clean as they looked.

Then she stared in horror, opening her eyes dinner-plate round. A deep gray smudge of dirt stained the material, exactly where she'd touched it.

Her hands!

She stared down, realizing what had happened. The dirt on her hands, her messy, grimy hands, had spoiled the pretty lady's clothes.

She stepped back, heart pounding, her glance darting from the smudge to the woman and back again. She wrung her hands and swallowed hard.

What had she done? The woman would get mad. She would go away and tell that school bus: *Do not come and pick up that naughty little girl. She got me dirty, see? Right here on my fancy blue dress that smells so nice. No, she cannot come to our school now.*

The woman angled her head, first at Cassie, then down at the telltale mark. She smiled. "My grandson is always messing me up. He can't seem to help it. I bet he's a lot like you, Cassandra. He likes to play outdoors and make messes. And he never wants to take a bath, but he likes how he feels once he's had one. Are you the same way?" Her look stayed soft and kind, even with the dark spot on her jacket that seemed to grow as Cassie watched.

"I don't know." Cassie looked at the woman, pondering the question. Was she the same as that little boy? How could she tell? She frowned. "Do we look the same?"

* * *

Shaking her head no, Susan McCabe made mental notes during the interchange. Timidity, lack of affect, hesitancy of speech.

Cassie had a deep, sonorous voice, a curiosity in a child, but there was a luster as well, a hint of sharp intelligence. Well shrouded, as if the girl kept it hidden. Sliding a glance to the disheveled man, now sitting on the weak-legged chair near the door, the social worker understood that maybe hidden was better in this case. She was pretty sure that bright, bubbly questions from a curious four-year-old wouldn't find a welcome audience at 1173 County Center Road. The child was playing the hand dealt her and doing an OK job of it.

Sue bit back a sigh. *Why should she have to, God?* she wondered, eyeing the child. *Why are so many couples barren, while this father gives no thought to the gift he's been given? The gift of a child, so precious. So prized.*

She had no answer, but that was the reason she'd gone into human services. To help the Cassie Carrutherses of the world. She directed her next question to the father. "I have a bag of clothes in the van, Mr. Carruthers. One of the teachers' girls outgrew them. Could you use them for Cassie, for school? They're all size four and five."

"Don't need no charity." He didn't bother shifting her a glance.

She kept her eyes trained on him and not the decrepit building at his back. "Not charity, sir. You'd actually be doing this woman a favor. She needs to get them off her hands. I think there's a pair or two of shoes in there, as well. Cassie needs shoes for school."

He humphed, but that consideration seemed to shift the matter in her favor. He gave a curt nod. "Just set 'em there." His glance indicated the listing stoop.

She extended a hand of invitation to the child. "I will, then. Come on, Cassie. I'll show you what I have."

Cassie hesitated. She slid her look to the left in case her father objected, but he was contemplating a cigarette with great interest. Quietly she followed Susan to the bright white van.

"These are the clothes," Susan offered, bending down. "From one pretty girl to another."

Cassie tilted her head at the words. Her pinched face went almost hopeful. "You sound like my mommy."

Susan's hands went still. She took a breath, grappling emotion. The child's longing tone tightened her belly. With a soft exhale, she shared a smile. "I bet your mommy was pretty. Like you."

Cassie regarded her, eyes solemn. "You're pretty."

"Thank you, Cassie." Susan let one hand graze the child's cheek with care. The girl didn't flinch. *Good.*

"Do you like pink?" At the child's nod, she held up an outfit. "So does Amy, the little girl who had these. And purple?" She proffered a pant set, the jacket flecked in pink and yellow flowers on a deep violet background.

"So beautiful." Cassie reached out a hand to the flowered softness, then yanked it back, remembering. Susan smiled at her.

"You're absolutely right. It would be better to touch them after you've washed your hands. Or had a bath. Do you know how to give yourself a bath?"

Cassie shook her head.

The social worker nodded. "I'll show you at school. We have a special room set up for that. I can show you how to take a bath and wash your hair. Would you like that, honey?"

Cassie started to nod, then shook her head. "I don't like bubbles in my eyes."

Susan agreed wholeheartedly. "Me either. I'll make you a promise. No bubbles in the eyes. Deal?" She stuck out a hand to the beleaguered girl.

The child looked at the hand, confused, making no attempt to take it. She slanted a sober gaze up, meeting Susan McCabe's eye. "Deal."

* * *

"What do you think?" Amanda Stanton poured Susan a fresh cup of coffee and sat down with her a short while later. "Can you help her?"

The school social worker picked her words with care. "I think it's a crying shame to have a child and not bother two cents for her. But there's little to be done. Jed Carruthers is within the parameters. He doesn't beat her, doesn't starve her. He just—" She paused, recalling Cassie's look of hope at the slightest attention, and sighed. "Ignores her existence, beyond the basics. Some food, some drink, a house to live in."

Amanda snorted and moved to the window, staring out. She was silent a long moment, arms crossed in frustration. Finally, she turned.

"It's not a house, it's a shack. A cold, drafty, infested shack. The only reason she eats is because he's drunk most of the time and Cassie tends herself, eating whatever's handy that a preschooler can find. She's dirty, unkempt, and lives in a hovel. That's not enough for the county to do something?" She aimed a look of irritation at her oldest friend.

Susan shrugged. "You can report it, sure. But they'll tell you the same thing I did. Neglect of this sort is not punishable. The rules are strict. A family is kept together unless the situation is out of control. There's nothing out of control at the Carrutherses'. Lousy, maybe. Stifling. But not dangerous or out of control."

"Human decency says otherwise." Amanda scowled, distraught. "With her mother gone, there's no buffer for Cassie anymore. No one looking out for her."

Susan thought of Sara Carruthers's death over a year past. Drunk, she'd been hit by a car on Lake Road after stumbling from a seedy bar. She wasn't too sure how much of a saving grace Sara had been, but she chose not to argue the point. Amanda had been Sara's only confidant, and she felt guilt-ridden by the woman's untimely demise. Susan shook her head as Jake's cruiser rolled to a stop next to her van. "Then human decency needs to handle it. Church. Neighbors. Much as you've been doing, Amanda. The Family Preservation Act won't allow anything of more import. The county might suggest counseling, but he'd plead lack of transportation, and they'd have to let it go."

Amanda made a sound of disgust.

Susan eyed her friend as Jake approached them. "Be careful. You could make things worse trying to make them better."

"She's making a good point, Amanda." Jake climbed the three wooden porch steps. "Poking a sleeping bear generally leaves the kids on the receiving end of stuff they don't need. Any of that coffee left, ladies?"

Amanda tossed him a pod for the single-cup brewer. "Dave said the same thing. That right now Jed's not a danger to Cass, but if we call the law in, we could push him over the edge."

Susan took relief in Dave's common-sense reaction. She'd watched well-meaning initiatives backfire too often in her tenure. "That husband of yours is a smart guy. Since there's not enough to remove her, she could end up becoming a target. That could be disastrous."

"Your talk went OK?" Jake made the coffee and accepted one of Amanda's molasses cookies. "He was all right?"

"Drunk and mellow for the most part. Mostly drunk."

Amanda sighed, her gaze turned outward once more. Beyond her, spring beckoned, the air filled with birdsong and the squawk of squabbling hens. Susan waited while Amanda weighed her options.

Turning back to her, Amanda gave a reluctant nod. "We'll do what we can, Sue. You know that."

The other woman nodded. "So will we."

"And we can make drive-bys a regular thing," Jake promised. "We'll get a better feel for things that way."

"I don't know how the occasional sheriff's car cruising by can help." Amanda looked at Jake, then his aunt. She shrugged, clearly torn. "I know it can't hurt. It's just..." She folded her arms, dissatisfied. "I think of how I felt when they first settled Addie into my arms. And then Brady." Her brow drew tight. "I fell in love at first sight, as if I'd just been given the most amazing gift of all. I can't imagine not feeling that way, so the thought of not caring..." She made a face. "I don't get it. But if we tackle this together..." She turned her face outward again toward the dusty road leading through the woods toward the Carrutherses' shack. "...maybe we can make a difference. I hope so."

Susan exchanged a look with Jake, then put her hand over Amanda's. "Me, too."

chapter two

"Kerry, on my word, aren't you just the prettiest thing!" Hannah Wilder clasped her hands to her elderly heart as if delighted by the sight of her twenty-seven-year-old tenant. Her over-the-top reaction made Kerry smile as she approached her landlady's screen door on Sunday morning.

"It's a cryin' shame that you're on the arm of an old woman headin' to church, and not walkin' beside a husband," Hannah continued, and Kerry couldn't find fault with her words. "What is the matter with that young man of yours?"

She meant Ryan O'Donnell, the on-again, off-again young oncologist who showed up at his own convenience, which really meant he wasn't Kerry's anything. "I have a young man?" Kerry teased as she took hold of Hannah's arm. "Do tell."

"Well, he runs hot and cold, so maybe he is and maybe he isn't," Hannah went on as they took the front steps with care. "In my day, if a man wouldn't commit, there were plenty of other fish in the sea. I don't expect that's any different now, is it? Of course, you have to be willing to cast that line in the waters, and women are singularly slow about doing that both now and when I was young and fleet of foot. We can be a downright foolish lot, if you ask me."

Kerry laughed and hugged the older woman's arm. "You think I should set a time limit on Ryan? Or stop by Walmart and grab myself a fishing pole?"

"It's worked before," Hannah declared. "It can work again. We women don't have the luxuries a man enjoys. We've got that biological clock thing tickin' right along, and it's a likely annoyance as the years go by."

Kerry knew the truth in that, although at twenty-seven, it wasn't a huge worry. More like a valid concern. "I've got a few good years yet, I think."

"It's not about good or bad, it's about supply and demand, darlin'. Mr. Wilder was in marketing. I do believe I've mentioned that."

Only a hundred times. Kerry nodded. "And he did quite well."

"Well enough, but that's because he understood supply-side economics better than most. And if a man's got a handy supply of this, that, or the other thing, he's not as likely to toss that aside and settle down."

The thinly veiled advice on promiscuity made Kerry wince inside, mostly because the aged woman was spot on.

"Did you know they did a survey with men about that very thing?"

Kerry was afraid to find out which "very thing" she meant. "About?"

"What made them settle down? What made them finally pop the question?"

"And what were the results?" Kerry asked as they crossed the final quiet intersection before getting to the church steps.

"Most all of them had been issued an ultimatum."

"Really?" Kerry made a face of displeasure. "There go my hopes and dreams of a fellow just falling so desperately in love with me that he can't bear to *not* pop the question. What's this world coming to?"

Hannah patted her arm, amused. "Oh, honey, that's how it should be, but these days, men are different. Not all, but a fair share. Less willing to commit. Why, I remember when this church was teeming with family men, pew by pew, proud to sit here and listen to the Good Word with their wives.

"But that was my generation and the one following. Now?" She swept the half-full church a quiet look. "Now it's old women like me and single-parent families, mostly. The men, the ones that used to dress up nice in their Sunday best and line the inner aisle, aren't here. Not now, leastways."

A few fathers had taken seats in the cozy, country church, but

Hannah was right. The percentage of men to women was low, and that didn't bode well for a community. "Maybe the farmer husbands are home, planting the fields now that spring's here. Getting things done when they can, as they can."

"Maybe."

Hannah glanced around once more, unconvinced, and Kerry understood why. She knew less than a handful of young men who went to church regularly, and while the town of Phillipsburg had a strong population of nuclear families, the surrounding countryside did not. Single-parent families had become commonplace, drug use in the hills was at an all-time high, and several of her students were being raised by grandparents for various reasons. As an elementary school teacher, she saw the everyday strain, and she'd lived the downside of a loveless, single-parent father, so she understood the effects firsthand.

"I pray a lot," Hannah murmured.

Kerry slipped an arm around the older woman's shoulders, thinking she'd need comforting, but then this was Hannah Wilder, and she was a tough old bird. She planted her hands firm on her hips and frowned. "I pray that we start seein' some common sense in how folks behave, in how they choose to lead their lives. And that starts with that young man of yours, no matter how good lookin' he is, and don't think for a minute I hadn't noticed. A woman would have to be blind and daft, and I'm neither."

Kerry slipped into her seat once Hannah sat down. "It's hard not to, isn't it?" Ryan O'Donnell was to-die-for good looking, but Hannah was right.

He was a player, or had been a player and maybe still was. In any case, Kerry didn't have time right now to fuss and bother about it. She'd face the issue once this school year was complete, her first year at Daystar, an ecumenical Christian academy housed in a former Catholic school. "I'm too busy doing my own personal restructuring on my teaching and writing career to dive headfirst into the fret-and-worry phase of romance run amok. First things first."

"Well, and that's the other thing," Hannah whispered before Reverend Stillman stepped up front. "Women work so much today. They're on the go, morning, noon, and night. Perhaps we were better off when they really needed their husbands. Nowadays, it's too easy to just toss the whole thing aside and start anew."

Kerry's mother hadn't worked.

She'd been completely dependent on the fairly heartless man who had fathered her two girls, Kerry and her sister, Jenn.

Kerry's parents had never married. And then her mother died young. Too young. That left two young girls in the care of a cold, self-righteous man who didn't want a wife and certainly never wanted children.

No, despite the higher marriage success rates of the nineteen-fifties, Kerry was determined to be her own person, to be able to make enough money to get by. She didn't want to be dependent on a man, any man. Ever.

But she didn't want to be alone, either.

"It's a conundrum, isn't it?" Hannah's words said one thing, but the gentle pat on Kerry's hand said something else. "And yet, with God, all things are possible! Although bringin' your young man around to God's way of thinking?" She arched an all-too-knowing look up at Kerry. "That might be the challenge that proves me wrong."

Her tart words made Kerry smile, but she'd have to deal with the truth behind the words at some point, because Hannah was right.

Ryan O'Donnell was a challenge. Kerry saw it. Recognized it. And she was pretty sure that despite all the self-help articles saying otherwise, she was the person meant to change him. His destiny.

If she didn't kill him first.

* * *

Kerry McHenry was driving Ryan O'Donnell crazy.

Positively, absolutely crazy, and it was his own fault. First, his father had married her aunt, otherwise their paths would have never crossed because Kerry didn't need a pediatric oncologist and she didn't party.

Ryan was a skilled physician with steady hands and an MLB player's visual acuity. He was born to either play ball or save lives, and a college knee injury tipped the scales. Med school won. But it was a shallow victory on nights like this.

"You heading out with us, Ryan?" Vic Sirianni tugged his sport coat into place over an urban black tee. A thin pewter chain finished his born-for-success look. "It's Ladies' Night at The Riverside. Cab's pulling up to the door as I speak."

Ryan hesitated.

Vic grinned. "That cute little school teacher's got you wrapped. It's about time."

He meant Kerry, and his words made Ryan's chest go tight.

She didn't.

She didn't have him wrapped because he wouldn't allow it. He called the shots, now and always. He didn't let anyone in that deep because when he did, it hurt that much more when they shrugged you off and walked away.

He stood, grabbed his jacket, and didn't care that he looked like a roughed-up James Dean against Vic's polish. Sometimes contrast benefitted the unexpected. "Let's go."

* * *

Kerry's phone buzzed an incoming text after church. She walked Hannah to her door and waited for her weekly gift, a zip-locked bag of cookies. This would be wonderful if Hannah could actually bake.

She couldn't, and she believed soft, chewy cookies were underdone and sure to cause Bad Stomach, a malaise to be avoided at all costs.

It was the one thing they disagreed on, but Kerry kept her opinions to herself. If Hannah wanted to reward her with bad cookies, she could. End of story.

She checked Jenn's text while she waited. *Memorial Day parade in town and picnic at Aunt Claire's tomorrow. You coming?*

She never missed the Memorial Day parade. Their two grandfathers had both served, and their Uncle Charlie. *Parade, yes. Picnic undecided.*

"Because of Ryan?"

Leave it to Jenn to get straight to the point. She texted back: *"Keeping it cool."*

"It will be a long life of missed events if you let him keep you away. We can choose friends. Can't always choose family. Come to the picnic."

She should.

She *would*, she decided, because she loved her Aunt Claire. Claire had been a voice of reason in an unreasonable existence, even though their father had tried to shut her out.

Claire had refused to allow that, letting the girls know they were beloved and beautiful and marvelous. She'd been a light in a long tunnel of darkness, so how could Kerry say no? *"I'll come."*

"See you tomorrow."

She tucked the phone away as Hannah reappeared. She handed Kerry the cookies, then peered up at the sky. "No rain forecast for today or tomorrow."

"Which means I can plant the new flowers around the house, if that's OK with you?"

"I was hoping you would!" Hannah's face beamed. "Maxwell and I always planted on Memorial Day weekend, weather allowin', of course. He'd terraced the gardens down the front slope at our old place, so pretty. Why, folks would stop all four seasons to take photographs of that house, it was quite special back then."

Kerry knew the story.

That house had burned, long ago. The weather-eroded skeleton still stood, unfixed, untended.

Hannah had lost her husband and grandchild in that fire. She'd never gone back and still never drove down County Road 32. Her daughter, the child's mother, hadn't spoken to Hannah in over fifteen years, a long punishment for a tragic mistake.

If Hannah wanted her flowers planted in her old tradition, then Kerry would plant the beds today because seeing the old woman's smile made her feel just plain good.

* * *

"Kerry!"

Ryan heard Claire's greeting the next day and fought the urge to turn. He kept his gaze trained on a pair of O'Donnell cousins scuffling by the pool.

"I'm so glad you came, and you brought cookies!"

"Dan's favorite, chocolate chip pecan."

Her voice...

Bright. Warm. Inviting. But strong, too, as if she'd had her share of practice being strong.

"Sodas are in the fridge, water in the cooler, and—hey, Aggie!" Claire's voice took on a tough edge. "No messing around like that near the pool. Trips to the ER are to be avoided at all costs, but especially on national holidays."

"Spoken like the true nurse you are." Ryan turned now. He moved toward them. "Hey, Ker. How's it going?"

Claire rolled her eyes at his lame attempt to act casual, then carried the cookie tray over to the food table set up under the portico.

Kerry looked up at him.

Those eyes.

Cornflower blue, only brighter, if that were possible. Eyes that looked like they were contact lens-enhanced, but weren't. Eyes that seemed to see beyond the image he presented, and maybe that's what bothered him most.

She saw too much, and Ryan didn't let anyone see too much.

"It's going well." She answered his question like she always did, straightforward and frank, never playing. That made him nervous, too. "I'm looking forward to winding down this first full year at kindergarten level."

"And moving back up here where you can get a job in a real district and make enough money to live on?"

She laughed, but something in her gaze said his words made her sad. "I'm not big on living high, and I've found my niche in Phillipsburg. The town, the kids, and especially the school."

"It's a back-to-basics sort, isn't it?" Dan O'Donnell came up behind Ryan, munching a cookie he held up in appreciation. "Best cookies ever, Kerry. I think being a country schoolmarm has done nothing but polish your culinary skills."

"Thank you!" Her smile to Ryan's father held none of the reserve she'd aimed at him. "I love that term, *schoolmarm*. It's delightful and totally apt. Maybe that's why Daystar is such a good fit for me."

Back to basics.

Yup.

That was Kerry, all right.

So why was he beguiled whenever she came near? What was the draw? If he could figure that out, he'd squelch it, because Kerry wanted it all and wasn't afraid to say so. Maybe that was the glitch, because Ryan already had it all. Everything *he* needed, tied up in one simple package. Great profession, great skills, easy life.

And then she turned her gaze his way.

Freckles dotted her Celtic skin. Her hair, thick, long, and full, lay braided down her back. Pale shoulders, with more freckles to match the ones on her arms.

Would they darken as the summer waxed on? Would her hair glow with more gold lights when it lay loose and long? And what would it feel like to weave his hands into that pretty gold hair?

He wanted to know.

He needed to know.

She started to move away. Jenn's kids were splashing in the shallow end, while Jenn sat on the pool's edge, watching.

"Kerry."

She turned back toward him and raised one brow, one perfectly sculpted golden brow.

"Are you free on Saturday night?"

"Yes."

He breathed easier, but his heart beat harder because if he pursued this attraction it was going to cause them nothing but grief. He knew it, and was pretty sure she knew it, too.

"For dinner?"

She held his gaze a few beats longer than needed. "I'd like that, Rye."

No one called him Rye, but when she said it, the name sounded perfect, as if all his life he'd been waiting for her to come along and call him that.

"Shall I meet you halfway?"

From some women, the question would be a trick, a test, to see if he was man enough to drive ninety minutes for a date that ended too soon. From Kerry, the question was a kindness, probably because he'd complained about the distance on the few occasions they'd gotten together. "I'll call you. We'll set it up."

"I'll look forward to it."

She crossed to her sister's side, confident and easy.

She didn't strut to hold his attention but held it anyway. She didn't flirt in the normal sense of the word; she simply treated him nicely, as if he mattered, and that made him almost wish he did.

But that would skate close to an edge he avoided at all costs.

He'd watched his father's sincere attempts to keep his mother happy, and it never worked. Nothing worked. It took a long time for Dan O'Donnell to move on with his life.

Ryan intended to skip straight to step three, living life on his terms, free to come and go as he pleased outside the office and the new upscale oncology unit at Children's Hospital. When not at work, he was a free bird, flying high, and that's exactly how he intended to stay.

No matter what.

chapter three

Cassie almost wet her pants, waiting. She heard the engine grind as the bus chugged up Adler's Hill, then saw the flash of yellow when it rounded the bend.

The bus wasn't big like Brady's. His was huge and looked like it could swallow a little girl whole.

This one was shorter. Maybe half the size. But it was shiny and clean, and rolled to a stop at her driveway. She twitched in anticipation. It was really stopping for *her*.

The door swung open. A woman sat there, her face big and full, the roundest face Cassie had ever seen. She gulped.

Then the woman smiled and about a hundred little dimples appeared. Creases here, folds there. Cassie stared, enthralled. She'd seen a TV show once that had lots of fat people. They talked about their feelings while a slim, dark-skinned woman nodded her understanding.

Cassie had stared then much as she did now. She'd never seen such big people before, but she'd read *Jack and the Beanstalk* with Mrs. Stanton. She was sure they were giants. She tilted her head, eyeing the woman before her.

"Come on, sweetie. First day jitters, huh? I've saved you a place right behind me. Have you ever been on a bus before?"

When Cassie shook her head, the woman smiled again. She had kind eyes. "Well then, this will be an adventure, don't you think? Walk on up those stairs and have a seat. I'm Mrs. Chapman, official driver of Phillipsburg Central bus number forty-two." Her nod indicated the black numbers over the window. She flashed Cassie a look of understanding. "Allow me to chauffer you to your first day of U.P.K, Miss Carruthers."

With a little shrug and one last tentative look around, Cassie followed the directions.

Once she was seated, the bus lurched, jostling her. She grabbed hold of the arm, then fastened her seat belt, just like Mrs. Stanton had shown her when she used to come around. As the engine churned, she stared out the front window, beyond the driver's head, watching the wonder of a world racing by.

There were other kids on the bus. She'd glimpsed them as she climbed aboard, but couldn't see them over the high cushion at her back.

She heard them, though. Someone was laughing while another scolded in a high-pitched, strange voice, like when music got mixed up.

Then something groaned. It was a low, deep groan like a growling dog, but not exactly like that, either. Leaning to one side, she peeked around the corner of her seat.

The scolder was two seats back, a boy with dark eyes and brown hair. His mouth moved nonstop, the strange, scolding words erupting in a screechy, girl-voice. Only he was a boy. Cassie frowned at that, perplexed.

At that moment, he spotted her and shrieked. "Keep away from Timmy, keep away, keep away. Timmy is a good boy, a good boy, a good boy. You keep away, keep away. Timmy wants his mommy, his mommy, his mommy." The boy tugged his hair, fingers tight in the strands, pulling hard. "Don't hurt Timmy. Don't hurt him. Timmy mustn't pull his hair. He mustn't pull his hair. There will be no snack for Timmy, no snack. He will have no cookies from Miss B., if Timmy pulls his hair. No snack, no snack, no snack."

The bus driver's voice broke in. "Timothy Randolph, stop that this minute. You're scaring this little girl. She was just looking at you, trying to get to know people. Take your hands out of your hair and fold them in your lap, or I *will* tell Miss B., and you *will* lose your snack."

Cassie shifted her look from Timmy to the bus driver and back. To her surprise, the boy paused. His face was still wretched, but his hands relaxed, then slowly fell to his lap. He wrung them together, but no longer pulled his hair. The bus driver's voice went on, "This is Cassie, everyone. She'll be riding with us 'til the end of the year. Then maybe summer school. Would you like that, dear?" The big woman's eyes met Cassie's in a shiny mirror above the front window. "Would you like to go to summer school?"

Cassie wrinkled her face in consideration. "I don't know." She contemplated the question at length. "I might like that. I might not."

The bus driver sent her a curious glance, but kept the smile. "Well, then, we'll just see, won't we? By and by."

Cassie liked the sound of that. She nodded. "Yes. By and by."

They pulled into a parking lot with the school spreading out to her right.

It was amazingly beautiful and unbelievably confusing, made of red brick and sparkling glass. Cassie gawked at the number of windows. Bright, shiny windows, not one of them covered in dirt or grime. Some had blinds; some were bare. Inside those windows were children. Lots of children. She could see them from the bus and heard them once she stepped down the three steep steps to the sidewalk. Grown-ups waited, smiling and talking.

One laughed a greeting as she helped ease Timmy out, fussing with his messed up hair, smoothing it gently back into place.

Then, something magical happened. The side door of the bus opened, swinging wide, and a bridge came out. A folding bridge, like she'd seen in movies. On the bridge was a girl with short, light hair. She sat in a chair with wheels and had things all around her very big head.

Cassie gulped. The girl's head lolled from side to side, cushioned by pads that must be there to keep her head from falling off.

Cassie stared. The magic bridge creaked and whirred as it lowered the girl to the ground. A thick woman with a flowered shirt and baggy pants waited on the sidewalk. "Come on, Jodi-girl. Let's see what you've got today."

The girl groaned in response, her head tilted, her hands jerking. But her eyes were bright as she gave a crooked smile to the woman with the forget-me-not shirt. She lifted a gnarled hand. "Booooo," she groaned, poking bent knuckles at the woman's blouse. "Boooooo."

"Yes." The woman rewarded her with a pleased smile. "The flowers on my shirt are blue. What color are the leaves?"

The girl worked to pull her head more upright as she studied the shirt. Her eyes narrowed, and Cassie saw her mouth work. A spot of dribble oozed down her chin. The woman wiped it away in a casual motion.

"Gaaaaweeen!" She sang the word out, her face breaking into an uneven smile once more.

The woman laughed, then tweaked her chin. "Yes, smarty. The flowers are blue. The leaves are green."

Cassie eyed them. The woman was teaching the girl, just like Cassie practiced at home. Only the girl was much bigger than Cassie, but not quite as big as Mrs. Stanton. Cassie drew her eyebrows together in wonder.

A touch to her arm startled her. She turned.

"Cassandra?"

A young woman stood before her. She had glossy brown hair, pulled back in a knot. Her eyes were yellow and brown, all mixed together, and they sparkled down at Cassie. Cassie swallowed and nodded.

"I'm Miss Becker, your teacher. Welcome to Phillipsburg Elementary. How was your ride?"

The woman smelled good, sweet and fresh, like a morning outside. Cassie sniffed. Maybe better. Then, realizing she hadn't answered, she stood straight. "Timmy pulled his hair."

Miss Becker didn't appear upset at the news. "I know, dear. He does that sometimes. Did you sit up front?"

She'd taken Cassie's hand and was leading her into the building, talking easily. As she swung open the door, she slanted a smile down. Cassie almost smiled back, but paused. It would be better to wait. "Almost in the front," she explained in a careful tone. "The driver was first, actually."

The teacher gave her a kind gaze. "Of course. How silly of me. You sat in the first seat meant for children."

"Yes." Cassie kept her voice serious. It had, after all, been a serious question.

Miss Becker squeezed her hand. "Well, we're glad to have you here, Cassie. I know this will all seem somewhat new. That's normal. After a little bit, you'll get used to how things are."

At that moment, they passed a classroom of assorted children. Some were in wheelchairs, some were on boards, and some wore metal things on their legs, hobbling like creatures in one of those early-morning movies. One talked like a robot, a machine at his throat. Cassie stared, lost in wonder, until Miss Becker guided her into a big, bright room filled with eleven other kids about her size. She breathed a sigh she hadn't realized she'd been holding. These kids at least kind of looked like her.

* * *

"So. What do you think?" Susan McCabe had waited until the end of Cassie's first full week before approaching Lisa Becker. The younger woman regarded her frankly.

"She can't stay here, Sue. I don't know why she was put in this room, but she's a fish out of water."

Susan's shoulders drooped. "Can we help her? Guide her? Give her some basics?"

"Basics?" Lisa hooted, then shook her head. "Basic what? Here's her workbook." She handed over the brightly colored preschool book and watched as Susan opened it.

"She did this?" Susan made no attempt to mask the surprise in her voice.

"The first day."

"No."

"Oh, yeah. And then proceeded to go through two weeks' worth of reading readiness work the following day. She's already reading simple words, sounding out phonetically, using independent thought contextually, and can count to a hundred. She adds basic numbers and sets them up on paper, stacking them properly. See?" Lisa pointed a softly curved fingernail to the diagnostic numbers worksheet she'd given Cassie. "I had her do fill-in-the-blank worksheets, to assess her levels. She not only did them, she then took a piece of scrap paper and set up her own little math lesson. Using the numbers, she made up problem sets, then solved for *n*. Where did you find this kid?"

Susan worked to close her mouth, then tapped the desktop thoughtfully. "In a backwoods shack that smells as bad as it looks. This"— shaking her head, she picked up the work before her, then set it back down—"is unbelievable. Cassie has almost no contact with the outside world, except for a kind neighbor who used to stop by occasionally." She surveyed the varied papers before her. The color chart, filled in and labeled, with only one spelling error—*purple* with no *e* finishing the second syllable. Written words, put in letter form: *"Dear teacher, I like your school. From Cassie"*

Susan eyed the missive. "No one helped her with this?"

"No."

"Or the math?"

Lisa sighed. "Again, no. Totally independent. She works within the group but doesn't mingle. Backward socialization skills. When lesson time is over, she doesn't run and play with the others. She studies. She picks up books and examines them. I thought it was her way of keeping to the outside, but then, on the third day, I sat with her and asked what was happening in the story."

"And?" Sue raised a brow of interest.

Lisa Becker sent her a look of quiet amazement. "She read it to me. *The Berenstain Bears and The Spooky Old Tree*. No affect. No inflection. Every word correct."

"Memorized?"

Lisa smiled and shifted forward, gathering papers into separate folders. "Exactly what I thought, so I pulled down Shel Silverstein's

The Giving Tree. She was curious; I could see that. Her eyes narrowed, and she scanned the pages carefully. Then she said, 'Can I read this?'

"I said, 'Sure, honey. Go ahead. I'll help if you need it.'" Lisa set the stack of folders aside and sighed. "She read it to me, Susan, cover to cover. Again, no affect or emotion, but every word correct with only occasional intervention."

"Autistic? PDD? Savant tendencies?" Susan threw out the familiar terms to the special education teacher.

Lisa shook her head. "I don't think so. I think the lack of emotion is psychological. Sometimes she wants to react but fights it. From what you've told me of her background, maybe getting too happy or too sad doesn't cut it. The low profile might be a defense mechanism."

Susan recalled the sight of the miserable, unkempt man perched on his wobbly chair. Yeah, she could see it. Sometimes less is better. She sat back in her chair, at a loss. "Now what?"

Lisa grimaced. "We don't have a choice. You know it as well as I do." She met Susan's look with an even gaze. "I can keep her until the term ends, but they'll never approve summer school funding for a child who's performing so far above grade level. They'll bounce her back to regular ed in a heartbeat, which is exactly where she needs to be. We don't want to slow her down. And you know I've got some challenges in my class. Cassie needs to be with normal kids, others who are developmentally on target or advanced. The social aspect can be augmented both inside and outside the classroom, but we can't keep her here."

Susan studied her hands for a moment, then rose. "I'm on it, Lisa. I'll get the paperwork going tomorrow. But," she paused, then swung back to the young teacher behind her. "That means she's with him the whole summer. What if something happens? How do we live with that?"

Lisa acknowledged the situation with a frown, but shook her head. "She's gotten this far, Sue. You can't fudge her paperwork, make her out to be less than she is. That would be wrong. Maybe we can visit her, drop by unexpectedly. Let her know we haven't forgotten her. Come September she gets on the big bus and heads off to Green Wing."

Green Wing was the segment of hallways designated for kindergarten through second grade classes at Phillipsburg Elementary.

Susan grimaced. "I know. And then she ends up with either Judy or Holly. Can you see Cassie thriving in either environment?"

The look Lisa gave her was empathetic. They both understood the limitations of the current Green Wing staff.

"Judy hasn't nurtured a child in the ten years I've known her, and Holly will be too busy planning her wedding and doing her nails to pay attention to a lost soul like Cassandra Carruthers. I wish…" Her voice faded on a note of resignation, then changed mid-beat. She sent Lisa a look of triumph.

"What?" Lisa wondered. "You wish what?"

"I was going to say I wish we had a kindergarten teacher like they do at Daystar Academy. The McHenry girl. You remember, don't you? We met her at a conference last year at the Holiday Inn. She authored that article you liked in *Education Magazine*."

"I remember her and the article. We had a discussion about the pros and cons of inclusion and seclusion. She's great. But she's at Daystar."

Sue grinned. "Luckily, the people in Phillipsburg are pretty tight, no matter what church door they darken." She stood and slung her bag over her shoulder. "I think I'll schedule a quick talk with the local pastors. Maybe with some prayer and promise, we can get Cassie Carruthers into kindergarten over there. I might have to smooth-talk her father, but if there's no money involved on his end, I can't imagine he'll put up a fuss."

Lisa looked relieved. "If you can engineer that, I'm all in to help. If they need pledges to offset her tuition, come see me. I'll be first in line."

"That kindly offer just made you head of the fundraising committee, my friend." Susan flashed her a quick, broad grin. "Discreet, of course."

Lisa was already jotting something in her smartphone. "I'll start scouting donations tonight."

Susan crossed the preschool classroom and turned the door handle with vigor. "And I need to go see some pastors about a girl."

chapter four

Kerry McHenry brushed her braid back over her shoulder and surveyed her freshly-decorated classroom in early September.

Primary colors? Check!

Alphabet present and accounted for? Done!

Numbers? Marching around the upper wall for everyone to see!

"This room screams *kindergarten* in bold, block letters."

Kerry laughed when the Daystar principal pretended fear as she walked into the room. "It scares me to death."

"Which is why *I'm* down here," Kerry waved a hand to the room at large, "and *you* run the school."

"Point taken."

Anne gave an indulgent smile to three friendly diplodocuses struggling to lift a giant *W* above their heads. Nearby, a triceratops hauled a hefty *e* on his stout back. In grand succession, differing dinosaurs bore distinct letters, creating a Mesozoic *Welcome* on the wall. Painted above the cubby corner, a cheerful elephant gripped a bright bunch of spectral balloons. Each balloon was boldly tagged until every shade of the rainbow was named in scientific succession.

"The guys did a great job painting this summer," Kerry noted as her boss approached. Anne held something in her hand, and Kerry moved forward, curious. "But I don't think you left your bustling office the day before classes start to talk about paint effects."

"Too right. Got a minute?"

Kerry noted the paper in Anne's hand and groaned on purpose. "Nope. Not one. On to the next question, please."

The principal waited, smiling, but if Kerry had learned nothing else in her time at Daystar, she'd learned that Anne Baxter was every bit as fervent about helping kids as she was, which meant Kerry would say yes even when she shouldn't. And Anne knew it.

"Whatever you have in your hot little hand, the answer is still no," she protested. "I can't head up any more committees or do any more tag-team than I'm already doing." She pretended to pout, then smiled instead. "I know you're the boss and all that, but have a heart."

Anne inclined her chin. "Ask the busy person to do one thing more." She handed off the innocuous-looking sheet of paper. Kerry scanned it with interest, then lifted her gaze to meet the principal's.

"She's five years old?"

"Mm-hmm."

"With these scores? Why wouldn't we just bump her on to first grade? Have her bypass the big K altogether?"

Anne offered a brief account of Cassandra Carruthers's background and the professionals who had intervened to get the child a slot in Kerry's kindergarten. "You've been handpicked to work with this child," the principal told her. "There's a quiet community fund to cover her tuition although I told them that wouldn't be necessary."

"Come unto me, all who are burdened."

"Well, luckily Father Joe over at St. Mary's is more pragmatic and insisted on putting together the funds for us," Anne admitted. "It seems the child's mother was Catholic, and while she hasn't been raised with any kind of religious experience, he felt compelled to jump in and make sure Cassie is covered."

"He's got a kind heart hidden under his down-to-earth spirit," Kerry noted.

"He does, and I fully support this whole idea, but there's a downside here."

"And that is?"

"The familial history and the girl's current living conditions," Anne explained. "She's been exposed to chronic alcoholism, drug dependency, and depression, and she's surrounded by what could best be called squalor. Concerns have been raised that her father might be slipping from neglectful and onerous to dangerous. That could jeopardize the school if he becomes problematic. Daystar has developed a diverse community, but we have to be careful. We can't afford to lose students."

Kerry's heart went quiet.

She understood dangerous conditions. She knew neglect firsthand. She understood the helplessness of a child in wretched circumstances, memories she'd tried to bury long ago. Having this child presented to her now brought that all back to the current light. She swallowed hard. "Let me get this straight. She's outrageously bright and focused, but has little expression, spontaneity, or social skills. She's unkempt, and the social worker at BOCES gave her bathing and hair washing lessons but didn't see much improvement."

"Right." Anne nodded. "Pretty understandable at age five. And she was actually only four when she was in their program last spring."

"Family?"

"Mother's deceased; father's indigent and suffers from alcohol abuse, possible substance abuse, and depression. He's been on disability for years. Child is not—"

"Cassie," Kerry corrected in a gentle tone.

Anne grimaced. "Of course. Cassie is not abused but has probably been overwhelmingly neglected since the mother's death at age three."

Kerry kept her gaze on the profile picture stapled to the fax.

Honey-gold skin set off green-gold eyes that should sparkle with childish glee but shone somber under unruly hair. The hair had dark undertones, but gold highlights brightened the tight mass of curls. A cute face, with a delightful point to the chin. The tilt of that chin won Kerry's heart instantly. It was determination at its finest, firmly set, the prim, unsmiling mouth above it a soft shade of rosebud pink. The shirt Cassie wore in the picture had a grunge stain sloping off the side of the chest, disappearing into the bottom of the digital shot. Kerry looked at the picture, then drew her eyes up to Anne's.

"People lobbied for her?"

"With great deliberation. They didn't want to see her get lost in the elementary school. I caved on the spot."

Kerry smiled at that. Daystar's principal had a heart of gold and a limited purse that never seemed of consequence to her. The finance committee thought otherwise, but if Father Joe and others had manufactured the funding, how could Kerry refuse?

"These women figured she'd have a better shot with us," Anne added. "They named you specifically after reading one of your articles on inclusion versus seclusion."

Kerry widened her eyes. "Nicest compliment there is, when other professionals want you on their team. She'll start tomorrow?"

Anne nodded and stood. "I know this puts you at twenty-six, but Rita Dumrese will be in to help you daily, and Jan Morehouse on occasion. And your room mother sheet filled up faster than anyone else's."

Kerry made a face. "Including Mrs. Perrotto, who seems determined to watch over Anthony by being as up close and personal as we allow her to be." Mrs. Perrotto was the full-on definition of *helicopter parent*, constantly hovering around her over-indulged son.

Anne pursed her lips. "If she causes a problem, let me know. I don't want your class disrupted."

Kerry gave a brisk nod. "Me, either."

Anne's focus on children was the primary reason Kerry had resigned her higher-salaried public school job. The academy offered less money but more leeway in a Christian environment. All kinds of kids came through their doors, with one commonality. Their parents wanted an old-fashioned school experience. Kerry would have given anything for that kind of chance as a child, so to her, the academy wasn't just a job. It was a mission within a mission.

At Daystar, children came first. Anne, Father Joe, and two other local ministers had worked to turn a struggling school into an accepted, now coveted, den of ecumenical education. Two years ago they'd contracted for an addition, allowing them to expand to two classrooms per grade level. Not bad for an out-of-the-way school in rural Phillipsburg. Outlying districts bused kids from all over, providing a growing base and a wonderful mix of normal. Kerry walked with Anne toward her office. "Left my lunch stuff in the teacher's room," she explained, noting the look of question.

"Your refrigerator isn't working?"

Kerry nodded. "Yes, but I just plugged it in so it wasn't cold. I'm mixing my tuna here, anyway. I like it fresh. Something about tuna sitting in the refrigerator makes me think of cat food."

"Appetizing thought." Anne's cringe indicated it wasn't the least bit appealing.

Kerry jingled the change in her pocket. "It costs me a dollar nineteen plus the price of the bread and a piece of lettuce to have a deli-fresh sandwich."

A frown creased Anne's forehead. "I wish we could pay you more, Kerry. All of you. Maybe someday that will be possible."

"I knew what I was getting into when I signed my contract," Kerry answered as she paused at the door of the teacher's lounge. "I'm getting by just fine. Hannah keeps my rent low in exchange for yard help, so we've got the perfect arrangement going. Don't apologize on my account."

"Still," the older woman made the turn toward her office, "it's different for some of the others. They have husbands making money as well. For you, on your own, it can't be easy to make ends meet.

It was and it wasn't. She had few bills, she spent little money, and she had carefully tucked herself into a quiet existence purposefully. She'd purposefully left her old life outside of Rochester and moved ninety minutes southwest to this quaint Southern Tier hamlet.

She loved it here. She loved the anonymity of her existence. In Phillipsburg, she wasn't one of Chad McHenry's girls. She was Kerry, plain and simple. She was OK with that.

The theme from *Jaws* rang out as she started back to her classroom. Anne poked her head out of her office door, surprised.

"My warning knell," Kerry told her as she withdrew the phone. "I chose this music because this guy has *high risk* written all over him. I figured I might need a constant reminder."

Anne burst out laughing as Kerry answered Ryan's call.

Yes, he was an amazing doctor dedicated to saving children's lives, and a smokin' hot date. That made him a dangerous mix for a woman who loved kids and still believed in romance despite a wealth of reasons not to. But pairing Ryan with romance spelled trouble with a capital *T*, so why did her heart ramp up when the warning notes sounded? Because hearts were untrustworthy organs, that's why. She answered the call as she retraced her steps down the hall. "What's up, Doc?"

"Long time, no see, Kerry."

"I know. It's been weeks." She didn't mention that ninety minutes wasn't exactly on the other side of the world; it was a simple car ride away. He'd either figure that out or he wouldn't. "How are you?"

"Lonely. Missing you. Wishing you were here."

Ryan's tone reflected his words. The guy knew how to work his voice, no doubt on that. She matched his manner.

"Me, too. Come see me."

"Wish I could. I'm on call, remember?"

"Um, no." Kerry thought back to their last conversation as she walked through her classroom door. "You were supposed to be on call tomorrow night."

"Dr. Amico asked to switch up. He wants to be home to get the kids off to school in the morning. His wife's out of town, and their littlest one gets first-day jitters."

A reality Kerry could understand. "How about tomorrow night? Can we meet in the middle? Have supper?"

"I'd like that," Ryan agreed before his voice went more serious, and she kicked herself for not making him drive the distance. If he really cared, would it be a big deal? No. "Tell me again why you have to teach three steps shy of the state line?"

"Because that's where they built the school?" She wouldn't spar with him. She had made her choices for her own reasons, none of which Ryan seemed to understand. To him a job was a job when it came to the education market, and nailing the best pay-to-performance ratio wrote the story. It wasn't that simple for Kerry.

"Very funny. Maybe I should ask why you have to work over seventy miles away at all. We have some of the best school districts in the state between Buffalo and Rochester, with lofty pay scales to boot. What *is* the draw out there, Kerry? I know it's not the paycheck."

His tone rankled, and Kerry had to put some old emotions on lockdown before she replied. "Money's not everything, Doc," she reminded him. "There's an intangible down here. An intangible I see reflected at Daystar. And it makes me happy. End of story."

"Hey, I'm the guy who helped roll your quarter jar two weeks ago so you could buy supplies the academy can't afford to provide. I'd just like to see you appreciated and properly compensated for all you do. Living on tuna and scrambled eggs has to get old after a while."

It did, but Kerry remembered Anne's words a few minutes before. How two professionals had lobbied for her to be a child's teacher, trusting her to do the job and do it right. Wasn't that what she worked for all these years? "Some rewards are intrinsic, Doc. Or spiritual."

There was a short silence. In a more subdued voice, Ryan acknowledged her statement. "I guess I'm just missing you, and being a jerk because of it. Where should we meet tomorrow?"

His change of tone lightened the moment. "How about the Steak House on Towle Road? I could get there by six thirty. Is that good with you?"

His voice relaxed a note further, probably because he only had to drive halfway. "It's fine with me. Gotta' go. Call coming in from the service. Tomorrow, Ker."

Kerry contemplated the phone before setting it aside to eat her inexpensive sandwich that suddenly didn't look all that good. What was she doing?

Ryan was suave, funny, focused, and hard working. He was GQ-model good-looking, no matter what he threw on. He loved the high life; he was quite comfortable being upper-income, single, childless and was always ready for a good time, almost her polar opposite.

So why the attraction? Was she trying to fix him? Tempt him? Convert him?

She didn't really know. Something in him called to her.

Sure it does, her conscience scoffed. *Your neuroses calling his neuroses and both discovering they're a perfect match. Let's get real, here.*

She mulled that as she planted fall-toned mums along Hannah's front walk later that day. She'd been attracted at first sight. Dark, curly hair. Gray eyes, both wise and cryptic. A quick smile that didn't always reach those eyes, and that was a problem.

He was ridiculously smart, and a nonbeliever in anything spiritual. What was she doing?

Taking it one day at a time, she assured herself. Sure, Ryan had issues. Who didn't? If she took her proceed-with-caution mental memo seriously, she'd be fine. Just fine. Right now she needed to focus on the looming first day of school, and seeing Cassie's picture today meant she better be on her A-game.

She'd lived the experience of being the castoff in a room full of normal kids. She could usually keep the old thoughts at bay, but not after seeing the picture of a sorely neglected child. Her heart had gone tight as she gazed into the girl's eyes, recognizing her needs. She understood the Cassies of the world better than most.

Ryan was right about one thing. Daystar Academy couldn't afford the public-school-sized paycheck that would make her monthly budget easier to manage, but Kerry had managed on so little for so long that her current lifestyle in Phillipsburg seemed almost opulent by comparison.

"Kerry!" Hannah's bright voice interrupted her thoughts. Her land-lady had walked to a neighbor's house an hour before, and now both elderly widows approached from the short, sweet Main Street a block away. "Oh, isn't this a sight for sore eyes. Maddie, what do you think?"

"I think I'd like to hire Miss Kerry to come do mine, if she's got time," Madeline Schultz declared. "I can't get up and down like I used to, but I appreciate pretty flowers as much as the next person. Would you mind, Kerry?"

"I'd love to help." She stood, brushed the dirt off her knees, and surveyed the hour's work. One hour of her time made such a difference to her elderly landlady. "Is Saturday morning OK? They're calling for rain on Sunday, so let's get them in. Do you need me to buy them, Mrs. Schultz?"

"Maddie, dear, just plain Maddie, and no, I'll get them myself when I run down to Wellsville with my son on Thursday. I've only got room for about eight or so, but what a joy they'll be through fall! I can hardly wait, I'm that delighted! Can I pay you in cookies, dear? Or does cold, hard cash work best?"

"Maddie Schultz, you old skinflint." Hannah folded her arms, insulted enough for both her and Kerry. "Both, of course. You know the pay over at Daystar isn't all that great; you're on the board for pity's sake." Hannah sent her friend a sharp look. "Now your molasses cookies don't hold a candle to mine, but those thumbprints of yours are the best around. Two dozen cookies and a twenty should suffice."

"Oh, now…," Kerry started to interrupt, but Mrs. Schultz took no offense. She laughed and waved off Kerry's protest. "When she's right, she's right," she said. "Cookies and cash and I'm still getting the better end of the deal. A pretty garden, right up to the first hard frost, and if this is the last autumn I see, it will be a worthy one."

The last autumn…

At twenty-seven, Kerry never thought in terms of "last" anything, but the women before her had different perspectives.

"I'll be there Saturday, first thing."

"Thank you, honey."

Hannah grinned and winked as Kerry gathered up the tools and stored them in the small backyard shed.

She liked helping others. Did that make her simple? Or special?

She wasn't sure, but it felt good, and for now, that's the feeling she'd embrace.

* * *

Ryan glanced at his dashboard clock hours later and scowled. Nearly ten. Hopefully the rest of the night would be quiet, but cancer came with no guarantees. He'd known that and had chosen it anyway. Proving a point? He worked his jaw and sighed.

Maybe. It didn't wipe away the past he abhorred, but it made him feel good to help kids in their hour of need.

Penance or payback? He wasn't sure, and it really didn't matter, did it?

As he pulled into the driveway of his townhouse, he let his thoughts wander to the earlier phone call with Kerry. He paused on the lowest step overlooking the upscale, lake-fed cove.

The girl was a cross between Eleanor Roosevelt and Joan of Arc, devout, energetic, opinionated, industrious, and downright beautiful. She pulled him like Ulysses to the Sirens. That intimated loss of control, *his control*, and Ryan didn't give up control. Ever. Where were Circe's words of warning when a guy really needed them?

He puffed a breath into the cool September night as he climbed the steps.

He didn't need a mythological Greek enchantress to steer him clear of Kerry McHenry and her staunch beliefs in a beneficent God. He was his own man, no ifs, ands, or buts. Ryan understood firsthand that fairy tales existed between the pages of children's books and animated DVDs.

He'd leave the Cinderella stories to them and take life one day at a time, solid and straight.

What more could a man need?

Nothing of consequence.

He'd figured that out as a kid, as his mother bounced her way in and out of his life, just enough for the courts to allow some level of visitation, something she used for her own good. Never his. He hadn't realized it then. As a kid, he'd just plain longed for his mother to love him.

Didn't happen.

He'd learned to use his intelligence to personal advantage. Long ago he'd set his sights on a good-paying career and a keep-your-distance attitude that had served him well so far. But it got him absolutely nowhere with Kerry McHenry, and that was beyond annoying.

Maybe that was it.

Perhaps the draw was because he was thwarted by lack of conquest. She played hard to get, and because that wasn't exactly the norm with women these days, his interest spiked.

Could it be that easy?

He wanted it to be that easy.

He wanted to find a simple reason behind this attraction, because the outdated notion of falling head over heels for a woman would never be his Achilles' heel. He'd watched his father try everything to keep his mother happy, and nothing had worked, and if a great guy like Dan O'Donnell couldn't make marriage work, Ryan didn't have a snowball's chance on a hot August day.

You called her.

You keep calling her.

What's your game plan?

He didn't have one where Kerry was concerned. Maybe that was the most aggravating thing of all. Without a plan, he wasn't sure which move to make and his erratic actions were probably exasperating her while they were frustrating him.

Those eyes...

That hair...

Her smile, so sweet, so kind, so inviting.

And an innocence he found appealing and maddening all at once.

She'd invited him to church.

He hadn't laughed. He'd wanted to, but he hadn't.

His father had taken him to church as a child, every week. More than that, actually, being Catholic. Holy days. Special services. Religious education classes. And then it came time for confirmation, and Dan had sat him down and said that being confirmed was a big step. An adult step, something a mature mind took seriously. That saying yes to God, to accepting Christ as God's Son was an affirmation to be serious about.

He had left the decision in Ryan's hands.

Had his father been brave or foolhardy? Ryan wasn't sure, but he walked away from church with greater respect for his father, because how many dads would put that decision in the hands of a kid?

Dan did, and that was a long time ago.

But now, old thoughts had begun to creep in.

His father never pressed, but he and Claire still attended the old gray-stoned church by Lake Ontario. He sponsored several fundraisers at the church, and Ryan gave willingly because his father believed and his father was a good man. A great man.

But he'd let a woman rule him for most of Ryan's childhood, and in retrospect, that made little sense to Ryan. His father should have cut and run at the first sign of trouble. As a physician, Ryan understood the value of a clean, sharp cut. Less pain, faster recovery.

He walked into the upscale, chic home he shared with Vic, another specialist.

Vic had just gotten engaged. He and Mandy would be planning a wedding, and Vic would move out. Start a new life.

Well, good for him. He'd worked hard and deserved whatever joy came his way.

Ryan wouldn't think about how empty the stylish digs would be once Vic left. It wasn't as if he couldn't afford the place on his own. He could, easily.

But for thirty-five years on the planet, he'd never been alone. Ever. And a part of him wasn't sure how that would be.

chapter five

Waiting at the road's edge, Cassie teased the hem of her shirt, then scuffed her toe in the dust-brown soil. Shifting her weight, she worried the woven fabric of the pink and purple top again. She bit her lip, watching. Maybe the new bus wouldn't come. Maybe they'd forgotten her.

But then engine noise warned of the bus's approach well before it rounded the upper bend, and there it was, bearing down on her, all orangey-gold with big black tires and crisp black letters marching along the side.

Cassie gulped at the size.

This wasn't the little bus with the nice, big woman in the driver's seat. This bus was huge and loud and could hurt a little girl if she stepped into the road and forgot to look both ways. Clutching her sack, Cassie stared as the bus rolled to a stop.

A man was driving. He had gray hair on some of his head and none on top. He wore glasses. He was big, but not really big. He looked at her, squinting. She looked at him, too, making assessment.

"All right, little girlie, I haven't got all day," the man offered in a booming voice. "Come on up here. I'm on a schedule, you know. I think Brady Stanton has a seat saved for you. That right, Brady?" The man's head tilted up. His gaze went to the mirror, a mirror just like the one on Mrs. Chapman's little bus.

"I do, Mr. Dennis." It was Addie Stanton's voice Cass heard as she climbed the first step.

The man before her nodded. "Well, good then. You head back by Adelaide, and she'll get you to your classroom at school."

Cassie stared at him, then down the long aisle. Addie poked her head around the corner of a tall seat. "Come on, Cassie," she called, her smile welcoming. "Come see what I have."

Cassie moved slowly, aware of the looks she was getting. One ugly boy pinched his nose when she went past, and crowed, "Smeeeeeeellllllllly. P. U.!"

She frowned at the phrase. Smelly p.u.? What was that? She sniffed audibly. She couldn't smell a thing except the fruity scent of someone's gum. She sat with Addie but made herself as small in the seat as she possibly could. Maybe they'd ignore her if she ignored them first.

"Here." Addie set something in Cassie's lap. Cassie looked down, then up, meeting Addie's smile.

"My mom sent it for you."

It was a banana, bright yellow, with no brown spots on it yet. Cassie didn't like brown bananas. They were yucky. Yellow ones were really good.

"And this." Adelaide handed her a pack of three cookies, the soft, chewy kind that reminded Cassie of Addie's mother. Her mouth watered, eyeing them.

"Can I have one now?" Cassie whispered. She didn't want others to hear; she didn't want them to guess how hungry she was. How the smell of that molasses cookie, all golden brown and chewy, was making her mouth water at just the thought.

Addie's look said she understood. She smiled down at Cassie. "Those are for later, at snack time. How about this instead?"

She handed over a wrapped rectangle with bright words printed across the front. Next to the words was a picture. A jug of milk stood next to a dark red bowl filled with flaky cereal.

"It's a breakfast bar," Addie told her. "It's like a bowl of cereal and a glass of milk all rolled into one. They're really good."

Cassie looked up at her, amazed. "I can have it? Really?" Just then her stomach growled in anticipation. She darted a glance around, embarrassed.

No one seemed to notice or care. Most were involved in chatter of one sort or another. Addie tore the top off of the wrapped bar. "Here you go."

Cassie savored that first bite.

Addie was right. It *was* good. Chewy and sweet, but crunchy, too. Relishing the blend of flavors, she tried to eat slowly, making it last, but hunger pushed her to speed. The delicious bar was gone quickly.

"Then there's this." Addie plunged a thin, yellow straw into the tiny hole of a silver pouch patterned with pictures of fruit. Cassie eyed the metallic sack, suspicious. Addie prodded her with a smile. "Try it, Cassie."

The fruity liquid was clear in the straw and cold and sweet in her mouth. Concentrating, she pulled on that straw again and again, feeling the sleeve relax in her hand. When the pouch was quite thin, she held it out and looked at it. The juice inside had to be the most wonderful thing she'd ever tasted. "What was that?"

"A juice pouch," answered Addie, taking the thin, aluminum sleeve and throwing it away in a sack to her left. "Mom thought you might be too excited to eat at home, so she said she'd send breakfast every day."

Cassie stared, then gulped. "Every day?"

Addie nodded agreeably, then turned away, her nose wrinkling. "Yup. Every day. If you'd like it, that is?"

Cassie almost smiled. She felt it touch her eyes but not quite curve her lips. "I like it. A lot."

Addie turned back and smiled. "Good. My mom will be happy to hear that. I'll bring more tomorrow."

When the bus pulled into the big parking lot, there were kids everywhere. Big kids, little kids, dark kids, light kids. Some in-between kids, like her. They were all over, milling about, jostling one another and shouting words of welcome.

Addie took Cassie's hand and led her through the throngs. They stopped at another big bus. Addie nudged Cassie forward. "Here we are."

Cassie hung back and looked wistfully at the brick and glass school. "We can't go to school? Why?"

Addie turned, her look puzzled, then shook her head. "This isn't our school, Cassie. This is Phillipsburg Elementary. We're going to the academy."

Cassie darted a look from the familiar building behind her and then back to Addie Stanton. "What is that?"

Now it was Addie's turn to frown. "No one brought you in for orientation?"

Cassie frowned more deeply at the big word. It wasn't one they used on *Daniel Tiger* or *Dora*.

Addie took her hand. "Our school is smaller, but I think you'll like it. Have you met your teacher?"

Cassie gave her a blank look.

Addie smiled and patted Cassie's head in a manner like her mother's. "Don't worry. I'll walk you to kindergarten when we get there. And you'll like Miss McHenry. She's young and pretty, with really long hair that she wears in a braid kind of like Elsa, and she wears really cool clothes." She retook Cassie's hand and led her up the bus steps. "Come on. We're blocking the way."

In no time at all, the bus pulled into a smaller lot near an old, ivory-bricked building. There was green stuff crawling up the side. Some kind of plant. Cassie furrowed her brow, staring. Plants grew on buildings?

The building looked strange to Cassie, but Addie stayed with her, leading her through groups of kids. Near the end of the hall, the bigger girl looked left and right, scanning lists on open doors.

"Aha." Addie's tone sounded happy. Giving Cassie's hand a reassuring squeeze, she led her into the room on the left. "Miss McHenry?"

A young woman raised her head and looked at them. She was so pretty that Cass had to take a deep breath, long and slow.

The lady's blue eyes sparkled. She did have a long, golden braid of hair lying thick across her shoulder, just like Elsa's. Only Elsa was a cartoon, and this lady was real.

"Addie!" the woman exclaimed. She crossed the room in quick, smooth movements, then reached an arm to the older girl and hugged her shoulders. "And who's this?" the woman asked, her pretty eyes focused on Cassie.

Cassie stared, dumbstruck. The woman crouched down to her level, the smile bright and friendly. She stuck out her hand. "I'm Miss McHenry, your new teacher. And you're...?"

Cassie stared at the hand. Grown-ups were always doing that to her. At least the ones in schools. They stuck their hands out. Was she supposed to give them something? She felt a tiny lurch to her heart. She didn't have anything to give the pretty lady with twinkly eyes. She knit her forehead, thinking.

"When I stick my hand out, you're supposed to grab it, like this," the lady explained. She took Cassie's right hand and placed it in hers. She shook Cassie's hand up, then down. Cassie looked up, confused.

The teacher kept smiling. "See? That's called shaking hands. We do it when we meet somebody new, or see someone we haven't seen in a while. It's a way of saying hello without the words."

"But you used the words." Cassie studied the woman's face as she spoke. This time her voice didn't bring a curious look. The lady only nodded as if Cassie were normal. For a brief moment, she felt normal.

"I sure did." The teacher laughed. "I usually use the words, Cassie, because I can't seem to stop talking." She patted Cassie's shoulder with a gentle touch. Cassie smelled something pretty, like a walk through the old orchard behind her house. "You'll get used to it.

"So, let's practice," the teacher continued. "I come up and say, 'Hi, Cassie. How are you?'" The teacher stuck her hand out once more. Cassie eyed the hand, then accepted the gesture. They shook, their gazes locked.

"Perfect." The lady's smile deepened. She gave a quiet nod to Addie but didn't let go of Cassie's hand. "Shall we find your desk?"

Her desk? Cassie Carruthers had a desk?

At preschool they'd had tables, long and thin, with rows of little chairs. Everyone chose the chair farthest away from her. If she sat next to them, they'd make funny faces and move, their noses scrunched. Sometimes they'd pinch their noses while they made faces at her. One time a girl with a pretty green dress put her hands on her hips and scolded, "Stiiiiiiiiinky!"

But this lady was nice. She smelled like fruit. *The lady smells good,* Cassie practiced to herself. *The lady smells fruity.* She narrowed her eyes at that thought. Could people smell fruity? Obviously so. But how? She sent a puzzled glance to the woman beside her.

"Ah, here it is." Still smiling, the lady paused by a desk near the front. "Cassandra Carruthers." She pointed a soft finger to the name on the desk. Cassie looked at the letters, tracing the shapes with her fingertip, mouthing them as she went. She nodded.

At nearby desks, children were unpacking loaded backpacks. Green ones, blue ones, princess ones, flowered ones. One was red and blue and had a big buffalo sprawled across the front. A blue buffalo? Cassie frowned in wonder. She'd never seen a blue buffalo on the Discovery channel.

A dark-haired boy with a sour face had a silver science bag. She stared at that one in particular. It wasn't like the others, silly and babyish. The shiny bag had cool, experiment things on it, like she saw with *Bill Nye, the Science Guy.* Cassie stared at the backpack, enthralled.

The lady drew her attention by saying, "Honey, you'll find some things in your desk. You can use a crayon or a pencil to write your name on them. OK?"

Cassie nodded, her eye still on the bag.

"Cassie?"

Tearing her gaze away, she refaced the lady. "Yes?"

The lady winked and passed a soft hand over her head. "Welcome to kindergarten."

As the lady moved away to see other children, Cassie cast one last, longing look at the cool, silver book bag, then bent to check her desk.

* * *

From across the room, Kerry kept a quiet eye on Cassie's reaction. The girl's eyes widened as she withdrew the thick, bright box of forty-eight crayons, then pencils, a tablet of writing paper, and folders. Bending deeply, she reached in again and pulled out a pair of purple-handled scissors. Kerry watched Cassie practice the cutting motion, her tiny fingers plying the scissors with care. Then, her attention diverted as three more children entered the room, Kerry lost track of Cassie until she heard Anthony Perrotto yell, "Get your filthy hands off that, ugly! It's mine!"

Turning, she spotted Cassie next to Anthony's desk as he snatched his silver bag out of the girl's reach.

Cassie's face was distraught. The harsh tone of Anthony's voice shook the girl's composure. Her normally flat countenance grew anxious. She wrung her hands, a silent plea. Her eyes hunted the room for a chance to escape.

In short steps, Kerry reached the pair of children. She crouched and laid a hand of comfort at Cassie's back. She kept her voice easy. "Is there a problem, Anthony?"

Anthony was never called Tony. His mother was adamant on that. A nickname wouldn't do.

"She put her dirty, filthy hands on my bag." His voice churned with righteous indignation in a tone similar to the one his mother employed. Kerry bit back a sharp retort and gave the boy a steady look.

"Where was your bag?"

"On my desk."

"And where was it supposed to be?"

He winced, caught. She'd given him explicit instructions to empty the bag and hang it under his cubby. He hadn't followed directions because he was pretty sure rules only applied to others. She arched a practiced brow meant to instill some level of self-control into five-year-old minds. "Well?"

He sputtered. "But she was touching it when she's not supposed to. It's not hers. It's mine! And it cost a lot of money!"

Kerry increased her pressure to Cassie's spine in a show of support. "Answer the question, please. Where was your book bag supposed to be, Anthony?"

He dropped his eyes more in anger than submission. His toe scuffed the carpet. "Hanging up."

"Exactly. Which is what you need to do right now." He grabbed the bag, chin down, and began to turn away. "And, Anthony?" Kerry paused and waited until the boy turned sullen eyes to her. "We don't yell at others, insult them, or talk to them in that tone of voice. If you do that again, to anyone in this room, there will be consequences." Her look told him the consequences wouldn't be good. He shuffled his feet once more before trudging across the room, bag in hand, muttering all the while.

Kerry turned her attention to Cassie and shook her head. "I don't like it when people yell at me," she confided, keeping her tone low and friendly.

Cassie hunched her shoulders, as if drawing herself inward. "Me, either," she whispered.

Kerry slid her glance to Anthony's departing back. "You like Anthony's bag?"

Her gaze moved to where the stocky boy now hung the backpack. "Oh, yes," she whispered, her fingers working together. "It has science stuff on it."

Kerry sat back on her heels, contemplating the reverence in the child's voice. Then she smiled and again passed a gentle hand across the head full of stringy, stressed curls. "And you like science?"

Cassie nodded, her eyes still trained across the room. "I do. I do like science."

"Well, then, you're going to love kindergarten, Miss Cassandra, because I love science, too. Would you like to see my microscope?"

Cassie's eyes went saucer-wide as she shifted her gaze to Kerry. "You have one? A real one?"

"I do." Kerry straightened and looked across the room. "Mrs. Dumrese?"

"Yes, Miss McHenry?"

"Can you take our little friend over to the science station and show her some slides through the microscope?" With her eyes, she sent a more silent communication.

Mrs. Dumrese smiled, crossed the room, and clasped Cassie's grungy hand. "Come with me, darling, and I'll show you the wonders of the universe."

Cassie hung back, her expression doubtful. "They'll fit?"

Mrs. Dumrese didn't miss a beat at the intelligence level of the question. Leading the way, she answered in a tone that stayed bright. "We'll target the smaller ones today. Cells and bugs and stuff."

Cassie gave a brief nod. Kerry noted the glimmer of excitement in her eyes, although her heart-shaped face remained impassive. *Cassie Carruthers,* she thought as the combined sounds of twenty-five other children waylaid her ears, *my goal this year is to have you run and play with other children. To see you smile on a daily basis. To get to know you better.*

She'd no more than finished the thought when Cassie glanced up, her green eyes seeking Kerry. Meeting Kerry's look of approval, Cassie's eyes grew cautious, then curious as she approached the mysteries of the microscope with Mrs. Dumrese. Almost indiscernible, her lips curved in a tiny smile as she contemplated her teacher and the scientific scope in front of her.

Winking, Kerry smiled back, considering the first day a resounding success.

The hour hand on the school clock hadn't hit the nine, but that didn't matter to Kerry. She'd made headway, first thing.

It was a great way to start a new year.

chapter six

Ryan watched from the far corner of the steakhouse dining room as Kerry followed the maitre d' through the maze of linen-draped tables. He tried to ignore the attention she drew from the male-dominated lounge as she passed through. He found it impossible, and that aggravated him.

Kerry seemed oblivious to the appreciative glances. He stood and opened his arms in welcome, sending a silent territorial message to single guys at large. *Taken.*

But she wasn't.

He inhaled long and slow before he relaxed his grip. Floral and fruity, soft and feminine. He slid her chair out, then sat next to her, leaning forward. He clasped her hand and brought it up for a kiss. "How was your first day?"

She raised her brows, amused. Her gaze moved from the hand that clasped hers to Ryan's mouth and back. She gave a brisk nod. "Great move, Rye. Well practiced?"

He laughed and squeezed her fingers. "Yes, actually. Polished on a regular basis. It's worked until now."

She slipped her fingers out of his with a knowing smile. "I bet it has. My first day was wonderful."

"How many kids?"

"Twenty-six."

"Boggles the mind."

Kerry shrugged. "Yes and no. I love it."

"I know you do." Ryan edged closer and took a deliberate sniff once more. "And you don't smell like crayons and glue sticks."

Kerry laughed. "That's why I said six thirty. I needed time to clean up, or that's exactly what you would have gotten, a girl that smelled like a kid's art project. I like that tie." The blue silk was patterned with multicultural kids' faces. "Did you wear that for me?"

"I did. But it's a favorite in the office, too. Glad it impressed you."

She twinkled up at him and laughed. "You could show up in gym sweats, and women would be impressed."

"Often are."

"Mmm-hmm."

He leaned forward and looked into her bright blue eyes, and for just a moment, he imagined a tiny girl with those same blue eyes, and maybe his curls. He shoved the notion aside and focused on the here and now, because that was his mode. "What would it take to impress you, Kerry?"

She met his gaze. This time her eyes were thoughtful. "Faith in God and a life-long commitment."

She was deadly serious, so he refused to be. He sat back with a *thunk*. "Foiled again."

She reached for her menu, undeterred. "And so easily, too."

"Lifelong commitments?" Ryan opened his menu and then slapped it shut. He was ordering prime rib, why waste time? "Scientific studies ascertain that only a few species pursue that particular practice. Today's more than 50 percent divorce rate indicates man's not among them."

"Pessimist."

"Pollyanna."

She grinned and closed her menu as well. "That's me."

He leaned her way again. "So, tell me. Why are we attracted to each other at all?"

There was nothing timid about Kerry. She looked right at him and met his gaze without a hint of hesitation. "Maybe I'm your destiny. Maybe I'm who God picked, and it's just taking you a while to recognize that."

His destiny?

No such thing. Ryan attacked everything with a course of action, ensuring a regularly scheduled good time on the side. There was no such thing as destiny or Providence or the "God's plan" schlock one of his medical partners waxed on about *ad nauseum*. People charted their own paths, right or wrong, good or bad. He was sure of that, but when she met his gaze with a long, cool look, a chill coursed up his spine.

He refused to let Kerry witness the effect of her quiet words. He flashed her an easy look that downplayed the rise of emotion, and raised one finger slightly. As the waiter moved to answer Ryan's silent summons, Ryan swung back to Kerry and offered his best rogue smile.

He swiped a hand across his brow in mock relief. "Now that we've got that settled, let's eat."

* * *

Cassie heard the furtive sounds that night and tried not to be afraid. Tiny noises. Tinier feet.

She shrunk beneath the thin covers and pulled them up, over her head. The rank smell of the unwashed bedding wafted into the room, dank and strong. If she didn't move, didn't wiggle at all, the stench wasn't so bad. But then her head would be uncovered, a target for whatever was running with such itty, bitty feet. When it came to a choice, smelling the sheets or being nibbled by rats, Cassie would pick the nasty sheets.

Any day.

* * *

"Did you have a good time last night?" Mrs. Wilder had been sitting on one of the front porch rockers. She perked up as Kerry shut the car door and started up the walk. "Your young man didn't see you home?"

"It's a haul from here to Rochester," Kerry reminded her. "Meeting in the middle works best."

The elderly woman didn't look convinced. "My Uncle George, God rest his soul, fell head over heels in love with Aunt Rita 'bout near the first time he laid eyes on her."

"Did he, now?" Kerry leaned against the sturdy porch rail because sometimes Hannah's stories were short…and sometimes they weren't.

"She was a pretty thing, not used to hardship with her daddy bein' in business and all, but she caught George's eye, and there was no holdin' him back. He was workin' just above Houghton, doing some sort of engineerin' or surveyin' for a company out of Albion." She sat back in her rocker, her dark eyes easy, remembering. "Rita and her mother had gone up to do some shopping. George, he fell, hook, line, and sinker, and it didn't matter one whit that it was a fourteen mile trip each way, and an older horse besides. Calling on Rita meant more than anything, and like George used to say, 'If I didn't have the gumption to do it, someone else would have.'"

"He went fourteen miles one way on horseback?"

Hannah nodded. "Nearly two hours there, two hours back. He 'bout had enough time for a howdy-do and a piece of cake, but George considered it time well spent. In the end, he won the girl, and that's what it's about, isn't it? Least it was back then."

Two hours, each way. On horseback. In all kinds of weather.

Ryan seemed reluctant to drive the hour and a half in an air-conditioned Beemer.

Sacrificial love.

She'd longed for that all her life, someone who cared enough to sacrifice for her, like she saw on all the best made-for-TV movies.

Perhaps that was the problem. Her problem.

She didn't want real; she wanted fairy tale sweetness rolled into a convenient package. If she was honest with herself, that would knock Ryan out of the picture right away. "They got married?"

"Had three kids, nice youngsters. Two live on the West Coast now with their families, and they're about my age, but I always used George as a barometer when young men came to call. If they weren't willing to ride fourteen miles each way to see me, I cut 'em loose quick. Why waste time?"

Why, indeed?

"But I do know that things are different now, not that it's necessarily a good thing." She stressed the word *good*. "Still, we have to go with the times. One way or another."

Fourteen miles.

Kerry went upstairs, assessing the distance, the time, the sacrifice.

Ryan O'Donnell didn't come close. Nor did he want to, and that was a disappointment. He was happy letting her drive halfway, and she was stupid enough to do it.

No more.

If he couldn't man up and behave like George, she wanted nothing to do with him. She went to sleep thinking of earnest men riding horseback for hours to court fine, young women.

Devotion, dedication, and loyalty. Were they too much to ask? If they were, she was ready to be done looking, because one way or another, she wanted the dream, the whole thing. And if she couldn't get it?

She'd settle for being the single, country schoolmarm in a quaint, hillside town.

* * *

Cassie was being ostracized because of the way she smelled, and Kerry needed to address the situation. But how? She met with Anne and presented the problem frankly. "The other kids are staying away from her, and they've all mentioned the odor," she told the school principal. "Which means she's on the outside of everything because no one wants to be near her."

"Kids can be cruel in their honesty."

They sure could. "So how can we fix this?"

"What about the shower in the nurse's office? I'm sure Terri would be glad to oversee it for you. You'd have to present the idea to Cassie, though."

Kerry took Cassie outside the classroom the next morning. She took her to a nook down the hall and explained the idea of taking a shower in school.

"Like right here in school?" Cassie wondered. "This school?"

"Yes."

Cassie's gaze turned serious. "When I was in that other place, Mrs. McCabe showed me how to do some things like that. Like how to turn water on, not too hot. And to be careful because wet things are slippery."

Her voice stayed deep and flat, as if there was nothing in life to get excited about. Nothing to look forward to.

Kerry remembered that all too well. "That was good advice, for sure. Let's go see Mrs. Johnson, OK? The shower is in the bathroom in her office."

Cassie took her hand, uncertain, but she walked beside her to the nurse's office just off the main hall. "Mrs. Johnson?"

Terri Johnson looked up with a welcoming smile. "Ladies, hello. What can I do for you?"

Kerry stepped into the room and brought Cassie along with her. "Cassie and I have had a little talk, and she was wondering if it would be all right to use the shower in your bathroom. She's not sure how to use hers at home."

"Can't see why not," Terri replied. "Have you ever given yourself a shower, Cassie?"

The little girl pushed herself more firmly into Kerry's side. "At school," she whispered.

"Cassie was with the BOCES program at the elementary school last year," Kerry explained. "Mrs. McCabe worked with her on some independent living skills."

Terri nodded. "And good skills they are. Come with me, Cassie. I'll get you started."

Cassie hung back. She clung to Kerry's hand, suddenly afraid. Her voice was a plea for salvation. "Can't you help me?" she whispered.

The fear in her voice weakened Kerry's resolve, but there were twenty-five other students waiting for her in Room Two. She stooped to Cassie's side. "I'd love to help you, but Mrs. Johnson is the shower expert around here. She knows how to get the water just right: not too hot, not too cold. Then she'll bring you back to me." Looking down into the face that had known so little but learned too much, Kerry fought her basic urge. Her nurturing side wanted to stay with the child. She'd be willing to bet no one had taken the time to bathe the child amidst a circle of bobbing tub toys since her mother's death and maybe not even then.

But she was Cassie's teacher, not her mother, and her job was to foster the girl's independence and strengthen her for whatever lay ahead. With that in mind, she extricated herself from the firm grip and turned Cassie's care over to the capable hands of the small, dark-haired nurse.

The class was doing prayer circle when Cassie returned. She had on a different dress, one from the cupboard loaded with cast-offs. Wet bottoms and torn knees were a given in elementary classrooms.

Kerry sent the girl a smile of welcome, then indicated a seat beside her. Cassie slid in looking uncertain and a little proud. Her thick, curly hair was wet and unruly but smelled of sweet summer strawberries, a big improvement.

A few of the kids offered her a look of wonder, as if trying to ascertain what was different. But Brian Voorhees was requesting prayers for his pet iguana. The reptile had disappeared three days before and hadn't been seen since. The idea of a large lizard lurking within the confines of a small, country home caught the collective attentions of the kindergarteners. Cassie's state of cleanliness was overlooked in the prayerful excitement.

At dismissal time, when everyone else went for their jackets, Cassie held back.

"No jacket today?" Kerry asked.

The little girl pressed her lips into a thin line. "It's not that cold."

Kerry wasn't sure which of them she was trying to convince, because it had gotten downright chilly the previous night, but she respected the girl's show of bravado. "And it's supposed to be warmer tomorrow."

The child's solemn eyes went round. "Yes."

"The bus is warm."

"Mr. Dennis gave me a little blanket this morning."

It took effort for Kerry to maintain a placid expression. It had been thirty-six degrees in Phillipsburg that morning; they'd had a killing frost in the valley. Driving the short distance to work, ice crystals had clung to the spent fronds of grass and flowers, painting the fields white. The season was officially done. What kind of father sent his little girl out in shirtsleeves at thirty-six degrees?

She gave Cassie a warm smile and a pat on the head. "Mr. Dennis is a nice man."

Cassie nodded, her voice grave. "Yes."

Once Cassie left, Kerry pulled up a cute jacket on the Internet, ordered it, and had it shipped to the school. *When I was naked, you clothed me...*

Clean clothes and a warm winter coat. Little things, greatly needed. She didn't think about her meager paycheck or her rent. She'd make do. She always did. The joy of seeing Cassie clean and warm was gift enough.

chapter seven

"Kerry, honey, you don't have nothin' better to do on a Saturday night than play cards with an old woman?" Hannah wondered the following evening.

"Hannah." Kerry met the older woman's frank gaze with a teasing smile, then laid down her hand. "I can't think of anything more rewarding than taking you to the cleaners. Gin."

Hannah peered at the table, then her cards. "Mr. Wilder never let me win, either."

Kerry laughed. "If you're not playing to win, there's no point in stepping on the field."

"I agree, which brings me right back to that on-again, off-again young man of yours."

"I wouldn't exactly call him *mine*." Kerry shuffled the cards and pretended she wasn't wondering the same thing. She'd prefer no relationship to sporadic. Games didn't work for her. Ever. "But I do believe you told me I should test the waters, right? Cast out a line or two?"

"Castin' is fine, but if the fish aren't inclined to bite, the smart woman pulls anchor and shifts locations."

"So I should shop around."

Hannah shrugged as she sorted her cards. "Keepin' options open is just plain smart. I always found a man committed to faith is more likely to be committed to his family."

Kerry's father hadn't committed to anything, ever, so the old woman's veracity tweaked a nerve. "I hear you, and I can't disagree, but it doesn't feel right to show interest in one direction while walking in another."

"Why is that any different from what that young man is doin'? I expect he's on call this weekend?"

Kerry was pretty sure he wasn't on call, and that reality irked her. "I'm not sure."

"Mm-hmm." Hannah played her card, eyes down.

"You think it shouldn't be this much work to reel a man in."

Hannah's expression softened. "If it's the right one, it shouldn't be any work at all. Temptin' a man to love us was not the good Lord's intention. The right man will love you simply because he can't help himself."

"In spite of himself."

"Oh, no." Hannah shook her head firmly. "I've seen unlikely matches work out just fine, but only when both are fully invested, not reluctant contributors."

"I think it's harder for some to commit, don't you?"

Hannah snorted. "That's a P.C. way of callin' a player a player. No matter how good-lookin' he is. And you wouldn't be the first woman to get herself into a boatload of trouble by thinkin' you can fix things. That you're just what he needs, if only he could see it."

Kerry winced because Hannah had read her mind.

"God's the true fixer." She drew cards, rearranged her hand, then peered over at Kerry. "Not you, not me, not random fate. We get ourselves into a mess tryin' to force square pegs into round holes. When the fit's right, it feels right. Anythin' else is settlin', but don't you be takin' too much of this to heart," Hannah added as she played her cards and laid down her hand in a surprisingly short number of moves. "You're young, you've got time, and I might just be tryin' to divert your attention so I win this hand. Gin."

Kerry conceded the hand with a frown. "Your strategy worked. And now"—she put the cards on the table and stood—"I must go. I promised the reverend I'd do a shift at the Harvest Festival after church tomorrow, and I've got some lesson planning to do. I'll see you in the morning."

"I might come help at that festival myself," Hannah declared as she walked Kerry to the door. "It's been a few years since I bothered, but this year I feel like botherin'."

"See if Maddie will come along, too," Kerry suggested. "I could drive us all down to the community center together."

"I'll call her first thing, she might be that pleased to get an invite. She gets crotchety, but she's less likely to be sour if we keep her busy."

"Then putting her to work is doing her a favor."

Hannah's face creased into a broad smile as Kerry went out the door. "That would be my take on it! Thanks for playin' cards with me, Kerry."

"My pleasure." She winked at the old woman and went upstairs to her apartment, determined to let things ride.

Ryan had a life. She had a life. The narrow overlap made a perfect Venn diagram, but was that how a relationship should be? Mostly one's self, then a smaller joining of the two?

Love does not insist on its own way…

She knew the Corinthians verses by heart, words of wisdom, strength, and grace, but were they real? Or just an apostle's poetic renderings of how he thought the world should be?

She was thinking too much. Hannah was right about that; a girl shouldn't have to think a thing to death. She jumped into her lesson outline for the next two weeks, sent out an e-mail to parents reminding them of the upcoming teacher conference schedule, and then typed a reminder letter to Cassie's father.

Would he come? Would he bother? She didn't know, but when she finally climbed into her nice, soft bed, a pang of remorse hit her, imagining the child's circumstances. There had to be some way to help Cassie, something more concrete than a standard classroom afforded. But what? And how?

She wasn't sure, but she went to bed determined to find a way.

* * *

Ryan showed up at his father's later than he'd promised on Sunday. Dan made his point by glancing at his watch, then at the empty dock leading into the water.

"You pulled the boat already?"

"Hours ago. I thought you weren't on call this weekend?"

"I'm not."

His father usually shrugged things off when Ryan messed up. This time he didn't. He held Ryan's gaze like he had years ago, and it wasn't hard to see the disappointment in the older man's eyes. "I went out last night, and one thing led to another."

"Ah." Dan turned away, shoved his hands in his pockets and started for the shore.

He said nothing more. Just that simple two-letter word that meant nothing and everything.

"Listen, Dad, I'm sorry." He was, too. His father had been nothing but good to him all his life. Why would he take that for granted when he saw kids without fathers all the time? "I know I promised to help put things up."

Dan kept walking, silent.

"Let me help with the dock. Then I'll order us pizza, and we can watch the late game together."

"Claire's making dinner. Jenn and her family are coming over."

"Good. The more, the merrier." He didn't mean that. Oh, Jenn and her farmer husband and two kids were fine, but he used to be able to just stop in at his dad's, help himself to anything, and wander back out.

Now he couldn't.

He liked Claire. He liked her a lot. She was great for his father, but this whole melding a family thing was a pain in the neck.

They brought the rolling dock onshore, then made sure the boathouse was secure, and when they were done, Ryan looked around.

He'd grown up here. His father's crazy restaurant schedule had meant weird sacrifices, but growing up along the shore, having the freedom to work the vastness of Lake Ontario, fish when he wanted, play when he could. His father had tried to make normal out of abnormal, and he'd done well. So why was Ryan never satisfied?

"Hey, Ryan, wanna see my art project?" Hallie raced his way from Jenn's car, and her little brother Ozzie was close behind.

"Sure do." He squatted and admired her handiwork while Ozzie scrambled onto his knee. "Hey, bud."

"I used the potty free times." The little guy worked to hold up three fingers, and it took a bit of effort to make that pinky stay down. "I got free suckers and a sticker."

"Whoa." Ryan widened his eyes, and the little guy did the same. "That's pretty cool, Oz."

"I know." He hopped down, so proud. So innocent. So cute. "My mom is so proud of me!"

"Hey, Ryan." Jenn waved as she carried a dish up the walk. "Nice to see you."

"You, too." He roughed up Ozzie's hair, making the boy shriek, then picked him up. "Hallie, your project's great. Nice job." He headed toward the house with Ozzie slung upside down over his shoulder.

"My mom e-mailed it to Aunt Kerry, and she loved it, too. She said she thought it was my best ever, didn't she, Mom?" Hallie skipped ahead, beaming.

"Those were her exact words."

"And she called me something." Hallie screwed up her face, thinking. "A funny name."

Jenn bent low. "She called you a bright little poppet."

"Yes!" Hallie smiled wide. "I'm a poppet! Here, Auntie Claire." She handed the project to Ryan's stepmother. "I made this just for you, to be so pretty in your house."

"Oh, darling." Claire stooped and made all the appreciative sounds a good mom or aunt was supposed to make. "It's absolutely stunning. May I put it on the refrigerator?"

"Yes!" Hallie clenched her hands together as if being displayed on the stainless steel door equated a Manhattan showing. "It looks so nice up there!"

"It does." Jenn palmed her head. "Can you go get that little box I had on the back seat for Aunt Claire? I forgot to grab it."

"Sure!"

"I'll go too!" Ozzie raced after her. The screen door slapped softly shut in his wake.

"I wanted to go over the Apple Fest schedule with you, if you're sure you don't mind helping again." Jenn grabbed a seat at the breakfast bar and laid out a couple of papers. "Kerry's coming up for the weekend, and I'm there, too, and I've got two of the farm stand girls helping in the afternoons, but if you could come join us for the mornings, that would be awesome."

"I'm glad to, and I'll wear old stuff to man the deep fryer," Claire said as she stirred a big pot of sauce, thick with meatballs and sausage. "And remember that we ran out of the fritter boxes last year, so we need more on hand."

"Ordered and in," Jenn agreed, jotting things down as Ryan watched nearby.

Family helping family. Promising to do a job and showing up to do it. He would be willing to bet that Kerry wouldn't arrive four hours later than planned. And she'd arrive with a good attitude, ready to jump in, with absolutely nothing in it for her.

Commitment. Why did he find it so hard in some things and so easy in others?

He'd aced undergrad, nailed med school, and then specialized after his residency. He'd done it all, on his own, step by step, determined to win big and win hard, and he had. So why did he suddenly feel half-empty?

Dan came in the back door with Jenn's husband, Will. Will clapped Ryan on the shoulder. "You think Buffalo's got a chance?"

He used to think that, but he'd learned his lesson the hard way after years of chronic football disappointment. "For my mental and emotional well-being, I'm refusing fan-hood from now on. I will only cheer from a fantasy football perspective. Losing a few bucks is way better than losing my heart."

"I hear ya'." Will commiserated and grabbed a couple of Claire's cheesy sausage balls, fresh from the oven.

Dan seemed disappointed by his words, as if putting it all on the line for football meant something. It did if utter disappointment at another's hands was the way to go.

It wasn't. Not for Ryan. He'd form his own happiness his way, thanks, and while that might not please his father, it pleased him. At least it had pleased him for years, but now— lately— he wasn't nearly as certain.

chapter eight

Monday morning dawned cold. The sky loomed ominous. A dark blanket of clouds hung low, heading east from Lake Erie. Lake effect snow was a common winter malady. The wind blew intemperate, a raw day for October, a portent of things to come. When the children arrived, laughing and shivering, Cassie sidled up to Kerry's desk. She looked scared.

"Hi, sweetie. How was your weekend?"

Deeper angst narrowed the girl's eyes as she proffered a shaking hand. "Here." She whispered the word in a voice so tiny, Kerry almost missed it. Taking the note from the child, she opened it.

"Nobody better be taking my girl's clothes off at your school."

Uh oh. Kerry frowned and sighed, then looked down at Cassie, trying to figure out what to do.

Should she go see him? Talk to him?

But what if that backfired and he got angry? Withdrew Cassie from Daystar and sent her back to Phillipsburg? Or worse, didn't send her to school at all?

The worried look on Cassie's face confirmed what Kerry surmised. The child had been in trouble over the weekend because they'd given her a fresh outfit to wear after her shower in the nurse's office.

Cassie handed her a ragged bag. Opening it, Kerry found the dress they'd used, wrinkled and crammed into the plastic sack. She accepted the sack and kept her voice low.

"Did you get in trouble, honey?"

"He was mad." Cassie's frightened look said the rest.

Kerry palmed her head. "Fathers like to take care of their own little girls. I guess I can understand that." Even as she said it, she wondered what to do about the little jacket that was tucked inside her desk. Deciding quickly, she rose, murmured to Mrs. Dumrese, and hurried to the bus loop.

John Dennis was still there. She rapped on the folding door and waited as he opened it.

"Miss McHenry. Come to visit, did you? Come on up here where it's warm. That wind has a bite to it." His face was curved into a smile, and the other bus drivers greeted her in kind. He waved an expansive hand toward them. "We have fifteen minutes before we start our last run of the morning. So here we sit, solving the problems of the world."

Myrt Anderson hooted. "Some problem solvers we are." She grinned at Kerry. "We can't even agree on what color to paint the town garage, Ivory Stone or Waterford Green. Puhlease! Have you ever heard of a green town building? Who came up with that?"

"I'm pleading the fifth on paint colors," Kerry told Myrt. "Whichever way they go will look nice with that evergreen forest backdrop, won't it?"

"You've got the heart of a diplomat," the woman declared. "Now come on, the rest of youse, Miss McHenry's got something to say to Denny, and I'm sure it's not a lick of our business."

Kerry waited while the drivers exited, then held up the small coat. "Cassie doesn't have a coat to wear."

Mr. Dennis folded his arms. "I've noticed that as well."

"She told me you gave her a blanket the other morning."

He shrugged as if being nice to a little kid was no big deal. Kerry knew differently. "I've got a jacket for her, but I don't think it would be wise for her to take it home. Could you—"

"I'll keep it right here on the bus," he interrupted. "It'll hang on this peg, alongside mine. She can grab it in the morning, nice and toasty from the heater, and hang it back there when I drop her off. That way she just has to run to the house."

"I'd appreciate it, Mr. Dennis. Thanks."

He exchanged a knowing look with her. "My pleasure."

At dismissal, she handed the coat to Cassie while the other students gathered their belongings. "Try it on, Cassie."

It was perfect. A touch big to allow for growth, the cute jacket would hold warmth to her body.

"Can I wear it?" Cassie's flat voice hinted emotion.

"You may. It's yours."

Big eyes regarded her. Cassie kept her voice soft. "But what about at home?"

Kerry squatted to Cassie's level. "Dad didn't say anything about a coat, did he?"

Cassie shook her head.

"Mr. Dennis said you can keep it on the bus if that makes things easier. He'll hang it on the hook next to his so that it's nice and warm when you get on in the morning."

Looking into Cassie's eyes, she knew the child understood what she was saying, that maybe it was better not to take the jacket home just yet. Nodding, the girl traced the embroidered flowers with the fingers of her right hand. "It's so beautiful, Miss McHenry."

"Just like you, kiddo." She winked at the little girl, then waved her toward the door. "Now, go on. Get out of here. That bus can't wait all day."

Watching the child work the zipper with capable hands, Kerry bit back a sigh at the forced independence and the lack of affection. What kind of person neglected a child and ignored their needs?

At least Cassie wasn't abused in a typical sense. Her father never struck her that anyone was aware of. Kerry watched for signs that would indicate such a change. So far, so good.

But starving the girl for affection was a crime in Kerry's book. To never know a hand of love, a warm embrace, the smell of fresh-baked cookies cooling on the counter, welcoming you home after a hard day at school? She'd dreamed of those things as a child, simple things. Caring things. The sort of family she saw on TV and never knew firsthand. That was her dream, her goal. To someday be that kind of wife, to be the best mother she could possibly be to a little brood of cherished children.

Cassie almost pranced to the bus, her jacket zipped snug against the crisp fall wind. Her hair was still ragged, and the dank smell of old urine was a detriment to five-year-old friendships, but there was a growing air about Cassie Carruthers. She had a survivor's nature. Kerry's heart fell just a little bit more when the child turned and lifted her hand in a shy wave. With a heartfelt smile, Kerry waved back.

Bless her, Lord, and watch over her. Keep her from harm's way. You've guided her to me. Let me be a channel of your peace, a friend to Cassie Carruthers.

"Kerry?"

Anne's voice hailed her from behind. She turned from the main door and started forward.

Whoa.

Over six feet of amazingly good-looking deputy sheriff stood next to Anne. He was saying something to one of the first grade teachers, then looked up.

His gaze met Kerry's. He paused. Wait, no, scratch that...

Pause wasn't a strong enough word. It was more like he came to a complete stop when he spotted her, the kind of reaction that set a woman's heart to doing all kinds of unexpected things.

And then he smiled.

She wasn't sure if her heart would stop, stutter, or simply race out of control.

She reached a hand to her hair, as if fixing it, but what was there to fix in a braid?

Anne set her hand on his left arm as Kerry approached, "Kerry, this is Deputy Jake Slattery. He's coming in to address the kids tomorrow. He'll talk to them about policemen and trust and doing the right thing. I have your class scheduled for nine thirty, right before their PE time. That way you can elongate your planning time if needed."

Planning?

While this guy was in the room?

Kerry wasn't a gambler, but she was willing to bet there wouldn't be a smidge of planning done in that thirty-minute time slot.

No ring.

She didn't mean to check, but as she'd walked forward, she couldn't help herself, so how lame was that?

He reached out a hand and clasped hers.

Electric.

Pure and beautiful and totally charged full-on sparks went through her system.

His grin deepened and so did the appreciation in his eyes. "Just call me Jake, miss."

"And it's Kerry," she told him.

He didn't let go.

She didn't try to break free.

The first grade teacher hummed and headed back to her classroom.

Anne cleared her throat. "So, about tomorrow."

Kerry slipped her hand out of his and tried to remember she was a professional. "That sounds fine, Anne. I'll prep the kids ahead of time, and is it all right if they ask you questions, deputy?"

"Jake," he reminded her in a warm, deep voice that resonated strength and kept her pulse erratic. "I've got a couple of boys at home. Questions are a constant, so yes, they can ask me anything."

Two little boys and no ring?

"Jake, I'm so glad you've got time to do this," Anne told him. "We really appreciate it. With the rising drug problems in the area, I want to foster a good student-police relationship early on."

"I agree, and yard work can wait. I expect we'll get a few more nice days before winter takes hold."

"You're doing this on your own time?" Kerry asked.

He shrugged. "It's better that way. Dedicated time. No interruptions," he made a pretend frown at the shoulder radio that came to life just then. "Like this one. Gotta go." He was already moving toward the door and keying his mike. "See you tomorrow, ladies."

He walked tall and strong and looked just as good from behind as he did from the front, and while she probably shouldn't notice that, she did. And he was coming in to build a relationship with area kids on his own time, a selfless act, and since Ryan had just blown her off for a whole weekend that he'd had free, Jake's sacrifice meant a little more.

"Widower."

"Stop reading my mind, Anne." Kerry scolded her with a look. "With two kids? Ouch."

"An accident on I-86 almost three years ago. Tragic. Abe was two, and Lorelei was expecting Ben. They delivered him unscathed, but Lorelei never regained consciousness."

"A newborn and a toddler?" Kerry stared at the door Jake had just walked through. "I can't imagine how hard that must have been."

"His aunt Susan and his mother are great helps, and his sister does daycare in Angelica, so when he's on days, Aria's got the boys. He's getting by. He's part of St. Mary's parish, and there's a bunch of people there that help out. Plus no small number of brownies and cakes that land at his door from single women."

"I bet." Kerry shoved the idea of baking him a cake way down the list and blushed that she'd even thought of it, but as she walked down the hall to her classroom, the warmth of his gray-green eyes called to her.

Warm caramel skin, not white, not brown. Short, dark hair under his sheriff's hat. A quick smile that didn't just meet his eyes; the twinkle lingered there, as if smiling at her meant something.

It didn't, of course, but it *felt* like it did, and as she drove back to her apartment after school, thinking about Jake's smile made her smile.

And that felt too right to be any kind of wrong.

* * *

Ryan's ring tone sounded as she walked into her apartment a few minutes later. She picked up the phone gingerly, as if talking to Ryan while smiling about Jake was unfair, no matter what Hannah told her. "Hey, Ryan."

A low growl greeted her.

"This is either a dog or my distinguished male friend. Maybe both."

"Ouch."

"Your own fault, Doc. You sounded like a dog."

"I'm growling because I'm lonely. Again. And hungry. Distinguished male friend?" He ended the last statement on an up-note. "Interesting description. What're you doing tonight?"

He'd been free all weekend, and now he was calling? When a call from the service could end their evening in an instant? "Aren't you on call?"

"I am, but I thought we could meet at Elm Creek. I can be back at the hospital in twenty minutes from there. How does that sound to you?"

A whole weekend had passed, and now he was trying to pack her into a narrow time slot that would most likely get interrupted. Kerry had been a gifted track-and-field runner in high school and college. Second place didn't work for her then. It didn't work for her now. "Sorry, Rye. Too many time constraints tonight. Another time, maybe?"

"Maybe?" Surprise and something else heightened his tone. "What about this weekend?"

"I'm at the Apple Fest all weekend."

"Volunteering again."

"Helping my sister, yes. Which I love doing, by the way. You could come to the festival and help us," she suggested. Would he do it? Would he even consider doing something like that?

He laughed it off, but it wasn't really funny. Not on Kerry's end of the phone. "Can't do it, sorry. I'm off next Monday, though."

She wasn't. "I'm working all day, then addressing the town council that evening about a drug outreach program we might implement. It's been successful in other rural areas, and I thought it might be helpful in Phillipsburg."

"You're a born do-gooder, Kerry."

He made it sound like it was a bad thing.

A stretch of silence went on too long before Ryan ended the call. "I'm getting a page, gotta go."

"All right."

He didn't say good-bye.

She'd irked him, but Hannah's advice and Ryan's actions had forged a wake-up call she needed. Their goals were different. They were on separate tracks, heading in disparate directions.

She saw the neediness beneath his polished veneer, but Hannah's advice rang truer this crisp October afternoon. He wasn't committed to her, or to anything, really. Except his job.

And she wasn't committed to him. She realized that now. Ryan called to the nurturer within her, but she'd watched her father do a real number on people with his noncommittal life. She'd lived the fallout of a parent who never cared about anything other than himself.

That wasn't a choice she was willing to ever make again.

chapter nine

Jake kissed Ben good-bye once Abe was picked up for school. "Mom, I'll be done at the academy by eleven or so. Then I'll come by and pick this guy up, all right?"

"I expect we'll be fine, won't we, Ben?" Ava Slattery winked at the little boy.

Ben scrambled up onto a chair and grinned back at her. "I 'spect we will!"

His mother followed Jake to the door, which meant she wanted to say something unsuitable for three-year-old ears.

Great.

"Hurrying out will not prevent me from speaking my mind, Jacob."

"It never has," he admitted and didn't pretend that was a good thing. "But I've got to get to Daystar by nine o'clock, and it's a fifteen-minute drive. Can it wait, Mom?"

"Can *you* wait is the question at hand." She folded her arms and pointed outside. "You are so busy helping change the world that you're forgetting your primary duty is to these boys. Your sons. Your flesh and blood."

She meant well. He knew that, but she'd never been a single parent, and worse, he was a single parent with a job that offered a particularly good overview of growing trends. The spike in drug-related arrests and deaths wasn't something that could be put on hold, even if she thought he was wasting his time. "That's not true. I'm trying to ensure that the community around them is as safe as we can make it, Mom. This isn't a Jake Slattery campaign. It's a county-wide outreach to teach kids to trust the police, to stay off drugs, and obey rules. That can't be a bad thing."

"Except that you're spending half of your only day off this week looking out for other people's children. I appreciate hard-luck stories as much as the next person, Jacob."

That was not true. His mother was a good person, but she had a pull-yourself-up-by-the-bootstraps mentality that rivaled an entire right-wing political conference. "Gotta go, Mom."

"I'm simply saying that your daily example of hard work and law and order should be enough for the community, unless you're doing something that also involves the boys, Jake." She set her hand on his sleeve and held his gaze, and Jake had learned a long time ago that respecting his mother was a smart thing to do. "You're their only parent, through no fault of your own. I love being here for them and with them, but don't let yourself get so blinded by what others need that you forget your first responsibility is to these two precious boys."

"I never forget that, and as much as you disagree, this is for them. A safe community is vital."

"I know." She put her hands on his cheeks, and she didn't scold although she probably wanted to, because they both understood why he was doing this. If he could keep kids from drinking and using drugs, maybe others wouldn't have to go through what he went through three years back, burying a victim of an out-of-control drunk driver. "I pray for you, Jacob. Every day."

He knew that, too, but she might as well save her breath.

He didn't say that out loud. Even a big guy like him wasn't stupid enough to dismiss a mother's claim to faith, but Jake had walked the walk and talked the talk for three decades. Then his world fell apart, his son survived because of a scientific medical miracle, and here he was, a decorated officer, wanting to make the world a better place for two little boys. "I appreciate it, Mom. But I appreciate the babysitting even more."

He headed to his car.

His words would worry her.

He didn't have the energy to care. His parents had brought him up to be a cornerstone of the church, to pray and sing and offer God praise.

But what kind of God snuffed out the life of an expectant mother weeks before she was scheduled to give birth?

Did God take her life? Or was it the three-time offender that climbed behind the wheel drunk to the gills four months after they suspended his license?

Jake backed out of his mother's driveway and headed toward Daystar. It might have been a conscience-less drunk driver who took Lorelei's life, but if there was a God, he had let it happen. And that was enough for Jake to swear off pew-sitting and Bible-thumping for life.

* * *

A soft tap on the kindergarten door indicated their morning guest had arrived.

Twenty-six pairs of eyes turned in that direction. Most of them looked excited to see Jake standing big and broad on the other side.

Not Cassie, and not two other little ones from rural addresses.

Kerry crossed to the door and scolded her pulse. Then her heart. Then her pulse again. By the time she opened the matte-finished oak door, she was pretty much at war with herself. "Good morning, deputy."

He tipped the brim of his hat ever so slightly. Just a tweak. Just enough.

And then he grinned.

Oh, be still her heart…clearly it was a ridiculous and fickle organ.

"Deputy is OK in front of our little friends." He kept his tone soft, but that wasn't easy to do with the deep timbre of his voice. "But Jake's fine, Kerry."

She blushed.

She knew she did because of the heat in her cheeks and the smile on his face, but she rolled her eyes at him because wasn't she already skating the edge of one smooth, practiced, polished guy?

Yup.

Which meant taking things slow and easy was her game plan no matter how wonderful the deputy sheriff looked when he eased that slow, warm smile her way. "Come on in." She swept the door wide. "Class, I'd like you all to meet a new friend."

She closed the door after he entered, then preceded him to the front of the room. "This is Deputy Jake Slattery, and he stopped by to tell us about police officers. What they do, how they help people, and how they work to keep us safe. Come on up here." She motioned to their circle area. "Let's show Deputy Jake how we can gather, learn, and listen together, OK?"

"OK!" Most of the kids hurried to the front.

Three moved more slowly, including Cassie.

"Can I show him my snake?" Peter Calabrese held up a clear plastic container as he stood. "I bet policemen like snakes a lot, Miss McHenry."

"Later," she promised. She glanced up at Jake.

He was eyeing the snake, the boy, then her, and then he smiled again, just a little. He leaned closer...just a little. And met her gaze. "Kindergarten sure has changed in the thirty years since I sat at one of these," he indicated the miniature desks with a look, then smiled right into her eyes. "For the better, I'd say."

He sank down to the floor to be more in line with the class, but even doing that, his size, his broad hands, and his deep voice kept the children watching in awe.

He didn't talk at them. He spoke to them in a deep, caring voice, gentle and strong all at once. He won their attention, a rarity in any grade, but especially when dealing with five-year-olds.

And as he smiled, joked, and teased the children, he won a good share of Kerry's attention, too.

All too soon it was time for him to leave.

The class groaned collectively, but when Kerry raised her hand for quiet, they calmed down, though not without several reluctant looks. "Can we thank Deputy Jake for coming by today?"

"Thank you!" A chorus of little voices rang out.

Not Cassie's. She stared, round-eyed, at the big deputy. And the two little boys from Cooper Road stared too, but they at least looked curious, as if maybe Jake was all right.

Cassie didn't relax. From the moment he'd walked in the door, she'd wrung her hands and stared as if waiting for something bad to happen. The fact that nothing bad happened didn't seem to help.

Rita gathered the class and took them to the gym for PE. Jake waved good-bye to them, then brought his attention back to Kerry. He pointed to the adjacent first grade. "I'm due next door."

She nodded, pretending to be calm, suave, and totally together while wishing he didn't have to hurry away.

And still he lingered, as if he was feeling the same way. He met her gaze and held it. "I've got kids at home, Kerry, so I'm not free to go out the way most guys are when they want to get to know a pretty woman."

He called her pretty and was concerned for his kids first and foremost. Mental checks in the plus column found their way next to his name.

"But my sister could keep the boys on Friday night if you'd do me the honor of having supper with me. They've got a couple of nice spots in Olean. If you'd like to think about it—"

"Think about a date? You?" She smiled up at him and was deliciously happy when he smiled back. "And me?"

"That's the formula I was considering. What do you say?" The first grade classroom door swung open, no doubt looking for him. "You can let me know—"

"Or I could just say yes right now so we can both consider how nice it will be," she supposed.

His smile deepened. "Definitely my preference." He tugged his hat into place. "I'll stop by when I'm done this morning to get your number. All right?"

"I'll be ready."

He moved to the next classroom, not as if he were in some big, all-fired hurry to get this done, but easy, like a lumbering bear, taking charge and having all the little bears look up to him.

Smitten.

She wouldn't have thought it possible, but clearly it was, and she might have to thank Mrs. Wilder or blame her. Right now she wasn't sure which.

*   *   *

You asked the kindergarten teacher out on a date.

His sister would think it was wonderful. His mother would take one look at Kerry and wince, not because Kerry was white, but because Abe and Ben were black.

Jake never saw color. Never had, and that was because his biracial parents raised him that way, but he had two dark-skinned sons from his beautiful wife, and he knew the idea of dating Kerry would tweak his mother's concerns. Could a white woman accept black children? And if that was a concern, why date her?

He knew why.

His heart beat harder in his chest the moment he saw her. It sped up, then thumped against his ribs, then sped up again.

Her eyes sparked with appreciation, and her smile just about did him in.

He'd stayed out of the dating circuit for a long time, but the moment he laid eyes on Kerry, he wanted to change that status.

Was he crazy?

Probably, but his parents' marriage had worked for nearly forty years.

Not that he was thinking about marriage.

The quick direction of his thoughts offered its own wake-up call.

But he wasn't stupid, and everything he did now affected Abe and Ben, so he didn't have a childless man's freedom to date whomever, whenever.

But he was sure of one thing later as he put Kerry's number into his phone.

He wanted to get to know this woman better, and Jake Slattery hadn't felt like that in a long time. He knew the rules; he understood the game plan of a single dad, dating. He'd get to know Kerry, then introduce the boys if all went well, a calm, systematic approach geared toward the boys' well-being.

Step by step romance? His conscience scoffed. *I'm pretty sure that's not how it works. Or maybe you've forgotten that part?*

Jake ignored the thought. For three years, he'd heard advice from all possible angles. Date. Don't date. Spend more time with the boys. Give the boys breathing room. Stay active. Chill out. And the constant of constants: Give it time.

He'd found out the hard way that time didn't come with guarantees, so while he appreciated the good intentions behind the mountains of advice, Jake was tired of other people's opinions, even the well-meant variety. This time, he needed no encouragement or convincing, because the thought of getting to know Kerry McHenry totally appealed.

His sister threw a wrench in his plans with a frenzied text on Friday afternoon. *"Norovirus! Two down, one to go. Sally Ann grabbed Ben and Abe to remove them from harm's way, but I can't watch them tonight. So sorry, Jake!"*

He dialed her back because kids with a stomach bug weren't fun. "Aria, I'm sorry. That's a tough weekend for you guys."

"It is," she agreed, "but I felt terrible telling you. And with Mom and Dad in Pittsburgh for that wedding…"

"Which means all your advice about finding a nice babysitter for the times when you and Mom weren't available should have been followed."

"I am smart," she agreed, and he had to smile. "And you're rock-solid stubborn sometimes, so this is like the natural consequence of your inaction. Of course the real test of a woman's character is how she handles the kids, so you could make it a foursome."

Jake had been thinking the same thing, then reminding himself that every self-help book advised an elongated process for the getting-to-know-you phase. The thought of having supper with Kerry and the boys didn't seem like a bad idea at all. She was a kindergarten teacher. They were little kids. How traumatized could the boys be from one simple supper? And yet… "I'm pretty sure that makes me a self-serving bad parent. The books advise against it."

"Did you really read those books?"

Not entirely, no. "I may have skimmed," he admitted. "Somewhat."

She laughed. "Listen, I might be wrong, I often am, but I can't see a huge amount of lifelong harm coming from one Friday night supper. But then, I'm the laid-back one of the family. Mom would lecture at length, but you're a grown man, and Mom's out of town. I say go for it. And have fun, Jake."

He couldn't.

He didn't say that to Aria. She'd want to scold him, and there was no time for that, but no. He couldn't put the boys in that kind of position. He'd skimmed the single-parenting books, yes, because he actually understood his role in all of this. He was a dad first.

He didn't sigh. He picked up his phone and hit Kerry's number. Breaking a date at the last minute wasn't a smart thing to do, but it was smarter than thrusting innocent kids into a first date scenario. He pulled the cruiser into a parking lot and waited for Kerry to answer.

Jake's number flashed on Kerry's phone as she walked out of school. Either he was calling to say he couldn't wait to see her or to break their date.

Pessimistic view, her conscience scolded.

Or a trained reaction after her on-again, off-again relationship with Ryan O'Donnell. "Jake, hey." Kerry held the phone between her ear and her shoulder while she groped for her keys as she approached her car. "What's up?"

"I've got to cancel, Kerry."

Be smooth. Be calm. Be cool. She started to pretend it didn't matter, but Jake jumped back in. "My sister's kids have come down with the stomach bug going around, my mom's out of town, and I don't have a backup sitter for the boys. And Kerry, I'd just bring them along, but I have to play that single-parent card again." He sounded truly torn, and that raised his status slightly out of the high-risk zone. "Once you and

I know each other, it's fine to include the boys. But I can't do that yet. I hope you understand."

She wished she didn't.

She wished she thought he was an insensitive lout for brushing her off and putting his sons first, but she actually liked the way he prioritized, even though she hated breaking the date. "I get it, Jake. Too many parents rank their dating life ahead of their kids, so it's actually nice that you put the boys first."

"Really? You're OK with this? Because my parents are due back midday tomorrow, so if we could rearrange—"

Kerry winced, unseen.

"I can't plan anything for this weekend. I'm tied up helping my sister at the Apple Fest tomorrow and Sunday. Jenn and her husband own an orchard west of Rochester, and this is a big deal for them. Fall is their crazy busy season, so I stay with them for the weekend and offer free help to keep the profit margin solid."

"That's good family stuff right there." The approval in his tone felt good. She hadn't realized how tiresome it was to have to explain her desire to help others. "Family helping family is important. You're there all day?"

"Until it closes at five." She climbed into her car and shut the door. "But I'll spend the night with them, then work until midafternoon Sunday. Then lesson planning Sunday night."

"Do they have kids' things at the festival?"

"It's geared for families, so, yes. Wagon rides, games, straw mountains to climb."

"It seems like the backup plan has been thwarted, too."

Bad timing all around. "So it seems."

"I'm sorry about tonight, Kerry." His regret sounded sincere. "But I want that rain check, OK? I'm working next weekend, and school nights are a bear with Abe. He's one of those kids who really needs his sleep, or he's a brat in the morning."

It wasn't the first rain check Kerry had given out lately. "We'll rearrange when we can, Jake. And I hope the boys avoid the bug; it spreads fast in schools." A tone signaled an incoming police call on his end. "I'll talk to you soon, OK?"

"All right."

He sounded grim, as if he hated putting her off. She understood his decision, but she'd been looking forward to an evening that included strappy shoes and an eye-candy escort.

In its place, she plotted two weeks of reading readiness and one third of the Christmas recital music needed for their mid-December school play. And while she worked, she pushed thoughts of Jake and a fun evening aside. Parents didn't come with the same set of freedoms so many took for granted.

Her phone buzzed a text from Ryan. "*Just heading home from hospital, kid in crisis. Miss you.*"

He'd spent a good share of the night trying to save a small life, so maybe she was judging him too harshly. Maybe the demands of his job kept him from committing.

You're making excuses for him. Again. Don't confuse dedication with bad choices.

That was the hardest thing of all. She saw the promise within Ryan, the depth he rarely tapped into. And she recognized the neediness. It drew the side of her that longed to help.

But was that love? Or simply the longing to fix things?

Another text buzzed through twenty minutes later. "*Boys asleep, tuckered out, no sign of sickness yet. Fingers crossed. Miss you. Still sorry about tonight.*" A sad-face emoji blinked at her.

The emoji made her smile. "*We'll reschedule, stuff happens, especially with kids. Talk next week?*"

"*Yes. Or before. Preferably before. Good night, Kerry.*"

Preferably before…

Two words that meant a lot, underscoring his regret. She finished packing what she'd need for the weekend and went to bed early.

Two men.

Two different men, each with their own agendas. The movies made this seem reasonably simple, how to juggle and choose between suitors. Kerry was pretty sure it was anything but easy.

* * *

Cassie pulled her blanket around her shoulders and tried to read the little book. Her room was dark, quite dark now that the days were getting colder and there was so little to do.

Miss McHenry had given her paper and crayons and books to bring home. And a little pair of scissors, just her size. And some glue sticks.

She made pretty pictures to decorate her walls. Maybe if she made enough pretty pictures, her house would look like other houses. Maybe she'd be more like other people. But when she tiptoed out of her room to use the bathroom, the depth of mess shattered her pretend world.

The man was snoring again. He slept a lot now, but that was all right. He wasn't angry or growling when he was sleeping.

She moved through the dirty kitchen. The smell wasn't as bad in the cold weather, but the house was cold…so cold. She hurried to the bathroom, and then made herself wash her hands, like Miss McHenry said, even though she didn't want to put her hands in the icy water.

There was no soap.

She closed her eyes, thought of the pretty-smelling soap at school, and pretended to squeeze a generous squirt onto her hands.

Someday she would have sweet soap, sheets that didn't smell, and pretty hair.

She tiptoed back to her room. The TV was on, and there were football players dodging back and forth. She didn't understand what they were supposed to do and didn't dare change the channel with her father in the house. He'd grown more angry lately, and she'd felt the sting of his hand twice in the past few weeks, and she never wanted to be slapped again.

She crept back into the dark room and left the door open just enough to let some light in.

She put some glue on the back of a picture and stuck it to the wall. The drawing was her and her teacher. It didn't look like them, at least not a lot, but she knew it was her with Miss McHenry, and she smiled.

She didn't draw a picture of the policeman.

She sank onto the bed, thinking hard.

The man said policemen were bad. Very bad. And that they'd do bad things if they ever came to her house. But Miss McHenry's friend didn't seem bad. He seemed big and strong and nice like Gordon on *Sesame Street*. As if he cared about little kids and wanted them happy.

So how was that bad?

Was the policeman fooling her?

Maybe.

She created a few more pictures until fighting the cold and the darkness wore her out.

She slept.

chapter ten

"Gentlemen, this is going to be crowded today," Jake instructed once he'd parked the car in a village lot. "Don't run off, don't misbehave, and don't let me forget to buy some of Miss Kerry's apples."

"This is a long way to come for apples," said Abe. "They must be really, really good ones."

Jake kept it simple. "I expect they are. But there's also some fun stuff to do."

"I hear music!" Easier to please, Ben looked around, excited.

"When in doubt, follow the music."

"Let's do it!"

Sales tents lined the street and three sides of the small town park, but the organizers had given the prime spots to local farmers. Decorated wagons and booths rimmed the spacious parking lot, with a petting zoo on one side and wagon rides through a nearby orchard flanking the other end.

A band played on a raised portable stage, a dance company performed on a ground-level stage, and beyond it all stood Kerry.

Jake's heart went tight. A broad farm wagon was pulled up along-side the booth, and an eye-catching display of apples, cider, and baked goods lined the wagon's edge. Whitewashed counters and graduated shelving stood under the booth's broad, red canopy, and the steam of a fryer plumed from the back, filling the air with the scent of freshly-fried donuts.

"Can we get cotton candy?"

"Can we go see the clowns?"

"Can we play on the straw mountain?"

"Yes, yes, and yes, but let's check out the apple stand first, OK?"

Abe rolled his eyes as if fruit ranked dead last on his list, but Ben squeezed his hand tighter. "Sure, Dad!"

One so easy to please and one who resisted any kind of change. Was this normal?

He started to ponder that but then locked the thought down.

It might be normal, but the boys' lives had been abnormal with Lorelei gone, so normal became atypical by default. They didn't have two parents to balance their equation. They had one somewhat stuck-in-his-ways father who got a little badgered by his own well-meaning mother.

But they were doing OK, and that was the main thing. He took each boy's hand and began to cross the last leg of the people-filled parking lot.

Kerry looked up.

Their eyes met.

And then she smiled, and oh...*that smile.* As if he'd gone and done something wildly marvelous by bringing the boys up north to the festival.

"Jake!"

He raised each boy's hand slightly higher. "We heard there were some of the best apples and cider fry cakes this side of the Genesee River, ma'am, so me and my little partners here decided to take a little drive and check the evidence." He raised his left hand higher. "This is Abraham Michael Slattery."

Kerry leaned over the counter and stuck out a hand. "Pleased to meet you, Abraham."

"Just Abe." Abe let go of Jake's hand and stuck his hands into his back pockets with all the swagger a five-year-old could muster. "My dad said these were the best apples ever."

"Did he, now?" She slanted a smile up at Jake but shifted her attention right back to Abe. "Well, we don't like to brag, but I think your dad is right. Here." She held out a sample plate. "Honey Crisp and Crispins. See what you think."

"I f-f-fink something sure smells very good!" Ben beamed a smile up at Jake, then at Kerry. "And I don't f-fink it's apples."

"And this is Ben." Jake palmed the littler guy's head. "He's got a soft spot for food."

"Well, who doesn't? And it just so happens you boys came at the right time because I need your opinion. Folks have voted these to be the best fried cakes in all of Western New York, but I want you to tell me what you think because your opinion matters a lot. As long as it's OK with your dad."

"We're happy to help, ma'am. In any way we can." He let his eyes twinkle into hers, and when her color rose, he figured he was doing all right for an out-of-practice guy."

"My 'pinion matters?" Abe looked unconvinced but intrigued by the idea.

"Cross my heart."

"Reawwy?" Ben wasn't only persuaded, he was ready, willing, and able to jump on the bandwagon. He took a bite and grinned before he was quite done chewing. "I fink it's the very best, yes!"

"Your good opinion is clutch, Ben. But Abe…" Kerry turned those baby blue eyes on Jake's oldest son, and her look of concern was Oscar-winning material. Or she was being utterly sincere, and that was a prize-winner in itself. "I need to know what older boys think, too. If you need a little time—" She waved like she had all day, like they weren't surrounded by throngs of people milling about, searching for goods, booth by booth.

"I've got time right now, I think." He looked up to Jake for confirmation, and Jake nodded.

"Take all the time you need, son."

The women in Kerry's booth were smiling.

A few folks who'd gathered around the booth were smiling.

And when Abe took a bite of that delicious cider-glazed confection and grinned, it was like the whole group breathed a sigh of relief. "It's good!" He held the rest of the donut in one hand and offered her a thumb-up with the other.

She waved her hand across her forehead in relief. "Phew! I was just that little bit worried, Abe Slattery, that you might not love these like I do, because when I make them on Mrs. Wilder's back porch, I like to share them."

"You make these?" Abe didn't have to pretend to be impressed, because not only were the donuts melt-in-your-mouth amazing, the thought of someone making them close to home clearly delighted him.

"I do, and it's the Gray family recipe, so I am sworn to secrecy, but yes, I can make these and share them with my Phillipsburg friends."

"Hey, I'm from Phillipsburg!" Abe's wide-eyed grin showed twin dimples. "That's where we live!"

"It's a small world!" Kerry smiled at him.

The boys looked happy. Genuinely happy, and Jake knew they needed to move on to show the boys the sights of the festival, even though he'd like to linger a while. See Kerry smile. Watch as they glazed the donuts in the back and brought warm, sweet trays to the front.

And then Kerry undid her apron, tossed it onto the back counter, and slipped out of the booth. "Jenn, I'll be back in a few minutes, OK?"

"We've got this." Jenn waved to her, then him. "Have fun."

And there she was, with him, with them, and it didn't seem to matter a whit that their skin tones didn't all match, and when Ben wanted to climb the straw mountain but shied away, Kerry went right up there with him, while Abe led the way. They sat at the top and posed while he grabbed a picture with his phone, the three of them looking triumphant and happy in the bright autumn setting.

Old emotions swept him, but not bad ones this time.

Good ones. Good feelings. A mix of joy and pride and fun. He had to give her back to the booth a short time later.

The boys requested apples, more time to play, and begged for fried cakes. "Yes, but we'll get the apples and donuts on our way to the car," he told them. "We'll stop back and see Kerry and her family on our way out, OK?"

"OK!"

"Sure!"

Abe was tugging his hand, ever impatient. Ben grinned up at Kerry, more easy-going than his older brother. "I'm glad you got to play with us."

"Me, too." She winked at him, then brought her attention up to Jake. "I'll see you before you leave, OK?"

"Will do."

"Jake?"

He turned back and caught her eye. "Yes?"

"Thanks for coming up here. For making the trip."

His smile started from somewhere indefinable, somewhere deep inside. "It was an absolute pleasure, ma'am."

His words pleased her, but that wasn't why he said them. He said them because they were true, but when she flushed, he knew he'd done well. "See you later."

"I'll be here."

It wasn't a date like they'd planned. It was life unscripted. With two busy boys, sometimes spur of the moment worked best, and when they piled apples and fried cakes and cider into the car later, Ben grabbed his hand tight. "This was like the best day, Dad! Thank you!"

"You're welcome." He ruffled Ben's short hair. "What about you, Abe-man?"

"The straw mountain was the best, and I'm probably the best climber there was today, don't you think? Like fastest and best?"

"Indubitably."

Abe's smug look reflected his competitive nature. Ben's contentment mirrored his more chill personality. They'd both had fun, and Jake was pretty sure he'd impressed the girl, which made the day special for all three Slattery men.

Perfect.

* * *

He drove ninety minutes to see her.

Wait. Fix that.

Jake drove ninety minutes with two kids to see her. And then he hung out, let the boys play, bought them some great food, and headed home after saying good-bye.

He didn't fuss, whine, or make her feel guilty about helping or being so far north.

She drove back to Phillipsburg late Sunday afternoon, happy. Jenn and Will had a crazy successful weekend, the family worked together to make that happen, and Jake Slattery had gone the distance when least expected.

Just thinking of that made her smile, because in her fun, make-believe world of romance, that was how it was supposed to be.

She liked it.

* * *

Kerry motioned her teaching assistant over a few weeks later. "I'm worried about Cassie."

Liz Morehouse nodded. "Me, too. What do you think is wrong? What's going on?"

Two rows away, Cassie sat, head down, engrossed in a Dr. Seuss book, but she hadn't turned a page in several minutes. "She looks depressed," Kerry whispered. "Worried. I know she's all right when she's here, but she watches the clock as if dreading dismissal. I'm going to drive her home today."

Liz lifted a brow. "Do you think that's wise?"

Kerry squared her shoulders and drew a deep breath. "Amanda Stanton gave me some things for Cassie. I can use delivering those as my reason. Her father didn't come to open house or parent conferences, so I've had no contact with him other than that first note."

"Would you like me to come along?"

Kerry shook her head. "No, I'll be fine. It might seem threatening to double-team him. Can you do cleanup and get things organized for tomorrow, though? That would be a huge help."

Liz gave her an easy shrug. "You've got it, boss."

* * *

Cassie shivered, but not from the cold. It was sheer delight.

She was in Miss McHenry's car, and it was all clean and nice. Cassie sat deep in the seat, feeling the cushioned back, imagining herself a special lady, riding in a grand limousine. *Carry on, James,* she would say as the long car came to a halt. She had no idea what it meant or who James was, but she'd heard it in a real good movie, and the woman had flowed into a palace like a princess, her head high and people trailing after her. Oh, yes.

Cassie squirmed, imagining.

She could be a princess.

As the house pulled into view, illusion shattered. Glancing at her beloved teacher, Cassie bit her lip in apprehension. Thoughts tumbled in her head.

Teacher had never been here. She'd never seen the house. She'd never met the man.

Cassie's house wasn't like other kids' houses. She'd figured that out when the going-home bus stopped to let children off.

Some houses had flowers and trees. Some had flags flying high. She saw toys in the grass and swing sets in backyards. No one lived in a house like Cassie's. Her inner fear mounted.

Miss McHenry would see the house and not want to come back.

She'd see the bugs and hear the rats and say, "I'm sorry. I can't have a messy girl in my class. I don't want a child who eats off dirty plates and doesn't wash the floor. I want clean children. I'm sorry, Cassie. You cannot come to my school anymore. You must stay home now."

Wringing her hands, Cassie bit her lip hard, the sharp taste of blood making her mouth curl. *Maybe Teacher should go away. Just drop me at the edge of the driveway, like Mr. Dennis does, and go away. Then maybe she won't notice the house. Or the man. Or the smell and the dirt.*

Maybe she should—

At that moment, Miss McHenry turned. Her eyes went all squinty, then she smiled and put out a reassuring hand, covering Cassie's small, twining ones. "It'll be fine, honey."

Just that. *It'll be fine, honey.*

Somehow Miss McHenry understood what Cassie was so afraid to say.

Please don't make me stay home. Please don't hate me because my house is dark and my windows are dirty and my father smells bad. Please let me come to school some more. Please.

* * *

Taking Cassie's hand once they'd stepped from the car, Kerry kept her expression calm as they approached the door. Cassie knocked, then plied the handle. She pushed hard, and the door groaned as it gave way. She stepped in and called out, "I'm home. Teacher came with me. Hello?"

Long seconds followed her announcement. Kerry glanced around as her eyes adjusted to the reduced light. Staying focused, she refused to dwell on what she saw. She would sort that out later, when time was on her side. Right now her job was to speak to the father and reassure the child. With a soft hand to Cassie's back, she asked, "Did he go out maybe? Shopping or something?"

"Who's there?"

A gruff, abrupt voice sounded from the back corner of the front room. Kerry peered, seeing no one, but answered, "It's Kerry McHenry, Mr. Carruthers. I'm Cassie's teacher. I wanted to stop out and see you, let you know how she's getting on in school."

"She makin' trouble?" The voice moved forward.

Kerry forced a laugh and hoped it sounded natural because nothing about these surroundings could be considered normal. "Cassie? No, sir. She's the most well-behaved child I have. An absolute delight in every way. May I sit down?" she asked as he shuffled into the circle of light, his slippers scuffing against the rough wood floor.

"Suit yourself." He indicated a chair at the table, moved past her, stared at the coffeepot as if in disbelief that it was empty, then eyed the also-empty can of Folgers beside it. He gulped, sighed, and turned back to Kerry, running a hand through matted hair. "You say she ain't causin' no trouble?"

"None at all, sir." Kerry kept a reassuring arm around Cassie's thin shoulders. "She's a breath of fresh air. Always wanting to learn more, to do more. She has a gift for learning, that's for sure."

"Like her mother." Looking broody, he sank into the chair across from Kerry with heavy eyes. "Sara was real smart. She went to college over in Columbus. Worked in a lab for some fancy doctors for…" He thought, then shook his head. "I don't know, for a real long time. 'Til the drink got her. Then she couldn't work there. She messed up tests and almost got someone killed. All that education wasted. Sure didn't need it at the Agway." He gave an almost triumphant snort. "They paid her eight dollars an hour to sell feed for animals. All that fancy schoolin' to make eight dollars an hour in the end. I guess she weren't so smart after all."

The triumph in his voice as he almost celebrated his wife's fall from grace hit old buttons for Kerry. How could he not see the amazing gift before him? The gift of a child, the first gift of Christmas? Why was this so clear to her, but ignored by people like him? Like her father?

Negativity rose up, resentment from long ago. She locked it down and refused to be deterred. "Well, Cassie is smart," she noted, keeping her look pleasant. She squeezed the child's shoulders as she spoke. Then an idea occurred, out of the blue, and she continued on impulse. "Like I said, Cassie is bright and inquisitive, but I need some extra time with her if it's all right with you, Mr. Carruthers. I'd like to keep her a few afternoons a week, with your permission. I'll help her with her lessons, then bring her back home in the evening. Can we start next Monday?"

Trying to seem open, Kerry angled her head at the scruffy man and resisted the urge to cover her nose when he spoke.

"Monday? Next week?" He sounded befuddled, as if wondering what was on his calendar.

"Yes, sir. We're going to be doing domestic lessons, teaching Cassie how to help out around the house. Sewing, straightening, cleaning. Things to help her take care of herself when the time comes. Would you mind if we did some practice sessions here as she becomes more skilled?"

"I don't understand." Mr. Carruthers scratched his head in apparent confusion. He gave Kerry an owlish look. "You're gonna come here and do some cleanin'? I don't like people messin' with my stuff."

Kerry nodded. "Me either. I'd like to do some off-site training with Cassie for a while, actually. Teach her the basics at my place and around town, if that's all right. She and I can practice. Once she's ready, she can help you out more here. As long as it's OK with you, of course." She sat back and kept her posture as unassuming as possible.

"I suppose…" His voice wandered as if he wasn't too sure what he was agreeing to.

"Good." Kerry stood and hurriedly stuck her hand out to shake his. She didn't want to give him time to change his mind. "I appreciate your faith in me, Mr. Carruthers. I've got this bag of things here, sent on by Mrs. Stanton up the road. It seems Addie grew out of them, and Mrs. Stanton would be glad for Cassie to use them."

His back straightened. His shoulders flared. Seeing that, Kerry threw her trump card. "With winter coming on, Cassie will need a new coat and boots. Luckily there are perfectly good ones right here."

She proffered the rose-toned nylon jacket with matching snow pants, then added the black boots with a pink string tie. "The boots are a touch big, but they should last all winter that way. That leaves your money for other things."

His eyes lit up. The less he had to provide for the girl, the more he'd have to spend at the liquor store.

At his gruff assent, Kerry gave a gentle squeeze to Cassie's shoulders.

"Thank you, sir. I'll plan on starting Cassie's extra lessons next week on Mondays, Wednesdays, and Fridays. And you," Kerry looked down into the jade green eyes of the winsome child before her. "I'll see you tomorrow."

"Yes." Trusting eyes looked up at her. Loving eyes. With a start, she realized they were falling in love with each other, woman and child.

Well. You could never have too much love. With a hug and a wave, Kerry left, waving again as she pulled away with the car. On the way home, she thought about what she'd done. And why.

Yes, she wanted more time with Cassie. That was a given. She wanted to teach her, enable her to deal more capably with her environment.

But mostly, when she was completely honest with herself, she wanted to get that child out of that house as often as possible. Show her another way like neighbors had done for Kerry so long ago.

With God's help, some elbow grease, and some odor killer, she could do it.

* * *

You're a jerk.

Ryan repositioned his body and hoisted the heavy weights up above his chest and back onto the bar rack. The workout was supposed to push Kerry from his mind, give him a clean edge.

Didn't happen. All he could hear was the hurt in her voice when he balked about the stupid festival, like it was his fault.

He wasn't the one who moved out of the area, who chose to hunker down in the thickly forested hills of Northern Appalachia and work where smart angels feared to tread. And how much prep work did a group of five-year-olds need to color a few pictures and recite their ABCs? Clearly more than he would have bargained for.

He shook his head, eyed the cold, fall drizzle, and chose to do his daily run on the treadmill instead of the street.

His conscience piqued him on mile one. By mile three, he was working his jaw, wishing he were a better person all around.

His patients loved him, but was that because of him, or because he was at the cutting edge of life-saving cancer treatments, unknown and unpracticed just a few years before?

Probably the latter, but he was good with kids. He knew that.

He was good with parents, too, but he'd seen far more single parents and broken marriages these past few years than he'd ever imagined. Was that because his father had kept him sheltered in Catholic schools as a kid, so his norm was skewed toward fairy-tale endings?

Except his reality had no happily-ever-after quality, and that made him the odd duck in a relatively small pond.

The current normal should make him feel less singular, shouldn't it? Growing up without a mother, knowing she valued drug-induced highs more than her family?

He wanted to move beyond the resentment.

He couldn't.

Why was that? He was a successful, hardworking professional. Why couldn't he just shrug off the past and move on?

Or maybe he had, and he was disappointed that moving on was a measure of disappointment in itself.

Kerry came to mind again. So beautiful, so funny, just cryptic enough to keep it real. In a game of players, Kerry refused to be played, and he loved that about her. She raised the stakes, and she did it openly. Was he falling for her? Or was it the challenge she offered? She wanted the package deal, the whole enchilada. A home, a husband, and a family.

Not him.

So why the attraction? Because Kerry was too nice to play games with, and yet…he couldn't move forward and wouldn't walk away.

She was uncommon. She was a waiting-for-marriage girl in a new-age society based on instant gratification. Ryan grimaced.

He'd been particularly fond of certain gratifications for a long time. That had all came to a screeching halt when he started dating Miss American Pie last spring.

His thoughts made him frown, and he scowled at his reflection in the floor-to-ceiling mirror. It wasn't like it was all about sex.

Right, O'Donnell.

He pushed a hand through sweat-dampened hair and flexed his jaw again.

OK, maybe it was. And holding out wasn't a game for Kerry like it was with some girls. Either that, or she was very skilled at the rules.

No. Not Kerry. And with his father being married to Kerry's aunt, things could get awkward if—

If what? If you mess her over? Break her heart?

Exactly. Thanksgiving dinners with the ex-girlfriend held little allure. Still, the thought of one girl and ever-after equated a walk down King's *Green Mile*. Nothing short of execution awaited.

He'd witnessed the reality of church-led vows. He wasn't a big fan. Women made promises only to break them when you least expected it. He'd had enough of that as a boy.

Marriage wasn't for him. Certainly not one with stakes as high as Kerry McHenry would expect. She longed for a world of promise and commitment, vows of forever.

Doesn't happen, Cupcake. Not anymore.

Ryan's world was reality-based. Stark. Simple.

So how come by mile five he was ready to head to Phillipsburg and apologize for not appreciating what a fine woman Kerry McHenry was?

He had no idea, but hoped the bouquet of bright fall flowers would smooth his way as he eased his Beemer onto the open road an hour later.

He was getting tired of being a jerk. Maybe he'd figure out some way to stop, but that would mean offering heart and soul. He wasn't sure that was possible.

Oh, he knew he had a heart. It beat quicker where Kerry McHenry was concerned.

He wasn't all that sure about the soul.

* * *

Kerry was in the middle of sorting time when Anne paged her to the office. Rita was working with Cassie and Peter at the science table. She left the pair with instructions to draw a five-year-old's rendition of what they saw and took over the sorting groups so Kerry could answer the page.

Kerry hurried out of the classroom. Anne rarely interrupted sessions; she was much more likely to tap on the door and leave a discreet message. For her to pull Kerry from class was unusual. She turned the corner to Anne's office and paused.

Ryan stood there chatting with Anne. In his hand, he clutched a stunning fall-hued floral arrangement. He turned as she rounded the corner and gave her that killer Celtic smile that had probably won many a heart in his time. It sure did a number on hers.

Remember his theme song on your phone. High-risk category for a varied number of reasons.

He moved her way, looking apologetic. "I didn't mean to interrupt your day."

She glanced at the office clock, then at him. "You must have meant to, you're here and I'm in the middle of lessons. How was that accidental?"

"I think he means he was going to just drop off the flowers to surprise you," Anne said, and from the smile on her face, she'd fallen under the Ryan O'Donnell spell.

Great.

"He was perfectly willing to wait until later," she went on, "but I decided to call you down to receive them personally."

She wasn't sure if she should thank Anne or scold her, so she redirected her attention to Ryan. "They're stunning, Rye. But you know that."

"I do, and I realize I've been short on time and short-tempered lately, and I wanted to drive down here and apologize. I'm sorry, Kerry."

He drove the distance and apologized in front of Anne. Was this progress or a well-constructed act? She wasn't sure, but he seemed sincere, and somewhat humbled, and that wasn't the norm for the Ryan she knew. "Would you like to meet my class?"

"Is that all right?" He looked from her to Anne.

"If it's all right with Kerry, it's fine with me. Maybe you could talk to the kids about what you do."

Ryan grimaced. "How do you talk to little kids about other little kids who develop life-threatening illnesses?"

"We can leave off the mortality end of it and just explain you're a doctor who helps kids when they get sick," Kerry suggested.

"That's a better idea," he admitted. "You don't mind if I visit, Kerry?"

She did mind. She minded a lot because she'd just tucked him into the has-been category, and here he was, contrite and carrying flowers. "I think this is an experience both the kids and I will never forget."

He started down the hall with her, glancing around. Was he noticing the scarred walls of the old building? Was he contrasting the decades-old structure with the shiny, taxpayer supported mega-buildings in his school district?

"This is nice," he offered, dispelling her negativity. "It's like Guardian Angel, the school I went to when I was a kid."

"Really?" Ryan attended a Catholic school? That was a revelation she hadn't expected, but maybe she should have. Dan talked about the church often, and he and Aunt Claire attended Mass there regularly.

"It wasn't fancy, but I got the best education. It was their standards that prepped me for college and med school. On the days I wanted to scrap it all and quit, I'd wonder what Miss Martin would do. She never quit anything, and if I gave it up or messed up, how would I explain that if I ever ran into her again?"

"And have you? Run into her?"

He shrugged as she reached for the classroom door. "A couple of times at parish festivals. Dad helps with things. Claire, too. A lot of things. So I stop by now and again."

But not to services or Mass, Kerry realized. Social aspects, yes.

Prayer might have been part of Ryan's life two decades ago, but it was nowhere to be found now. *I always found a man committed to his faith is more likely to be committed to his family.* Hannah's sage advice, timeless wisdom, and yet…

And yet…

When Ryan was around, her heart was tugged in his direction, no matter how stern her warnings. Was she simply a foolish romantic?

She admitted that possibility to herself as she introduced Ryan to the class, much like she'd done with Jake two weeks before.

Beyond the romanticism, something about this man called to her. He needed help. She saw that.

But it wasn't hers to give. Was it?

It's yours to pray about. To champion before the Lord your God. To rail the heavens. Stop being a wuss.

He charmed the children instantly. He sat on the floor, teasing, talking, and laughing with the kids. Not one held back; even Cassie giggled out loud as Ryan told them stories about helping children and being a kid. Maybe his tales of early childhood delighted them most of all.

He charmed her too, but life was more than surface behavior. Life was deep and motivated and challenging, and when she gave her heart—*if she gave her heart*—her soul mate would have to understand the depths of that commitment. She and Jenn had spent over a decade in a situation similar to Cassie's. No matter what the attraction, she'd never risk that kind of rejection again.

chapter eleven

Cassie wiggled with excitement on the bus that afternoon. Mr. Dennis's eyes went kind of little and puzzled-looking, and he looked at her through the big mirror. "What's got you so giddy, Miss Carruthers?"

She had a hard time containing herself. She leaned toward him and offered a tiny smile. "I think teacher's got a boyfriend."

"Really?" His brows went up, and he smiled back at her in the reflection. "It wouldn't surprise me any, a pretty thing like Miss McHenry. Did she tell you?"

Cassie shook her head and wriggled some more. "He came to see us, right in our kindergarten. He brought her flowers. He's a doctor who takes care of people. And…"

Mr. Dennis creased his forehead. His eyes crinkled as he waited for her to finish. When she didn't, he raised up one eyebrow, encouraging her to continue. "And?"

"I think he likes me," Cassie confessed. "He shook my hand and smiled right at me. Maybe…" She let her voice trail off, imagining.

"Maybe what, honey?"

She glanced up and met Mr. Dennis's smiling eyes in the mirror. "Maybe they'll get married. Maybe I could go to their wedding. Maybe—"

But this last was too wonderful to say out loud. That maybe they would want a little girl all their own. A curly-haired little girl with pretty green eyes. Miss McHenry always told her she had pretty green eyes. And Miss McHenry did things with her. They worked on special projects while the other kids finished their letters and numbers. Mrs.

Dumrese and Miss Morehouse showed her special things sometimes, science things, explaining how everything worked together. And now Miss McHenry took her home with her sometimes, and she helped her cook and clean and play and read.

It was a world of magic and wonder. When Cassie thought about Miss McHenry and her house, science and school, she could forget everything else. For a little while.

It wasn't easy as the days grew colder and the nights longer.

This was the scary time of year. The time when daylight thinned and the rains came. Nothing was bright or cheery at the little house. Day after day of dim, dirty light made by two lamps, a ceiling light in the kitchen where only one bulb worked, and whatever glow fought its way through dirt-crusted windows.

The house was dark and sad. The shadows held furtive movements.

With short days and long nights, it was impossible to avoid the shadows altogether, but Cassie tried.

Miss McHenry had taught everyone to pray. She told the whole class how her mama died when she was young, and how she cried because she missed her mama so much. Just like me, Cassie thought, but then corrected herself.

Cassie didn't cry. Not much, anyhow. The man didn't like crying. Crying made him angry. When things got bad or she got hurt, Cassie would catch her bottom lip between her teeth and squeeze hard enough to feel the pain. Doing that kept her from crying. Quiet was her best choice. She'd figured that out a long time ago.

Miss McHenry told the class that she prayed to God when her mother died. She still missed her mom, but talking to God helped. She said praying made her stronger and better. Cassie couldn't imagine anyone stronger or better than Miss McHenry, and she longed to be just like her someday.

So Cassie prayed.

* * *

She liked the flowers, Ryan decided once he'd left the school. She liked him, but probably wished she didn't, and she didn't like being surprised.

Or maybe it's half-baked measures done at your convenience?

He understood the somewhat bitter truth in that.

He had almost an hour to kill before Daystar released the kids to go home. He did an Internet search for a coffee shop, found one in Angelica, and drove there and back before school let out. When Kerry approached the parking lot, he was there, holding one of her favorite coffees in his hand. She reached out and sighed, then tipped her gaze up to his. He'd read the phrase *twinkling eyes* often. It never meant much, a romantic's twist on the commonplace. But today, gazing down at Kerry, it meant a lot, a phrase come alive before his eyes. "This could be a game changer. Is it a—"

"Caramel macchiato with an extra shot of espresso and caramel."

"To offset the extra coffee, perfect. You remembered."

"My memory's never been a problem," he admitted. He swept the school a look as several of Kerry's colleagues called good-bye while giving him the once-over. "The other teachers are scoping me out."

"They're all mothers; they're protecting me."

"From me? What have you told them?"

She laughed and brushed that off. "I'm not a talker when it comes to affairs of the heart. That's totally TMI in the workplace. Now at home, that's different. Hannah Wilder is my new confidante, and that's because she figures things out before I say them."

"Grandma O'Donnell was like that." Ryan thrust his hands into his jacket pockets as the wind picked up. "She always knew what I was up to and loved me anyway."

"Best kind of grandma to have."

They'd been walking back toward her car, but now he stopped. "Do you have a grandmother, Kerry?"

"I did, of course. Not now." She stared off before bringing her attention back to him. "My mother's mother passed away when I was little. My father's mother was gone long before he met my mother. I've never really looked into it. Claire and my mother were kind of like me and Jenn, only they had a great dad. Aunt Claire tells stories about him, and they're so vivid you can see him. I've always wondered if my mother tried to replace him by marrying an older man. That maybe losing her father pushed her to marry the wrong man."

"How can you tell the right from the wrong when you fall in love with someone?" He almost didn't want to ask the question, but he had to, because there wasn't a litmus test for character assessment, was there?

"I think that's where the smart person, man or woman"—she added pointedly, and he wondered if she was referencing his mother. She'd have heard stories from Claire and his father, no doubt—"steps outside the romantic attraction and analyzes the situation."

"I thought you were supposed to be the romantic?" He pretended surprise because she was making too much sense. "Analytical assessment blows the rest of your happily-ever-after stuff out of the water, doesn't it?"

"Not in the least. I think one without the other is rather foolhardy."

He was pretty sure the romance trope was too confining, and that made the whole thing rather foolish to begin with. "I was hoping you might be free this weekend." He waited at her car while she stowed her teaching bag in the back, and he tried not to notice the worn tires, the dings and dents, while wondering when she'd last had the brakes checked. Not to mention the battery, timing chains, oil…

He shoved that aside, waiting for her response.

"I've got some time." She faced him now, and when she turned those baby blues his way, it was all he could do to not declare himself and ride off into the sunset with her, like an old-style western. Although in those they often left the girl and took the horse. "But my little friend Cassie is with me this weekend, so anything I do has to include a really cute kid."

He frowned, then remembered the unkempt little girl from the classroom. "Green eyes. Shy. Odd man out."

"Correct. Her father's agreed to let me work with her after school, and I pushed for weekends occasionally, which is code for I get to rescue her from hours of squalor and neglect."

Squalor and neglect? Ryan swept the little school a curious look. "The unlikely scenario of that setting and a private school says there's more to this story."

"There usually is."

"Got time for supper?" He pointed out his car next to hers. "We can drop your car off and grab food down in Wellsville."

"Homemade pie at The Texas Hot."

"You've got to be one of the most reasonably priced dates around, Kerry."

She laughed, unoffended. "There's an attribute for you." She stopped laughing and shook her head. "I can't tonight."

He was so sure she'd go to supper with him that it took a minute for her refusal to register. "You can't? Really?"

She looked torn. Was that good or bad? He wasn't sure.

Then she looked straight at him. "I've got a date."

A date.

Something buzzed. His ears? His fingers? His toes?

He recognized the adrenaline rush because while he'd been messing around partying the last couple of months, he'd been stupid enough to think Kerry would be so wound up in saving the world that she'd be there waiting when he finally got some common sense.

Clearly he was mistaken.

He wanted to walk away, but another part of him wanted to get over stupid, adolescent behaviors. He drew a breath, then shrugged. "My bad for being too casual. But are we good for Saturday, Ker?"

"With Cassie?"

"Absolutely. If I get out here around ten, we can spend the day together."

She hesitated before she agreed, but she did agree, so that meant he wasn't out of the running yet. But was he in the running? Did he want to be in the running, or should he man up and let the girl get on with her life?

"I'd like that, Rye."

"All right, then." He waited while she got into her car, made sure it started, then resisted the urge to follow her back to her apartment on the other side of the village.

He'd had competition for women before, and he'd always considered it a game he excelled at and generally won.

As she drove away, he realized he wasn't playing with Kerry. It wasn't a game or a contest. This was different, and he wasn't sure if that was good or bad for either of them. And he wasn't at all assured of victory, and that bit deep.

* * *

"You're ready." Jake's smile widened in appreciation as Kerry met him on the front porch.

"I figured we'd need to make good use of the light, but then I realized this pumpkin farm is lit up at night."

"The front part, yes. And the boys will get such a kick out of picking their own pumpkins. You warm enough?" Jake reached up a hand to her cheek...

And her heart sped up.

The warmth and strength of his hand warmed more than her face, so why had she said yes to Ryan forty-five minutes before? She wasn't a player, but this was starting to feel like a game.

She hated games, so when Jake dropped her off after a wonderful time at the Great Pumpkin Patch, she put her hands on his arms and blurted out the truth. "I have a date with someone else on Saturday."

He looked surprised, then a little amused. "Confession time, huh?"

She winced. "Yes, kind of."

"Are you in a relationship?" he wondered aloud. "You can't be, Kerry, because you'd have said so up front."

"I'm not." She frowned, then shrugged. "But there's something there, Jake, and I can't be dishonest with you."

"You're not exclusive, obviously." He motioned between the two of them and raised one eyebrow, teasing because clearly she'd gone out with him.

"No." She frowned, half wishing she was exclusive because none of this felt right or smart.

"Then there's no problem."

"There's not?" She stared up at him, because Kerry was 100 percent sure there was a problem. A big one.

Jake didn't ask, he didn't hesitate, he didn't wonder. He leaned right in and feathered the sweetest of kisses to her mouth, her face, and then her hair. Then he breathed deeply, nuzzled her ear, and stepped back, but he left his hands on her shoulders. "Just means I have to try harder, Kerry, and a man not willing to try harder isn't worth having."

A sound of approval from next door said Mrs. Wilder was listening… and approving.

Jake's grin softened. "Listen, Kerry, we just met."

"Yes."

"And I haven't dated much since I lost my wife, so this is uncharted ground for me, too."

He was being nice. Truly nice.

"So let's just see how things go. Are you in a hurry?"

She shook her head.

"Me, either. And no matter what happens, I want my boys happy, so let's take things as they come. But if I get a chance to arrest the guy, you know I'll do it, right?"

His teasing broke the tension. "Well, he's a cancer doctor, so we can't put him in jail. Folks depend on him to save their lives."

"Man, you go big, woman." He held her gaze, then gave her shoulders a quick squeeze. "Now I have to go home and reassess my strategies based on new information."

"You're really OK with this?"

He started to step away, then didn't. "No, of course not, but that's not the issue, is it? You need to be OK with this. All of this." He waved toward the car. "Because I come fully equipped with a ready-made family, and I understand how that can be a game changer."

He thought the boys were a negative? That she'd be scoping out other guys because she couldn't mother those two precious and precocious children? "Abe and Ben are amazing and wonderful, and any woman would be honored to care for them."

He waited a moment but didn't say anything more before he left to get the boys home.

She'd told Jake.

She'd told Ryan.

So what was her problem? And why, when she was a younger woman, did she ever think it would be good or fun to have more than one man vying for her attention? Because now that she was caught in that scenario, she absolutely, positively hated it.

chapter twelve

Cassie watched the bird-shaped fabric dip and bob in the brisk wind. She chased down the beach, laughing with delight. "Faster, Ryan! Go faster!"

Ryan yelled to her from across the deep, soft surface edging Lake Ontario's Charlotte Beach, "I'm thirty-five, kid. This is as fast as it gets. Especially in sand."

Cassie laughed louder. "It looks like a real bird. A giant one."

As Ryan released more and more string, the kite arched its fabric wings and soared. Cassie clutched her hands together. Her heart rose with the kite. "I never, ever saw one of these for real before. Thank you, Ryan!"

Kerry laughed as Ryan dashed across the sand, tugging the kite this way and that.

Cassie marveled at the sight.

It was an amazing day. A wonderful day. She had stayed overnight at Kerry's clean house. Then Ryan met them at a farm where Cassie touched cows and pigs, sheep and goats. It smelled funny, but the animals were warm and friendly.

Then Ryan took them to lunch at his father's restaurant by the lake. Cassie ate chicken strips and drank a tall, frosty chocolate milkshake that Ryan's father made just for her. Never had she tasted something as creamy and good as that milkshake, all bubbly and smooth. Her mouth watered remembering it.

And now they were at the beach, bundled against the chill, flying a kite that looked like a giant bird.

She'd seen kites on *Sesame Street*. People raced through a green park, tugging strings, their kites waving above the trees. But not one of them had a kite as high or cool as the one Ryan flew today. His was so high that Cassie could no longer see the markings on the bird's belly or its wings.

"What do you think, Cassie?" Kerry snugged an arm around Cassie's shoulders.

Cassie clenched her hands and stared upwards. "I think it's the most wonderful thing I've seen in my whole life."

Kerry planted a kiss on Cassie's hair. "Just the way it should be. Wanna give it a try?"

"Me?" Cassie stared up at Kerry. "I can't. I'm little."

"Not so little." Ryan had moved closer. His eyes were trained on the kite and the string, working his hands to steer the kite clear of the park trees just south of the beach. "Come on, Cassie. Give it a try."

He reached out a hand and drew Cassie close. Then he let her fingers slide along the string above his until their hands met. "Now the other hand."

Cassie brought her left hand up to the string and gripped for dear life.

Ryan stepped back. "All yours. Let's see what you've got, Munchkin."

Munchkin? Cassie frowned but forgot the word in the excitement of holding the kite.

The wind tugged the fabric bird. Cassie moved right then left, but the wind pulled harder. As the kite soared toward the trees, Cassie panicked and tried to move the other way, but the buoyant kite fought her.

"Like this." Ryan's hands closed over hers. His hands felt big and warm. Gentle. "We have to work with the wind. Not against it. It's like sailing a boat. The kite's our sail, and we let it fill with wind to make it fly."

"The wind is strong."

Ryan nodded. He worked the string with her, easing the kite away from the broad, leafless trees. "It is. But so are you."

Cassie smiled. She felt strong with Ryan's hands over hers, the kite high in the sky, the trees now a distant problem.

Was this what it would be like to have a family? A mom and a dad who loved you, who cared for you? She heard Kerry's laugh and sensed Ryan's smile behind her.

For a minute, it was just like TV, all the families she saw there. The ones that loved one another and did things together. For just a moment, she felt strong and loved. Normal. One of the crowd.

She was a kite flyer, and it felt good.

* * *

Mrs. Wilder poked her head out the door on a brisk late-November afternoon as Kerry exited her car. "I've got somethin' for you. It just got delivered, and where's Miss Cassie? I thought she'd be with you today, like usual, and I made cookies."

"Hannah, how nice." Cassie never seemed to mind Hannah's over-baked offerings, and Hannah thrived on the girl's enthusiasm. Kerry stepped into Hannah's little vestibule and closed the storm door against the sharp wind. "Cassie wasn't in school today. I'm about to check out why. What was the delivery?"

"Flowers. Came ten minutes ago. Glad I was here."

Kerry almost asked, "From whom?" but the incongruity of the question made her wince. There was something wrong about garnering the attentions of two men at the same time. Wasn't there?

It had to be wrong because it felt wrong, and yet these were both good men. Solid men. Strong men.

And they both profess faith in our Lord Jesus Christ, the only begotten Son of God, right?

Well, no. One was mad at God, and one didn't believe at all. Since that was a huge deal with her, why were they both still on the list?

She opened the card and realized why right off. *"I know you're busy this weekend with the drug-free rally, and I'm working, but I thought if you looked at these flowers whenever you're at home, you'd think of me…and then we wouldn't feel so far apart."*

She lifted her gaze and noted Hannah's smile. "You read the card."

"It was here, I was here, and it does an old woman's heart good to see romance in the air. So sue me."

Kerry laughed and hugged her instead.

"Last week it was Jake, this week it's the young doctor…You have taken my advice to great lengths, and so excellently, too!"

"I didn't mean to. It's just they're both so…" Kerry mulled the choice of words, came up blank, and shrugged. "I'm attracted to both of them, and that sounds so lame."

"Oh, honey, you're not the first person to run into this problem. And land sakes, I remember times when this sort of thing happened with others, and neither one ended up being Mr. Right. Or Mrs. Right in one case," she amended. "You just have to remember that this is not a measurin' contest. It's not a competition. It's life, and it's sacred, a vow and a sacrament if you've a mind to sit in St. Mary's, so it's nothin' for a bein' to take lightly. You take the time you need. Ryan's been jammin' 'round for fifteen years of adulthood. He's been on his own agenda for a while now."

That was true and possibly part of her hesitation. Ryan's busy past wasn't something she wanted to have sneak up on her, and she'd considered that more than once.

"Our Jake, now he's a different story, because there are two little children ridin' on his decisions, and he can't take anything lightly, bein' a single dad and all, but if you bow out of the picture, there is no shortage of Southern Tier lovelies dyin' to take your place. Now that he's finally steppin' out again."

"He didn't date before me?" He'd alluded to that, but he was offhand about it, and she hadn't delved.

"He was heartsick with his hands full and barely time to breathe, so no, not to speak of, although no small number of women tried to tempt him. You're the first he's shown interest in, but I suppose it would be too much to ask the good Lord to make his first move as a widower his last move as a widower."

"Hannah." Kerry rolled her eyes. "I think I know which way your scales are weighted."

"Not so." Hannah crossed her arms and had her say. "I'm just sayin' a man's got to prioritize, same as a woman. I expect those boys are crazy about Christmas, aren't they?"

They were excited, and thinking about that dimmed the hues of Ryan's bouquet. "Crazy excited and too cute for words. I told them we'd bake cookies next week, with all the sprinkles they want. They're pretty psyched." She lifted the flowers slightly. "I'm going to tuck these upstairs and take a ride out to County Center and check on Cassie, see what's going on."

"I'll get my coat."

"No, Hannah, it's—"

"You are not drivin' out there to that house with dark comin' on without someone alongside, and that's that."

"I take Cassie back home all the time now," Kerry reminded her.

"Jed's expectin' you then. I reckon he's not expectin' anyone right now, and that can be a dangerous situation if he's edgin' the far side of the law."

Kerry couldn't argue the truth with her landlady, although what help she could be was another thought entirely. Still there was comfort in both of them going. She put the flowers upstairs, topped off the water in the vase, and returned to the porch as Hannah stepped out. "We've got some wind comin' on, and that means lake effect by morning this time of year."

"I'll get up early and shovel if we need to," Kerry promised.

"You're a blessin', darlin'." Hannah drew her wool coat more closely around herself as she settled into Kerry's front seat. "Our arrangement has been so good that I don't know if I dare hope for you to find the right man, because who will be shovelin' me out then?"

Kerry laughed. "We'll cross that bridge when we come to it." Her phone buzzed. She tucked her Bluetooth onto her ear and answered. "Hey, Jake."

"Snow tonight, pretty heavy. Were you planning on going out?"

"Are you worried about me, Jake Slattery?"

"It's possible that your well-being crosses my mind about a thousand times a day, Kerry. No pressure."

She laughed and made a face at Hannah when the aged woman clapped her hands together, gleeful. "None taken. I'm actually heading out to Cassie's right now. She didn't come to school, and her father didn't answer his phone."

"Never does. You're not going out there alone, are you? He's gotten worse, Kerry, from what I see, and—"

"Hannah's with me." She interrupted him as she rolled to a stop just outside of town. "And don't disparage the idea of two women walking face-first into a situation, because I'm on speaker and she'll hear everything you say."

"Hannah's got good sense. I'm glad you're not alone. Listen, I'm on C sector patrol, but I'm going to let them know I'm heading your way. I won't show up at the Carrutherses', but I'll be close by at the Stantons' if you need me, OK?"

"That's a good idea!" Hannah called out. "We'll stop there after Carrutherses'. I've been meaning to get Amanda's peach pie recipe for two years. Before you know it, I'll be gone, and I still won't have made that pie, and that would be a shame."

"I'll call you, Jake. And, Jake?"

"Yeah?" His tone, deep and husky, like warm velvet on a cold, cold night.

"Thank you."

He laughed softly. "It takes a village, darlin'."

Darling…

Her heart and hands went soft. When he talked…when he said her name, when he gazed at her, it was as if she was the most precious thing on earth.

And when he did that, she felt like the most precious thing on earth and melted inside. What could be better than that?

Nothing.

She parked in Carrutherses' driveway, and she and Hannah hurried to the door. She knocked briskly, the strong west wind pounding their backs.

No response, and the dingy gray shack was dark, inside and out.

She knocked again, harder this time.

Still no answer. She looked at Hannah, but Hannah wasn't the type to hesitate. She took hold of that door, wrenched the handle, and swung it wide. "Jed? Jed Carruthers, are you here?"

Silence answered them.

"There's no car here."

"He doesn't have a car half the time, so that's not exactly news," Hannah muttered. They moved into the front room.

Something moved to Kerry's right, something small, furtive, and darker than the shadows it sought. *Dear God...*

"Cassie? Cassie, are you here?" She strode forward, hating the conditions, hating the memories this wrought, and wanting to find and rescue the little girl who had done nothing to deserve this kind of squalid existence. She reached for a door handle and turned it. "Cassie?"

The stench of the room hit her first, but that all disappeared the moment she spotted the fevered child on the bed. "Hannah!"

Kerry crossed the room, laid a hand on Cassie's head, then pulled back. "High fever. Rash. Flushed cheeks."

"Let's get this sweet child back home."

Kerry lifted her while Hannah pulled the dirty bedding from the bed, then from the room. She bundled it all and toted it to the car, and when Kerry popped the trunk, she laid it all in there. "Nothing a good washing or two won't fix." She climbed into the back seat and held out her arms to hold Cassie close.

"If you mind her tonight, I'll come up to your rooms tomorrow and look after her, poor thing. I might be on in years, but I'm a darn sight better at nursin' a wee thing back to health than an old drunk like Jed Carruthers could ever hope to be. Call Jake and tell him what we found. The man should be horsewhipped," Hannah whispered harshly, cradling Cassie in her aged arms. "Jed, of course, not Jake. God's given him the most exquisite prize, the most beloved gift of all, and he takes it for nothing. Shame on him."

Kerry couldn't disagree. She called Jake and told him what they'd done.

"You took her?" Jake's normally calm voice shot up.

"We had to."

"Kerry, you can't just do that," he started, but she cut right in.

"Human decency says otherwise. So does the Bible. And wherever her father is, he might not have even known she was there."

"What do you mean? Of course he knew she was there if she didn't go to school this morning."

"She gets herself on the bus every day."

"She's five." His voice went flat and firm as if he doubted her assertion, or doubted that anyone could be that careless with a child.

"He's always asleep according to Cassie, and the bus driver has never seen the father."

"So you think he might have left, thinking she was at school."

"And she usually comes home for supper with me on Wednesday nights, so he wouldn't expect her home until eight o'clock."

"Are you excusing his actions, Kerry?" He sounded surprised and not too happy. "Because frankly, they're inexcusable. I know Aunt Susan and Amanda have been worried, but I never thought he'd leave her there, sick. I'm coming to your place to write a report. Then I'll head back to the Carrutherses' and see what happens when Jed shows up."

"We need a report? For tending a sick child? Is that necessary, Jake?"

"Unless you'd prefer a kidnapping charge."

"What?" Was he kidding? His next words assured her he wasn't.

"Your little agreement with Jed is shaky at best, but if he thinks his weird, self-absorbed lifestyle is threatened, he's liable to come out swinging. And you don't need that."

She didn't, but would Jed do something like that? He might, she realized, remembering how quickly he assessed her help with Cassie. Free shoes and clothing equated more liquid refreshment, a scenario she'd known well. "Of course you're right. I'll see you there."

She drove fast but not too fast because old tires and rural roads weren't the best pairing, and when she pulled along the curb in front of Hannah's village house, Jake pulled up right behind her. He met her by the rear passenger door and held out his arms. "I'll carry her up. You go unlock the doors." When Kerry hesitated, he did too. "You did lock the doors, didn't you?"

"I will. I promise."

"Kerry." He scolded her with a look, but his expression softened as he lifted Cassie from Hannah's arms. "Oh, baby." He leaned his lips against her forehead in a move so natural anyone watching would think she was his. He followed Kerry upstairs, and when she turned the bed down, he set Cassie down with the utmost tenderness. Then he reached into his pocket and withdrew a bottle. "Children's ibuprofen and acetaminophen for the fever. You can alternate them if needed."

"How'd you think of this?"

"I've got it on hand with the boys." He shrugged and didn't try to wipe the worry from his gaze as he watched Cassie. "I passed the pharmacy on the way and ran in."

"Thank you, Jake. I never thought of that."

"Well, once you have kids, it's a staple. I'm going to ask you a few questions, but it can wait until you've got her settled. A warm bath can help, too."

He didn't mention the smell, but Kerry understood both sides of the warm bath. Cassie woke up as she undressed her. She stared at Kerry, then saw Jake.

She screamed.

It was a tiny scream, weak and frail, but there was no doubt that the sight of the big sheriff's deputy scared her.

Jake kept an easy expression, but Kerry read the hurt in his eyes. She saw the knowledge, too. Kids that were scared of cops were generally taught to be afraid, which meant Jed didn't want police around. Was he using illegal drugs? Or dealing them? Or was it something else?

Hannah bustled out of the cozy bathroom. "I've got a warm tub for her, and two towels on the heater."

"Thank you, Hannah."

Then while Jake waited in the living room, Kerry and Hannah dosed Cassie with the fever reducer before bathing the little girl. When they were done, Hannah brought the thick towels in so Kerry could wrap her up.

"We have no clothes for her."

Hannah snapped her fingers. "Denise Madison runs the clothing closet in the back of St. Mary's. I'll call her. Maybe they've got something we could use. Size six?"

"Five or six," Kerry told her. "She's small for her age. Either will do."

Hannah bustled out to make the phone call.

Kerry slipped one of her T-shirts over Cassie's head. It made a perfect nightgown, just long enough. Then she tucked Cassie into her clean, soft bed. The little girl's eyes flew open, as if alarmed. She stared at Kerry, then at the room, and then she sighed and settled into the thick, soft pillow.

Contrast.

She'd plucked Cassie from a dank, dark, cold room with foul-smelling covers, running a high fever.

And now the child lay clean and more comfortable against bright white cotton on plump down pillows that were a gift from Aunt Claire.

She couldn't take her back to County Center Road. Would Jed listen to reason and let the child stay here, with her, surrounded by cleanliness and warmth and joy?

"And lose his government payments?" Jake shook his head as he made a few notes when she offered that suggestion a few minutes later. "He's probably getting disability for himself, social security survivor benefits from his wife, and a payment for Cassie. Trust me, he's not going to give up that money, Kerry. It's not going to happen."

"If I appeal to his decency as a father?"

Jake stopped jotting long enough to stare at her. "You saw the conditions she's living in. He has no decency, or she wouldn't be in that kind of setting. You said Hannah brought the bedding with her."

"To wash it, yes, but I can't imagine allowing Cassie to go back to that place. It's a hovel, and no child should be treated like that. Ever."

Jake studied her. He looked concerned, but not for Cassie. For her. "Kerry, the likelihood of the county removing Cassie from his guardianship is slim to none. He'll plead that he didn't know she was there and left assuming she was in school."

"The fact that any judge would deem that all right at age five says our system needs an overhaul."

Jake moved closer. He settled his hands on her shoulders, but it wasn't a romantic gesture this time. She knew it, she felt the difference, because Jake was going to tell her there was absolutely nothing that could or would be done.

It wasn't right.

She couldn't stand by and watch this same thing happen again, to another little child, when she'd happily open her home and heart to Cassie. Why couldn't it be that easy?

"Kerry, let's not argue about this. We both want the same thing." Jake's radio alerted him to another call. "I'll check in at the Carrutherses' when I've taken care of this, and it's not that I don't agree with you, Kerry." He lifted his gaze to the small bedroom beyond. "She'd be better off here for sure, but in the end, these things come down to money and the law. Families don't get broken up, and money talks."

She hated him right now.

She hated that he was right, that he understood the law and the ramifications of domestic situations, but what she wanted at that moment was someone to assure her there was a chance, even if there wasn't.

"I've got to go. I'll call you later to see how she's doing, OK?"

She nodded but didn't look at him.

Cassie moaned from the bedroom. She turned her back on Jake and hurried to the room, and when Hannah returned from the church, she had two cans of ginger ale, some saltines, and a bag of clothing. She set the cans of soda down on the nightstand next to the crackers. "I had these downstairs in case I got the Bad Stomach, but I never get the Bad Stomach, so that's good! The soda and the crackers will get us by until we can get to Salty's in the morning." Salty's was the little convenience store attached to the gas station just west of the village on Main. "How's she doing?"

"More comfortable," Kerry whispered. "How about if you go get some sleep, and then you can take over in the morning when I go to work. Are you up for that?"

"Takin' care of one of God's children? Oh, honey, there ain't a day been made when I'm not up for that task." Hannah slung an arm around Kerry's shoulders. "We'll get her healthy first. Then we'll see about the rest."

"You heard Jake."

"Well, when you've been on the planet for this many decades, you watch stuff go 'round and come 'round. Now in this case," she leveled her look to Cassie's rosy cheeks and messy hair, "I think we can try to talk sense into people. But times are different now, mm-hmm. In the old days, a rapscallion like Jed wouldn't have much cared about passin' a child off, one less mouth to feed and all that. But Jake made a point, such a good point. Nowadays there's money involved, and I've watched folks do what they will for money. And that's the truth and the shame of it, Kerry. And of course it's not Jake's fault; he's not writin' laws, but he's got to follow them."

Kerry knew that in abstract, but right now, when it was Cassie's health and well-being on the line, things were different.

She was different. And she was angry that even with today's circumstances, Jed would most likely keep his hold on the child, and that made her spitting mad for Cassie, for herself and her sister, and for every other little kid born to parents who didn't care.

"You've gone and bonded with this child, and that's a good thing, but we've got to keep it so's you can help her in times comin' up, no matter what happens after today. And that's where you have to keep your focus, Kerry. Today's situation is temporary." She stressed the last two words, and Kerry knew she was right. "And then we'll see about the days to come."

"All right." She couldn't hold Hannah up any longer. The aged woman was tired, and if she was going to watch over Cassie in the morning, she needed to rest tonight. "Will you pray, Hannah? Pray that we can figure out a way to help her before it all goes bad?"

"I've been doin' that, and I'll do it some more, and I'll put it right where it belongs, right there in the Lord's hands, because if you and me and Jake aren't strong enough or fierce enough to change things up, he is." She pointed up. "I'll see you in the mornin'. And if you need anythin', anythin' at all, you come and get me. I'm old, and I wake up mighty quick these days."

"I will," Kerry promised.

She checked Cassie again. Her fever was still down, and she slept sweet and solid, tucked inside the thick, layered covers of Kerry's bed. Jake called as Kerry was making up the couch with blankets and a pillow. "How's she doing?"

"Still sound asleep, and her fever's still down. Should I set the clock to give her more when it's time? Or let her sleep?"

"I'd set the clock and try and stay ahead of the fever overnight," he told her. "Jed just came home."

Eight o'clock, when he'd be expecting Kerry to drop Cassie off.

"He was driving under the influence."

Taking more lives for granted. Of course.

"I wanted to kill him, but I couldn't, so I called for someone else to come and ticket him. It won't stop him, of course."

She recognized the battle in his voice, a battle he'd already lost once. "I explained that Cassie was sick and staying with you. I didn't go into detail because he was in no condition to understand what I was saying."

"So you were right. He is getting more dangerous and careless. And with winter coming, that shack's got to be so cold, Jake. It was freezing in there."

"I know." She heard the helplessness in his voice and felt the same way. "I'll have a chat with Aunt Susan, see if there's a chance to change things up."

"Will you, Jake?" Just knowing someone would do something made her feel more in control.

"Don't get your hopes up, though," he warned. "I've seen this kind of thing too many times, Kerry, especially in the hills. There's a forgotten population up there, and a lot of kids like Cassie. I don't think the county will step in, but it's worth a look."

Of course there were other indigent children in the area. Kerry understood that. But this one was in her care right now, and that's where her fight to help would begin. And to think of Jed using or dealing drugs around a small child…getting wasted daily.

One thing at a time. Jenn had always told her that, and she'd set a good example to her younger sister. "We'll start off like that boy who saved the beached starfish by throwing them back one at a time. And when the man questioned if the boy's actions would make a difference, the boy shrugged and looked at the water and said, 'It made a difference to that one.' So that's what we'll do, Jake. We'll see if we can make a difference. One by one."

"That works for me."

She set the clock, then curled up on the sofa. She wanted to sleep, but tonight's events brought up too many old thoughts, memories she thought she had laid to rest long ago. Finally she called Jenn and told her what happened.

"Kerry." Jenn breathed out a sigh, then paused. "I don't think a lot about what happened when we were kids. I make it a point not to think about it."

"I know. I think that's wise, and I do it, too, but working with Cassie has stirred it all up. Walking in there tonight, finding her in such wretched conditions, and so sick…Jenn, if he'd been there, I honestly don't know what I would have done. I wanted to punch him. I seriously think I might have wailed on him if he'd walked in that door, I was so mad."

"You wouldn't have because you'd have put her first, Ker. That's your nature. But there's a lot of old anger in us, and sometimes when those buttons get pushed, it rears up. But we can't let it control us, and we can't let it mess up the present. The past is gone. It's over. If we're smart, we let it shape us into stronger, better women, like Aunt Claire says. To let it mess up our lives just gives him back the power he had when we were kids, and I'm never going to let that happen again."

Jenn's words soothed Kerry's angst. "You're right, of course. I needed that reminder. Thanks, Jenn."

"You're welcome. Now get some sleep. And just know that it was no accident of timing that brought Cassie to you in school, or you to her tonight. I see God's hand all over this, and I'm going to trust in that."

No accident. No coincidence. God's timing.

Kerry relaxed a little more. "Love you. Good night."

"Love you back," Jenn told her, just like when they were kids. "I'll talk to you tomorrow."

"Yes." Kerry hung up the phone and sank down against the worn secondhand couch cushions and the extra pillow.

She slept.

chapter thirteen

"Are you getting your girl a ring for Christmas? I heard you ordering flowers today. Sounded pretty serious." Dr. Sam D'Amico eyed Ryan from across the locker room that evening. Ryan had just roughed the senior partner up in a game of racquetball, so he couldn't be rude and tell Sam to mind his own business.

Ryan tugged his shirt over his head. "We haven't been dating all that long."

Sam seemed unimpressed. "So?"

Ryan busied himself with tying his shoes. "Plenty of time."

"Really?"

"Yup."

"Does she know that?"

Ryan glanced Sam's way. "Know what?"

"That you're more than willing to waste her time?"

The hairs on the back of Ryan's neck stood up. "Taking time isn't the same as wasting time, Sam."

"It is if your intentions aren't honorable." Sam's know-it-all tone stirred Ryan's antipathy. More than that, the grain of truth in Sam's unsolicited advice bit deep. "This is the woman you brought to the summer party at Phil's place, right?"

"Kerry. Yes."

"She seems like a nice girl, and you seem nicer when she's around."

More hairs rose along Ryan's neck because Sam was right, and he hated that.

"Marry her. Make some babies. My wife will throw you a shower. Make that two showers."

That thought added goose bumps to Ryan's already agitated skin. He averted his gaze. "I'm in no rush."

Sam nodded. His eyes narrowed. "I see that. What I'm wondering is why."

Now Ryan threw caution to the winds. "Mind your own business, Sam." He closed his locker door with more emphasis than necessary.

Sam was silent while he adjusted his collar. Ryan had the evening off. Sam was on call. As Ryan started for the door, he looked over his shoulder. "Thanks for the game."

"The shellacking you gave me, you mean."

Ryan dipped his chin, acknowledging his win.

Sam eyed him, his gaze thoughtful, then snapped his fingers. His look sharpened. *A Christmas Carol.*"

"Huh?" Ryan frowned in confusion.

"Dickens. Scrooge. His girlfriend. The one that married the other guy and had a passel full of kids because Scrooge wouldn't propose. Kept waiting for everything to be just right. It never was so she married someone else."

"Sam—" Ryan's voice edged up in warning. Sam might be the boss, but Ryan's personal life was exactly that. Personal.

Sam clapped a hand on Ryan's shoulder, then fell in step with him toward the exit. "You're a great doctor, Ryan. You see the new edge of cancer-fighting therapies that are changing the landscape daily. You cut your medical teeth on research that's saving lives. You care, you're smart, you do the job right. I couldn't ask for a better professional."

Before Ryan's head could swell with the compliment, Sam shook his head. "But with the way you feel about women, I'd keep you far from my daughters if they were of age. Luckily they're not."

"I like women." Ryan met Sam's gaze. His tone was indignant. He made no effort to soften it.

Sam gave him a long look, then opened the door. "Of course you do. How silly of me to have thought otherwise." He moved through the door and didn't look back. "Enjoy your night, Ryan."

* * *

Scrooge.

Marry her.

Lose her to someone else.

Sam's words swam in Ryan's head as he drove to the bay. The eastern ends of Lakes Erie and Ontario were expecting lake effect snow tonight, but his area was only due for a dusting. He was all right with that, but his thoughts went to Kerry.

She was in the middle of a Lake Erie snow belt. Conditions east of the lake could go from sunny to squall with no warning. Visibility became negligible, and roads were made impassable in blizzard-like conditions. Luckily, the school wasn't far from her apartment. He called her from the car.

No answer.

He left a message, wondering if she liked the flowers, and was a little insulted that she hadn't bothered calling. He checked the phone when he got home in case he missed the call.

Nope. No messages.

He didn't like being taken for granted, but as soon as that thought touched old buttons, he squelched it.

Kerry didn't take anyone for granted, ever. If she didn't call or text to thank him, there was a reason. With that in mind, he texted her. *"Everything OK? Are you all right? Let me know, worried."*

He stared at the words. His finger hovered over the *send* icon. Then he brushed it, ever so lightly.

The message sent.

He'd admitted he was concerned. That was a novelty for him, except with his father.

It felt weird, and almost a little scary, which was absurd, but as he plugged the phone into the charger, he knew that while it might be irrational…it was also true.

* * *

It was a dream, such a nice dream that Cassie didn't want to wake up. She refused to wake up, and that was all right.

Soft, sweet sheets surrounded her.

Warm, clean air filled her with every single breath.

She rolled over and almost peeked around, but didn't dare. If she opened her eyes and saw her regular room, her normal bed, the dream would go away and might not ever come back.

The dream bed was nice. The dream feeling was good, and as her head started to ache once more, she closed her eyes tight, popped her thumb into her mouth, and rolled over, going right back to sleep

* * *

Jake came by the school midday, during Kerry's lunch. He looked big and official and none too happy. Kerry moved his way when she spotted him down the hall. "No luck, I take it."

He shook his head. "Not as yet. I tried calling, but your phone must have died."

"I'm milking my worn-out battery, so yes. It died sometime last night and is now on my charger in the classroom. You talked to Susan?"

"Yes, and she gave a quick call to the county while I was there, and they agreed that under the circumstances, Jed's actions were repugnant, but not enough to get Cassie removed. Their concern is that if they try and fail, he'd most likely pull back and pull her from school and you. That's a big risk, Kerry."

It was. And she knew that. But which risk was greater? Cassie's existence in that house or Jed's reaction?

"We're right back there between that rock and a hard place."

"That's exactly what I said to Hannah when I stopped by with cookies and fresh milk, but she told me to remember who was really in charge."

Kerry acknowledged that with a rueful smile. "She's mentioned that to me, too."

"It's a tough decision, Kerry."

"What would you do, Jake?" She gazed up at him, longing for his advice. He wasn't just a wonderful man she was growing to care deeply about. He was a professional who dealt with all kinds of people daily, and his opinion was invaluable. "I'd let it go and keep working to build Jed's trust in you."

Trust in the Lord with all your heart, and do not rely on your own insight…

She loved that proverb, mostly because her do-gooder side liked to take charge, jump in, and fix things.

Trust in the Lord…

She accepted Jake's words and wisdom and nodded. "Hannah said the same thing. I'll keep doing what I'm doing, and maybe he'll loosen up even more. I should be grateful he lets me take her as often as he does."

"That's my girl."

She blushed, but when he reached out a big, broad hand to her cheek, his touch made her long to step closer. Be closer. "Am I your girl, Jake?"

He held her gaze. "If it was up to me, the answer is yes, but then I see pretty flowers in your apartment that I didn't send, and that makes a guy tread carefully."

Ryan's flowers. She'd never given them a thought after finding Cassie. She sighed and made a face. "I won't say it's complicated, because it's not. It's just me, taking time because a wise old woman told me it's a smart thing to do."

Jake smiled and frowned at the same time. "Hannah's smart all right, but I might have wished she'd mind her own business on this particular topic. Oh, here." He withdrew his phone and pulled up a picture of Cassie sitting up, coloring.

"She looks better."

"She looks wonderful," he corrected her. "And that's your doing, Kerry. You've made a difference to this child, and that's a marvelous thing."

She had. She could see that, and with God's help and a little more patience on her part, maybe she could help Cassie's home life. And if not…she'd cross that bridge when she came to it. "Thank you for showing me that picture. It made my day."

"Good." He tipped his hat, then paused. "I expect the personal delivery added to the experience."

She laughed because he was right. "Without question."

"See you later." He strode out, and as he did, her heart did a funny little jig, as if it didn't want him to leave. She watched him go, and the longing grew…

She was falling in love with him. The realization made her smile, inside and out. When she got back to her classroom, her phone had finished charging, and it signaled a message. She picked it up, and the first thing she saw was Ryan's message that he was concerned for her. Worried for her. And the short, sincere message made her think twice.

She was quick to hold his inattention against him, but *she* was the one who moved away. She was the one who had created a physical distance, purposely.

Was she selfishly following her own dreams, or was she being smart, knowing Ryan's past and doubting the sincerity of his future?

She studied the message, unsure again, then closed the phone as busy feet hurried her way.

She'd figure this all out later, and she might just put the whole romance thing in God's hands too, because right now, Kerry was right back where she started. Torn and confused. And that didn't just feel wrong, it felt stupid.

* * *

Soft. So soft.

Cassie snuggled deep beneath the covers and breathed deeply. She wanted to inhale the difference, to absorb it and make it like a part of her. Soft, clean, sweet…oh, those were things she saw on TV commercials, and here she was, living just like that!

But when she took a deep breath, the cough started and wouldn't stop. Mrs. Wilder helped her sit up, and she rubbed something sticky on Cassie's back.

Now she smelled funny again, but not bad. Just...different. Like cough drop different.

She tried toast.

It didn't taste good.

She tried some of the pale soda and liked it, so Mrs. Wilder didn't fuss at her to eat. She just let her snuggle in the big, soft bed with all the covers she could ever want, and drink soda from a straw cup.

She fell asleep again midday, thinking that if she weren't sick, this might be the best day ever.

* * *

"How's she doing?" Kerry slipped into the apartment quietly, but she didn't need to because Cassie's voice hailed her right away.

"Kerry! I almost feel better!"

Kerry hurried into the bedroom. The twenty-hour transformation made her smile. "You look better. And you smell like chest rub."

Cassie wrinkled her nose. "Mrs. Wilder said it would help me, and it did, but it smells funny."

"As long as it helps, that's the important thing, darling. And Jake brought me a really sweet picture of you. He stopped by the school to tell me how you were doing."

Cassie's face clouded. "Why does he always come to see me?"

"Because he likes you. And he likes me. And you and I do a lot of stuff together now."

"Are you in trouble, Kerry?" She stared up at Kerry with rounded eyes. Her gaze flicked from Kerry to Hannah, then back. "You can tell me if you are."

"Why would you think that?" Kerry sank down on the edge of the bed. "Of course I'm not in trouble, honey.

"My father says if police hang around, that means trouble, and I'm not supposed to cause trouble or tell things that the police want me to say."

Remembering Jake's advice, Kerry spoke with caution. "The sheriffs are here to help us. So are the other policemen and women. Jake helped us rescue you last night, and he went back to tell your dad that you're OK."

Cassie went pale. "He went to my house?"

"Just to tell your dad you were sick and staying here."

"Was he mad?" Her voice went tiny. Her expression grayed.

"I expect he was worried 'bout you, and hoped you'd be OK soon," Hannah cut in. "Nothin' to fret about, doll-face. Nothin' at all."

Cassie looked from one to the other, then said, "When do I have to go back?"

The unspoken message rang clear without words. She didn't want to go back. She dreaded going back. And Kerry had no choice but to send her, and that broke Kerry's heart.

Trust in the Lord...

She took a breath and waded in. "I'm going to keep you here tonight and tomorrow, and I'll see if your dad will let you stay with Mrs. Wilder and me for the weekend. By Sunday, you should be well enough to go back."

Cassie didn't cry. Kerry was pretty sure she wasn't allowed to cry, so the fact that she didn't meant little. Cassie glanced around, as if memorizing the pretty, clean room, then nodded. "OK."

She yawned, and Kerry stood. "You might want a little nap again, darling. I've got some soup and chicken nuggets for tonight if you're hungry, but if you're not, we won't worry about it. Once you're feeling better, your appetite will come back."

"OK." Cassie leaned up when Kerry bent to kiss her cheek, and then she did something she hadn't done before.

She twined her arms around Kerry and hugged her, hugged her tight.

Kerry sat back down onto the bed and held her. Just that, holding her, cuddling her, rocking slowly on the soft surface, until Cassie's even breathing said she'd fallen asleep.

And then she laid her back down between the smooth, clean covers and tucked her in, dreading Sunday...but understanding the inevitable.

They had a few days to get Cassie strong again, as long as Jed agreed, and then they'd do what they could. For the moment, she'd have to pretend that was all right.

* * *

Kerry knocked on Jed Carruthers's door at seven thirty-five Sunday evening and deplored the action.

Cassie clung to her hand, and Kerry didn't dare look down. If she did, if she focused on the fear and longing in the girl's face, she'd put her right back in the car and take her back to the village, but she didn't have that option.

Jake was waiting in the car. They'd brought his car and the boys, and they'd had a fun time at a movie in Wellsville, then supper at The Texas Hot.

Cassie had been better with Jake when he was out of uniform. And she'd gotten along well with the boys for the time they were together, although Abe gave her strange looks a couple of times. Overall, it had gone all right, but now the moment of truth had come.

The door finally opened. Jed stared at her, then at Cassie. "She got sick?"

No welcome home, no hug, no kisses or daddy pulling her up into his arms, cuddling her. "She did, but she's doing better now. May I come in, Mr. Carruthers?"

He frowned but opened the door a little wider, a stingy move. "I guess."

She stepped in and didn't look around. If she did, she might lose it on him, and that wouldn't be good. Steeling her nerves, she faced him. "Remember how I said I'd work with Cassie about straightening up? Cleaning things?"

He looked befuddled, not angry. "Kinda."

"Back in the fall, before it got cold."

"Mebbe."

"Well, Cassie's done well with her lessons, and I'd like to continue them with your permission, of course."

"You mean take her to your place now and again, like you been doin'?"

"Yes, but also showing her how to help here, if that's all right. I can show her how to run the washing machine and the dryer. How to put things away so she knows where they are. Just simple, organizational skills we all need. Would that be all right?"

A part of her wished he'd refuse because the thought of coming there and helping reenforce his wretched lifestyle made her angry, but from Cassie's perspective, being able to do things would give her more choices and open more doors.

If she could wash and dry laundry, that would help her be more accepted in class. And if she knew where clean clothes were, little hands could withdraw them in the dark mornings and put them on. As long as she focused on helping Cassie, she'd do all right. She hoped. "So would that be OK? If I came by with Cassie a day or two the next few weeks and showed her how to do things here?"

She wasn't sure if it was his scrape with the law a few days before, or realizing that he'd left Cassie home alone, but he was unusually cooperative. "I guess. Don't stay long."

"Just long enough to help her," she promised, then bent low.

She'd come to the hardest part of all. Saying good-bye and walking away, knowing how happy Cassie had been at her place. "Cassie, I'll see you tomorrow, OK?"

"K." Cassie didn't look at her. She looked away, not daring to make eye contact, and Kerry knew why. It would just make the parting worse.

She wanted to hug Cassie.

But she didn't dare because they'd both start crying, and she might mess up the leeway she'd created. She touched Cassie's head, the clean, wiry curls soft beneath her hands.

And then she left, wishing there could be another way.

But there wasn't.

chapter fourteen

The next weeks flew by. Christmas and kindergarten equated chronically busy. Kerry had songs to teach, a Nativity play to arrange with the other kindergarten and first grade teachers, art projects, class projects, and a weekly ecumenical vespers service hosted by St. Mary's Church.

She shopped for Jake's boys, Jenn's kids, and Cassie. And then came the moment of truth when she had to face shopping for two men.

Was she crazy?

Yes.

Because this was insane, like a day of fishing with nothing to show for it, only she'd been doing this for months…and felt the strain.

Ryan ignored Jake's existence. He didn't mention him and didn't acknowledge that she was seeing anyone else, or that she was free to see anyone else on the few days they got together.

Jake was the polar opposite. He stood straight and tall, caring for her, for the boys, for Cassie when she was around, and for the community, and every once in a while, he'd tease her with a look or a phrase at Ryan's expense.

Jake didn't act threatened or insecure, but he didn't act like the victor either. Was he satisfied with half a relationship?

But if that's all she allowed him, then that was her fault, right?

Ryan called her mid-December to invite her to his office Christmas party. Kerry stared at the calendar and winced because she was pretty sure whoever organized an evening at the country club hadn't thrown it together at the last minute. That meant Ryan either hadn't planned on going, planned on taking someone else, or was just too caught up in himself to ask ahead of time.

"This Saturday?" she repeated. She was supposed to help decorate the church on Saturday, and Cassie was staying overnight. "That's not a lot of notice, Ryan. I've invited Cassie to spend the night with me. Then we're going to Jenn's on Sunday to make cookies with her and the kids."

"So you're not available? Again?"

"I'm not available because I have prior commitments," she replied. "You're giving me a three-day notice for a party you've probably known about for a while. And it's Christmas time, in a small town, in a Christian school. I'm swamped, Ryan."

"No problem."

He tried to sound cool about her refusal, but Kerry knew better. Ryan wasn't used to accommodating others, and she wasn't at anyone's beck and call. "We're putting on our play at school next Tuesday night. If you're free, I'm sure Cassie would love to have you come see her."

"What time?"

"Seven o'clock."

"I'm working until six, barring emergencies, so there's no way for me to get down there by seven. Tell Cassie I'll be sorry to miss her."

"I will." She hung up, glad she'd stood her ground, but sorry it had to be a choice.

Not your fault. If he'd called a few weeks ago, it would be on the calendar. You snooze, you lose, and who wants a man who gets so tied up in his job and his life that he forgets you? Note the red flag warnings, please.

The internal scolding was correct.

She didn't want to be second place or second fiddle, and maybe this was the wake-up call she needed.

Saturday afternoon an e-mail popped into her inbox. She saw the return address, and her heart went on instant pause: *j_fredrickson@U.S.Teacher. com.* She clicked it open, scarcely daring to breathe, then sat back in her chair, grinning like crazy.

"Dear Ms. McHenry, on behalf of U.S. Teacher, *we'd like to offer you a contract for your series of articles "Inviting Functional Dysfunction into the Classroom," with the possibility of naming you as a regular* U.S. Teacher

columnist. I would like to do a telephone conference interview with you after the holidays. Please let me know if the attached terms are agreeable to you, and if you have an agent, please attach their name and e-mail to your reply.

"Looking forward to hearing from you and congratulations from the editorial staff of U.S. Teacher.

"Juanita Fredrickson, Senior Editor"

Four thousand dollars for the original four articles, and the possibility of an extra thousand dollars per month if she signed on as a regular columnist.

She stared at the screen so long, Cassie grew worried. "Are you all right?"

Kerry turned, grabbed her up, and hugged her like crazy. "I'm more than all right. I'm quite possibly rich!"

Cassie laughed. Her eyes went wide. "So you can get a pony!"

"Well, not that rich. We'll just have to keep on having you ride Dundee up at the Stantons' place," Kerry told her, then hugged her again. "But this means you and I are going out for supper, kid."

"With Ben and Abe?" Cassie looked excited by the prospect, but Jake was working all weekend, and the boys were staying with his sister.

"Not this time, but I'm glad you like being with Jake and the boys. They're good kids."

"Am I good, Kerry?"

"What?" The concern in Cassie's voice made Kerry stoop low. "Of course you are, darling. You're very, very good."

"Really?" Cassie gripped the hem of her shirt, nervous. "I want to be good."

"What brought this up, Cassie?" Kerry searched the little girl's gaze, puzzled. "Why would you worry about being good?"

Worry dragged Cassie's face down. "Sometimes I'm naughty when the man is sleeping."

A child, left to her own devices, trying to amuse herself for hours. Oh yes, Kerry could see it. "What do you do?"

"I sneak things sometimes." She glanced over at Kerry's Nativity set, and the pieces of straw piling up in the little wooden manger. "And touch things I'm not supposed to. And maybe I want to cook sometimes."

"Oh, honey, you can't be playing with stoves and fire and that kind of thing. That's so dangerous, Cassie."

A tear slipped down Cassie's cheek, a tear that meant she'd probably tried to use the stove in the past. "I will make sure you have cereal and granola bars to eat when there's no supper, OK? Stuff you can do all by yourself, but you've got to promise me you won't play with the stove or matches or anything. All right?"

Cassie nodded, grim but sincere. Then she looked at the Nativity again. "Do you want me to take my straw out of the box?"

For every good deed Cassie had done, Kerry had let her add a piece of straw to the manger so the Christ child would have a warm, soft bed on Christmas Eve. "Oh, no, of course not, darling! You earned every one of those."

"Even if I'm naughty?" Cassie's expression clouded with confusion.

"You earned those by being super good or nice or helpful. They never come off. We all make mistakes, honey. That's normal."

"It is?" Cassie gripped Kerry's hands and leaned in close. "I was scared that we would have to take the straw away, and the baby would get born, and he would be cold. So cold."

Cassie knew cold. Kerry saw it in her eyes and read it in the way she hugged herself. "Well he was born a long time ago, and his mommy and daddy took very good care of him. But he smiles in heaven when he sees all the wonderful things you do, Cassie Carruthers."

"I make him smile?" Delight replaced the momentary sorrow. "For real?"

"For real. Now let's go get some supper, and tomorrow morning we'll ride up to visit Jenn and make cookies. Sound good?"

"So good!" Cassie clapped her hands in delight, joyful again, but her confession worried Kerry. A cold and hungry five-year-old was big enough to get into dangerous circumstances while unsupervised, and most of Cassie's existence fell into that category. But what could Kerry do besides provide easy-to-reach food? Not much, and that reality drove Kerry's concern deeper.

* * *

Ryan was going a little bit crazy, and it was his own fault. Well that, and the stupid holidays.

Had he ever loved Christmas?

Maybe, as a child. A young child. But he didn't have conscious memories of that, just the later ones where his mother promised to come see him but then didn't.

Year after year he'd let her build his hopes, only to shatter them. By the time he was ten or eleven, he knew better. He knew better, and still he hoped.

She was a party animal, and nothing got in the way of Maureen O'Donnell and her good times.

Remind you of anyone?

Ryan shut the thought down, because there was one major difference. He was a respected professional who saved lives, and he had no children to disappoint. That made his grown-up habits of no concern to anyone but himself. If he wanted to go out and have a good time on his time off, he could, no harm, no foul.

The stupid Christmas party was circled in red on his desk calendar. And he'd set a reminder on his phone to call Kerry and invite her, and when the reminder clicked in, he'd silenced it because he was at a club with friends.

He'd messed up again, his fault, but that didn't stop him from being mad at Kerry for standing up for herself.

He lifted the desk phone to call her, then smacked it back into the cradle, hard.

Anger coursed through him. Why did he bother? Why did he care? Miss Goody-Two-Shoes could have her God, her faith, her stupid little low-paying job, and her Podunk town all to herself.

He was done. Through. Women didn't shove Ryan O'Donnell aside. They waited for his calls. Hung on his words. Gave him that come-hither look he used to love.

Until Kerry. She wasn't afraid to call him on his actions. To make him want to be a better person, a better man.

But he was tired of being told no. Enough was enough.

Familiar writing caught his eye from the stack of envelopes the office manager had set on his desk.

Zoe. A fellow peds doctor who'd gotten the call from Stanford Children's Oncology.

They'd had a thing several years ago. She'd left to do specialized training on the West Coast, and Ryan had stayed here. End of story.

He'd heard she'd come back. The splayed-out script on the envelope in front of him was confirmation. He sliced the flap and read the folded note snugged inside an irreverent Christmas card sporting a picture of two drunken reindeer.

"Back in town at last! The old gang is getting together Saturday night at Bayside. I'll be there. Learned some new maneuvers in California. Innovative people on the West Coast. Stop down. We can get reacquainted. Zoe"

Maneuvers, huh?

Ryan felt a dual thrust of shame and interest.

He hadn't enjoyed a maneuver of any significant sort in a very long time. Maybe it was time to get back in a game he was good at.

He stared at the silent phone and mulled his options. A thumping-music, longneck-studded night with a former lover or a staff holiday party on his own.

His shoulders clenched. Not a difficult choice.

* * *

Kerry glanced at her dashboard clock, then the upcoming expressway exit, and curved right instead of left. She had an extra half-hour before Jenn was expecting her. Why not use it to share her good news with

Ryan? A significant check and a possible monthly position was nothing to scoff at.

Maybe now he'd understand her work ethic. Maybe now he'd appreciate the time and effort she was willing to expend as a writer, as a teacher. As a giver. Even Ryan O'Donnell couldn't brush off an e-mail like this. She pulled up to the curb outside the townhouse door. Cassie was busy tracing a Christmas tree in the backseat, so good at amusing herself. Too good, actually. Kerry hopped out of the car, excited to share the news. "Cassie, I'll just be a minute, right up those stairs there, OK?"

"Sure!" Head bent, she kept right on working, unbothered.

A light snow fell as Kerry hurried up his steps. She smiled, knocked on his door, and rang his doorbell, all at once.

No answer. Kerry frowned, glanced at her watch, and pressed the doorbell once more. He wasn't supposed to be on call this morning, but maybe the Christmas party celebration had changed things around.

Heavy footsteps sounded from within. Kerry stepped back, waiting. He *was* here. Good.

Vic opened the door. He looked sleepy and confused to see her. Really confused.

"Kerry. Hi. What're you doin' here?" Vic rubbed a tired hand across his eyes and squinted.

"Nice to see you, too, Vic. I came to see Ryan. Where is he? Still sleeping?" Vic looked befuddled. "He's with you. He told me last night he was ditching the Christmas party because he had a really hot date and don't expect him back until sometime Sun—"

The look Kerry gave him stopped Vic cold. His voice trailed off. He fumbled for words but only managed a brief stutter.

Kerry recovered first, but then she'd been awake longer. "I see."

She backed down a step, still clutching the acceptance letter in her hand. Suddenly it didn't mean quite so much.

"Kerry, I—"

"No." She held up a hand and shook her head. "I'm embarrassed enough, Vic. Don't say anything more."

He stepped forward, his face full of concern. "Can I do anything? You want coffee or something?"

The thought of walking into Ryan's apartment, chatting with Vic over a cup of coffee while Ryan was sleeping with another woman held scant appeal. "No. I've got to go. Cassie and I are baking Christmas cookies today. A whole other kind of fun, I guess."

As she turned, her heel slipped on the slick step. She grabbed for the rail. When she did, the acceptance letter fluttered to the frosted ground.

Vic reached out a steadying hand, then bent to retrieve the letter. He eyed it, then her. "Is this what I think it is?"

Kerry breathed deeply. "It's an acceptance letter from *U. S. Teacher*. They're buying a series of articles I wrote."

Vic whistled at the prestigious name. "That's wonderful, Kerry. You must be thrilled."

Kerry gripped the rail with one hand. With the other, she accepted the paper Vic had retrieved. She looked at him. The expression on his face said he realized that he'd just experienced another severe lapse in judgment. Kerry let out a long breath. "I was."

chapter fifteen

Ryan filled his days with work and his nights with more work.

His roommate apologized at least once a day until Ryan made him stop. Even now, weeks later, Vic still brought it up from time to time.

"Vic, enough. It's over. Done. Let's move on."

Vic shook his head. "But I am sorry, man. I can't believe I messed up that badly."

A now-familiar stab punctured Ryan's heart. Vic had blurted what he thought to be true, and Kerry had had no trouble believing him. With good reason, it seemed. Vic's inadvertent admission had pushed Ryan's tenuous relationship with Kerry over a steep edge.

Ryan shook his head and pressed his twenty-pounders with repeated precision. "It's history, man. Things happen."

Vic eyed the phone. "Have you called her recently? She's had time to cool off."

Were weeks enough time to forgive a betrayal of trust? Ryan glanced at the phone and continued to work out. "I'm not what Kerry needs. She needs a guy who's in it for the long haul. Really." Ryan gave Vic an understanding look. "You probably did me a favor."

"By telling her you spent the night with someone else?" Vic hit a punching bag with vigor, still upset with himself. "Some favor. Did you try to explain that nothing happened?"

Ryan paused. He stared out the window for long seconds. Would it matter to Kerry that nothing happened in actuality? He'd gone to the bar hoping to spend the night with an old flame because he was angry. Five minutes in Zoe's company made him realize how much he had to lose. Kerry's love, her respect. He'd kept his distance the rest of the evening, tipped back more than a few beers, and spent the night on a buddy's couch because he was in no condition to drive.

Kerry was a girl of promises. She said what she meant and meant what she said. He'd sinned in the spirit of the law, if not the letter, and she was better off without him. "Kerry wants a man of faith."

"Mandy and I are going to the early service at Grace Community on Sunday. Come with us."

"You? Going to church?" That announcement made Ryan take notice. He raised a skeptical eyebrow Vic's way.

Vic didn't squirm. "She wants the wedding there, and it seemed stupid to plan a wedding in a church I've never seen. Mandy likes going there. You might, too."

Ryan thought of his childhood church, the blue-stoned building near the shores of Lake Ontario. "I have a church. I just don't go."

Vic kept punching, hard and steady. "Then you might want to rethink that decision, old man. I've got to head back to our place and grab a shower. We're registering at department stores this afternoon."

The flash of envy surprised Ryan. He tucked it aside and kept his expression placid. "That's cool."

Vic grinned. "It is. Like the ultimate Christmas list. I get to pick out anything I want, and people buy it for me. On top of that, I get the girl. Doesn't get much better than that."

"I guess not."

Ryan headed outside for his run. There was a winter storm warning issued for parts of Western New York, starting that evening. He wanted to get his run in before the wintry mix arrived.

He missed Kerry, which was ridiculous because she wasn't his to miss. And yet…

Her absence was a constant ache in his heart. He hadn't realized how much he had to lose until he'd looked into Zoe's sassy brown eyes at the club. She hadn't changed. Still bright, aggressive, an in-your-face kind of woman who thrived on action scenes. No, Zoe hadn't grown up at all, but he had realized something within the first two minutes of conversation.

He had.

Ryan swiped a hand across his ribs to ease the stitch in his side. He kept his running pace even, ignoring the protest from his quads.

He wondered how Cassie was doing, but didn't dare call. Why set in motion a chain of events with no purpose? Kerry thought he was a lying, cheating fornicator with no thought to her wants and needs.

He wasn't any of the above, but he was smart enough to know he didn't deserve Kerry's love in his current state.

Could he change?

He passed a hand across his brow and looked at his upscale watch.

Pretty slow. No surprise there. His legs felt like lead, and his calves ached.

The question repeated itself. Could he become the man she wanted him to be? Would it do any good now that he'd ruined everything?

Shouldn't you just do it with or without the girl? Couldn't you do it for me? Remember me? The Way, the Truth, the Life?

Scripture came back to him from a seventh grade lesson, intentionally thrust aside all these years. He'd studied John's Gospel and the wisdom of the apostles, until his mother left him high and dry once more.

She'd abandoned him repeatedly, so he abandoned faith. The immature response had struck him as reasonable back then, but he was twelve at the time and pretty mad at the world.

Let what you heard from the beginning abide in you.

John's Gospel, well said, and he'd done nothing of the sort. He'd walked away in a childish funk and repeated the action short weeks ago, ruining his chance with a wonderful woman.

Fix yourself first. Let God handle the rest.

Reason won. With or without Kerry McHenry, Ryan had serious adjustments to make. He didn't like who he was on the inside, but he had no clue how to change.

Sure you do.

OK, maybe he should rephrase that last. Was it gratuitous to search for faith in order to get a girl?

Men have sought my peace for lesser reasons than that. Try it and see. What have you got to lose, Bozo?

Good point. He'd already lost everything with a wicked slap upside the head. But what could be gained by seeking the intangible? His scientific mind had a problem with that.

Nothing major.

Ryan perked an ear to the inner voice. He recognized sarcasm when he heard it.

Faith. Hope. Eternal life. The voice that tweaked him paused an extra beat. *Maybe I'll throw in the girl for good measure.*

Ryan decided to head to his father's home on the lake when his workout was complete. He'd brushed off his father's common sense for a long time. Too long.

He thought of Cassie. He pictured her pinched face, the aged worry that clouded her somber green eyes, and then gave himself a metaphysical smack.

Cassie had been handed a raw deal, just like him.

She didn't whine about her fate. She didn't fuss about her circumstances, not out loud.

With clearer vision than he'd known in over a decade, Ryan realized that maybe God had plunked Cassie into the middle of his life to help him heal and help her thrive.

Suddenly it all made perfect sense.

He took a deep breath and tried not to hurry back. His legs wouldn't appreciate the additional stress. They weren't all too happy with the current level, but the other option was to walk, and Ryan was in way too much of a rush to consider that.

He wanted to make things right with Kerry McHenry. He knew it, heart and soul. The loss of her companionship darkened his days. The lack of her voice, her bright blue eyes, haunted his nights. He wanted her back, once and for all, for better or worse, and all the other euphemisms that rang true when a man loved a woman.

He needed to become a better man.

As Ryan crossed beneath a leafless oak, a stalwart squirrel jumped for the tree next door. When his tiny feet hit the maple, he scrabbled for purchase and slipped.

For just a moment, the rodent's paws beat nothing but air until he brushed the edge of a lower branch. With Olympic speed, the creature scrambled for footing on the thinner appendage.

The narrow branch wavered, sank, then settled with the squirrel maintaining a delicate balance.

Ryan watched.

The squirrel didn't look right or left. With faith and purpose, he made a leap to the thicker limb above.

Ryan eyed the squirrel with appreciation. The rodent's success was all about timing. If he jumped too soon, the skinny stem would give way, and he'd fall to his death at Ryan's feet.

The squirrel needed a perfect blend of faith and fortitude. The upper limb had waited, arms extended. All the thick-tailed rodent had to do was trust himself to reach it.

A smile of recognition tugged Ryan's mouth. He gave a quick cheer when the squirrel found his feet firmly planted on the targeted limb.

The critter hadn't given up. He'd taken a chance and attained greater height and security because of it.

Did he weigh the options and recognize the possible downfalls? Who knew? Ryan wasn't exactly a squirrel soothsayer.

It didn't matter. If the squirrel could face death and destruction with his leap of faith, Ryan could find the courage to face childhood fears head-on.

He'd lost a lot already, but maybe he had more to gain. The least he could do was take that chance and see what happened.

Kerry said she prayed for him, every day. Did she still?

He had no way of knowing, but something had chipped at the wedge of anger lodged firmly inside him. If she was still praying, then maybe all wasn't lost.

Just maybe.

chapter sixteen

Cassie eyed the upcoming road with trepidation. She hated this part. For nearly two days, she'd been able to pretend. As the curve ahead announced her return home, she cringed.

There was no pretending here. She tried, but all she could think of was Kerry's fresh, clean apartment. The soft blankets, sweet smelling. The box of toys and dolls that sat ready, waiting for her.

Kerry said the man was trying harder. Maybe he was. He let her go with Kerry more often now. That was good.

But then she had to come back, and she didn't want to come back. She wanted to stay in town with Kerry. The thought of waking up in the dark, smelly bedroom made her chest hurt. Her throat tightened. She clamped her lips and pushed back the feelings that rose as Kerry swung the car into the drive.

Here was where the dream always shattered. Cassie narrowed her eyes, swallowed hard, and pushed herself out of the car.

Rusting equipment littered the muddy yard. When it was snow-covered, things hadn't looked so bad. With the snow gone, everything took shades of brown and gray. Dull. Lifeless.

It matched Cassie's feelings as she approached the house.

She understood time now. Tomorrow morning the bus would come, and she could pretend again, at least for the day. Maybe if she went to bed really early, morning would come quicker.

The smell hit her as she walked in the door. Familiar and sour, she didn't have to look to know the clear bottle was pretty empty again.

"You're back."

She nodded and set her backpack on a small table that she and Kerry had polished Friday afternoon.

"I expect those dishes done."

Cassie stared at the kitchen.

He hadn't lifted a finger since she left on Friday. Half-scorched pots littered the stove. Dirty, unscraped plates sat in greasy, cool water. Bits of old food floated on the top.

"Scrub 'em hard. Ain't no good you gettin' all kinds of ideas, goin' off with your friends in their fancy cars. This is where you belong, where you're from, girl."

It's not. Cassie wanted to shout the words.

She didn't. With a deep breath, Cassie pushed the dreams into a safe corner of her heart, rolled up her sleeves, and dragged a chair to the sink.

She didn't look at the man. She didn't listen to the TV with its whining sound of engines as race cars roared around a track.

She prayed. Talking to God had helped before. It made her feel peaceful, like someone was watching out for her even when Kerry wasn't around.

She eyed the clutter of dirty dishes, sucked in some air, and plunged her hands into the nasty water to find the drain plug. She set it aside and let dirty water drain away as she scraped hard, crusty food into the garbage can.

Kerry said Jesus loved the poor. That when the men in charge bossed him around, he went out of his way to help the people no one liked.

Would he do that for her? Could he?

She didn't know.

She knew he sent Kerry. Kerry told her that. As she refilled the chipped sink with warm, soapy water, Cassie almost smiled, remembering.

Kerry said God sent Cassie to her classroom so they could be friends. In the soft glow of Kerry's house, that was easy to believe. There, among the shining windows, the tucked-back curtains, the warm smells of good food cooking, Cassie could imagine herself a regular girl. Even special, sometimes.

Here, in the late-day shadows of her real home, faith didn't come as easily. Here she was Cassie Carruthers, the dirty daughter of a drunk.

Two drunks, Cassie corrected herself. Her hands shook at that thought.

She'd thought her mother wonderful. She was nice to Cassie and hugged her a lot before she died. She laughed with her. Cassie remembered that the most.

But the man said Sara Carruthers was a no-account drunk for all her high-and-mighty ways.

Cassie was older now. She understood the comment. He meant her mom pretended to be normal even though she was a drunk.

Cassie wasn't even sure what a drunk was, but it wasn't good, she could tell that much.

Out of the corner of her eye, she saw the man's head roll back against the upper pad of the old reclining chair. Soon he'd be snoring.

Cassie scrubbed, not wanting to take a chance he'd wake up and her work wouldn't be done. Sometimes he liked that she went away with Kerry, other times it made him mad.

She didn't like people to be mad at her. If she could be very small, very little inside, then maybe he wouldn't notice her when he woke up.

Help him to sleep a long time, Jesus, she prayed as her fingers scrubbed at a stuck-on piece of old egg. *Help him to be nice when he wakes up.*

It was a long while before the dishes were washed completely. By the time she was done, the light had long since gone from the sky. The dark, cluttered kitchen was lit by a single bulb that hung in the middle. Kerry had changed the bulb on Friday. The new one wasn't dusty and gave Cassie more light.

She emptied the sink, then threw away clumps of food caught in the silver drain.

She tiptoed past the man. Sometimes he would sleep all night, but other times he would wake up after a little nap. He was always mad then. Cassie made it just beyond him when his voice made her pause.

"Them dishes done?"

"Yes."

"Done right?"

"Yes."

"Do I need to be checkin' 'em?"

"I don't know." Cassie hated the shiver in her voice. It was always better to show no fear.

His voice dropped a level. Not a good sign. "You think I got nothin' better to do than check up on you?"

Cassie worked to keep her voice steady. He liked to see her scared, so she tried not to let it show. "No."

He stared at her. "Get yourself back to that kitchen and check them dishes. Then sweep up that floor. You think 'cause you got all kinds of rich friends, you don't have to do your share around here?"

Cassie didn't answer. She set her book bag down and trudged back to the kitchen on quiet feet.

She'd almost made it. So close.

Tired hands seized the worn broom. With small strokes, she worked the broom around the floor, between chairs, under the cupboards. There was no dustpan. It took long minutes to find something that could catch the debris. A piece of newspaper folded one time worked OK.

She eyed the dishes, sighed, then dragged the chair back to the sink. She stifled a yawn, then glanced at the clock.

The long hand was on the eleven. The short hand was on the ten.

Almost ten o'clock, then. She yawned again. When she did, the pan she was holding slipped from her fingers and clattered to the floor.

The man shot out of his chair. "What are you doin'?"

He strode to the kitchen, his face angry. "Can't a body sit and watch TV on Sunday without some brat of a kid makin' a racket?"

Cassie froze.

The man rarely hit her, but he seemed very angry now. She didn't look up. "I'm sorry."

"Get to bed."

Thank you, God. Cassie eyed the dishes she was supposed to check but didn't breathe a word.

"And don't make no noise in the morning. I need my sleep."

Cassie slipped off the chair and skirted the table to get to her room.

Her heart beat hard against her chest as she leaned her bedroom door closed.

Once in here, she was safe. He never came in here.

With care, Cassie slipped into clean pajamas and tucked herself into bed. She pressed the button on the radio Kerry had given her for Christmas. A dot of light told her the alarm was set.

She didn't usually need the buzzer. She liked to wake up and leave for school, but it was late tonight. She didn't want to oversleep. Kerry would miss her.

She tried to say her bedtime prayers the way Kerry showed her.

It didn't work here. The words wouldn't come. Finally, she sank into the pillow, her hands folded. "Thank you for letting the man send me to bed."

Would Jesus understand what she meant? That she was tired and glad to go to sleep?

Cassie sighed. Her eyes fluttered shut.

She hoped so.

chapter seventeen

"That's great, Cassie. Do it again." Kerry offered the compliment as Cassie guided Brady Stanton's roan gelding around the Stantons' inside arena the following week. Amanda watched with a look of pure pleasure on her face.

"She's doing better."

Amanda wasn't just referring to Cassie's improved seat in the saddle.

"I think so, too." Kerry flashed her a quiet smile. "This girl has beauty and brains, and I have every intention of seeing her get full benefit of both. Her father is letting me take her to church with me."

"Really?" Dave Stanton didn't hide his surprise.

"Mm-hmm. And Cassie and I have been doing Friday field trips to her house."

Dave looked confused.

"To clean," Kerry explained.

"Ah."

He gnawed on the toothpick and made a face at Cassie. "Light hands, please."

Cassie nodded and eased her grip.

Dave turned back to Kerry. "He doesn't mind the intrusion?"

Kerry frowned. "I keep the sessions short so I don't crowd his space."

"He's still drinking."

"Yes." Less? More? She had no idea. "Sometimes he seems more cognizant of what's going on. He's fixed up some things around the cabin that I don't think he's noticed in years. Patched up holes from rodents, then set out traps to help clear them. That was a huge step."

"Mice?"

"Not mice."

Dave cringed, watching the smile of delight on Cassie's face as she circled the paddock in an easy lope. "I hate rats. Mostly because they smarten up too quick." He switched his focus back to Cassie. "Straighten up, Cassie. Don't hunch." He gave a brisk nod of approval when Cassie followed his direction. "Much better."

"Are you warm enough, Kerry?" Amanda pointed to the far wall. "Extra barn coats over there."

"I'm fine. It's not bad in here. But it looks like we've got a taste of real winter coming up again, and I can't pretend I don't worry about her when she's home. That shack's cold on a normal day. I can't imagine it in a storm." She walked forward and held up a hand to Cassie once Dave had finished the lesson. "That's it, Munchkin. Gotta cool the old guy down now."

Cassie leaned into the horse's neck and gave him a big hug. "I love you, Dundee."

"I think he loves you right back." Kerry reached up to offer help. "I'll give you a hand."

"I can do it."

Kerry accepted the surge of independence. "OK."

Watching as Cassie grasped the horn, she saw the moment of hesitation followed by quick decision. With a firm grip and a shove, the girl half-slid, half-vaulted from the back of the roan.

Kerry handed her the reins. "Good job. Let's put the tack away and give him a nice walk."

Cassie accepted the reins and started moving forward. Dundee matched his pace to the child's, his head nodding in easy rhythm. When they got to the other side of the ring, Cassie looked up at Kerry. "I like Addie's dad."

"He's a good guy."

"I like him a lot," Cassie continued. "He smiles at me, and he shakes his head yes, and he makes faces sometimes, and they never scare me. Do you think he's like that with Addie and Brady? Like nice to them?"

The question in her voice indicated where the conversation was heading. Kerry faltered, then said, "Yes."

Cassie trudged forward, chin down, with the easygoing horse alongside. And then she peeked up toward Kerry again. "Will my dad ever be nice?"

Oh, man. How could she reason that to a small child? Kerry searched for positives. "Your dad's been doing more around the house lately, right?"

Cassie didn't look all that impressed by Jed's efforts. "I guess."

"And he lets you come with me."

Cassie shrugged. "Yes."

Kerry nudged the child's shoulder. "That's a big improvement, Cassie. Remember when you first started school, and he wouldn't let you go with me at all?"

Cassie's hesitation said too much. Kerry paused. "Does he get mad because you're with me, Cassie?"

Cassie looked away. Her mouth tightened. "Maybe sometimes."

Kerry's heart stutter-stepped. She bent to Cassie's level. "Does he yell at you? Hurt you?"

Cassie kept her look averted, and when she spoke, she whispered the words. "He yells. Kind of a lot now."

Kerry stared at her, unsure what to say. If Jed was growing more agitated because she had Cassie so often, maybe she was making a bad situation worse. "I like having you with me, Cassie, but I don't want to make trouble for you."

Cassie turned frightened eyes her way. "You mean you wouldn't come get me?" The dread in her voice matched the fear in her eyes.

Kerry shook her head. "No, honey, of course not. But maybe I shouldn't take you so often. I don't want you to be in trouble at home."

"Do I have to go back there?" Cassie's expression implored Kerry to offer a reprieve.

Kerry's heart plunged. Her principal had talked to her about this very thing as she resupplied her classroom the week before. Cassie's attachment to her was strong. Maybe too strong. Kerry's goal had been to help Cassie become self-assured, less ostracized.

Had she crippled the child by making her more dependent?

No. She couldn't believe that. She loved the girl. Not having her around wasn't an option. She grabbed Cassie into a firm hug. "We'll try not to make your dad angry, OK?"

Cassie nodded against her shirt. "How?"

That was the question of the hour. Kerry had no idea. She puffed out a breath and kissed the girl's soft cheek. "I'm not sure. I'll think about it."

Cassie's head bobbed once more. She cuddled her face into Kerry's neck. "I love you, Kerry."

"I know. I love you, too."

Kerry straightened and handed Cassie the reins again. "Come on, kid. Enough of this emotional stuff. I'm starving, and we've got a horse to tend."

Cassie's dimples flashed. "OK." She looked around the horse paddock and the barn. "I like coming here. When I was little, Mrs. Stanton sent me things. Brady would put them in my mailbox. It was sneaking, but it wasn't bad sneaking, she told me. It was surprise sneaking, and that was OK." She followed Kerry's lead and aimed for the far paddock. "She was like my fairy godmother. Her presents made me feel really good. So does coming up here to ride Dundee."

Kerry sensed the growing conundrum.

There was little they could do about Cassie's home life, but as Cassie observed other options, she'd become more discontented. "Dave and Amanda love having you here. We're blessed to have so many good neighbors and friends, Munchkin. Let's finish up with Dundee, all right? I'm hungry, and Amanda makes the best chicken stew around."

Cassie's stomach picked that moment to gurgle. She tipped her chin up. "I'm hungry, too! Maybe we can take some home with us."

Kerry knew what the girl meant. She thought of Kerry's home as her own when they were together. Kerry pushed the feeling of guilt away and smiled. "Maybe we can."

chapter eighteen

"Again?" Jake deadpanned a look of disbelief at Abe, Cassie, and Ben as they clamored for one more ride down the long, sloping, snow-covered hill. "All three of you? For real?"

"Not me, Dad!" Abe squared up his shoulders and started hiking up the hill. "I can go up all by myself!"

He made it eight steps before his feet went every which way and he sprawled onto the slick surface.

"Abe!" Cassie tried to hurry up the slope after him, but her boots slipped and slid on the slick hill.

Jake settled Ben onto the sled, tucked Cassie in behind him, and by the time he got to Abe, the boy was scrubbing snow off his face with two snowy hands.

"Allow me." Kerry took the end of her soft scarf and dusted Abe's face. And then she touched his cold cheek and asked, "Are you OK? Are you hurt?"

Abe stared up at her. He stood like that, just like that, for long beats of the clock, then a tear slipped down his cheek.

Abe wasn't a crying kind of kid. Never had been. But right now he was staring at Kerry, and his whole face looked sad. So sad.

She bent low and hugged him. And when the five-year-old hugged her back, Jake's awareness grew.

Abe was falling in love with Kerry.

Well, so was Jake.

But stepping out, moving forward with two kids wasn't a process a man should take lightly. Except there was nothing about Kerry McHenry that he took lightly, including the old boyfriend that seemed to crop up at the most inconvenient times.

His mother disapproved.

Jake ignored her advice.

He understood her concerns, but these were new times. Mixed-race families were more normal now than when she married his dad nearly forty years before.

He spotted Abe's snow-crusted mitten in the snow. He bent to retrieve it, knowing his boy's little hand must be icy cold.

Kerry whipped her gloves off and tugged them into place over Abe's hands. They were huge, but Abe didn't care. "These are warm!" A happy grin split his face as he gazed up at her. "Now my hands feel better, Kerry!"

"Good." She leaned down and kissed his cheek, laughing. "I've got another pair in the car, so you keep those on, OK?"

"OK! Thanks!" He hugged her, all on his own, and the sight of his little boy being cherished and mothered by a wonderful woman seemed to open doors and windows in Jake's brain.

Abe let go, and Kerry put her soft, pale hand along his cheek. "And now would you like to ride on the sled with Cassie and Ben, or walk up the hill with me?"

"With you." Abe stuck his hand into hers, then made his way up the long incline beside her.

She fit.

They fit.

Watching the two of them push their way up the softer snow alongside the sleeker sledding trail, Jake didn't see his mother's concerns. He saw possibilities. Joy. Laughter. And when Abe tipped his face up to Kerry, talking a mile a minute, his little son didn't see skin tones. He saw Kerry's warmth, her smile, her humor…her love.

She turned just then and flashed an over-the-shoulder smile for him. Just him.

He'd picked her up after church, skirting the fact that he took the boys sporadically, when the mood hit.

Maybe next week, they could go together. Him, the boys, Kerry, and

Cassie. And Hannah, if she wanted to. Why not?

Watching Kerry with Abe, hearing Cassie and Ben giggle as he tugged them back up the hill, he realized he'd stopped being angry.

He wasn't sure when it happened, but as he drew abreast of Kerry at the summit, he was glad it did. "So, Miss McHenry?"

"Yes?" She tipped her face up toward his, and he had no choice but to kiss her. And then, as the kids scrambled into position for one last ride, he held the sled rope in one hand and the beautiful woman with the other. "What do you think about going to church together next week? Like all of us?"

She held his gaze, then leaned forward and gave him butterfly kisses across his chin, and then his cheek. She increased the distance slightly and smiled. "I think I'd like that, Deputy Slattery." When he grinned, she smiled right back and tapped his chin with her now-chilled bare hand. "I'd like that a lot."

So would he. "Go get your gloves. I'm going to take them for one last ride…"

He ignored their collective groan.

"And then we can go home and make hot chocolate. OK?"

"Oh, yeah." She smiled up at him, a slow, enchanting smile, the kind that made him feel taller, stronger, and warmer. "Very OK."

* * *

Ryan strode through the near-empty church parking lot early the next Tuesday and hurried up the steps to the rectory door. It swung wide almost immediately.

"I was watching for you tonight," the reverend explained. "Wicked night. Snow, sleet, freezing rain. It's like Mother Nature can't quite make up her mind and decided to just come packing her entire arsenal. How were the roads?"

"Not bad yet, but I expect that's going to change. Did you make coffee? Because I sure could go for a cup, Father."

The pastor gave him a nod and a grin. "Just like I've been doing. Have a seat. Tell me what you thought of Jacob's story."

"He was a manipulator, a liar, and a cheat." Ryan hung his coat on the row of hooks inside the rectory door, then followed the pastor into the sitting room. "Why would God have anything to do with him, much less bless him?" He sank into the corner cushion of the sofa and reached forward to take the hot mug from Father Cummings.

The older man laughed. "Why, indeed? But then, why bother with any of us? Who among us hasn't lied?"

He watched Ryan's face and nodded. "Cheated? Manipulated?"

Ryan waved a hand of acknowledgment. "So Jacob is any man."

"Jacob was specific," the priest corrected. "He was the man for the job at that place and time, but his sins are those of any man."

"I can relate to that." He offered the rector a wry look. "He sought the love of his life a long time."

Father Cummings's expression indicated he understood the correlation. Ryan had filled the older man in on the details of his faith quest from the beginning. He was determined to move forward, one way or another. Meeting with a man of God seemed a sensible way to start for a guy who hadn't graced the inside of a church of his own volition in nearly two decades.

The pastor contemplated Ryan's words as he sipped his coffee. "He did. He believed it was meant to be, and so he waited and worked."

"While he slept with others." The irony of that wasn't lost on Ryan.

"Yes." The older man acknowledged that with a bob of his head. "In those days, it was not uncommon to have more than one wife."

Ryan shook his head. "Managing to keep one woman happy is a task modern man messes up regularly." He thought of his parents. "How would a simple man manage two? Throw in a couple of handmaids, besides. And all of them having babies." Ryan gave a mock shudder. Then he leaned forward, serious. "Jacob was a sinner. He was a man who engineered things to his own ends. In today's terms, we'd call him a player and ridicule him."

"Yes," the pastor agreed. "Until he was thwarted by God. It took Jacob a long time to realize his choices could have been a whole lot better a whole lot sooner."

His words gave Ryan a personal stab of truth. "I've told you about Kerry."

The pastor folded his hands.

"Her faith is strong. Unshakable." Ryan pressed his lips into a line and shook his head, eyes narrowed. "I can't imagine trusting something abstract to that extent. Even God. Maybe especially God. Sometimes I sit in church among all those believers and wonder why they don't question their own actions? Are they simply sheep, following one another? Do they realize the unlikelihood of their beliefs in a scientific world?"

"The Thomas syndrome."

Ryan frowned.

"A common malady among the learned," Father Cummings assured him. "It's what makes the simple faith of a child difficult to accept."

Ryan flushed.

The pastor regarded him with a slight smile. "You want to witness the wounds in Christ's hands and feet before you believe, Ryan. Probe the pierce-mark in his side. Like Thomas." He sat more upright in his chair. "Your lady friend believes because God has put it on her heart. He's imprinted her soul, and she offers her love and trust without promise of proof or payment."

Ryan pressed a hand to the arm of the couch. "So how do we Thomas-types figure this out? How do you believe without doubt?"

"Faith with no doubts?" The pastor's eyes lightened. He sat back. "A rarity." He hoisted his mug in a mock toast. "Let me know when you find it."

"But—"

"Faith is a gift."

Ryan slumped his shoulders.

"Pray for it, Ryan. Pray for the insight, the ability to believe. Pray for his guidance, his eternal love. Faith will come when you turn yourself over to Christ fully. But I can't promise there won't be doubts." The pastor mulled the idea and shook his head. "Life isn't easy. Doubts come. They're part of the package."

Ryan sat forward. "I see miracles all the time, Reverend. Especially these days."

The rector inclined his chin. "You're in the right line of work for it."

Ryan nodded. "I used to attribute them to quirks of science or phantoms of nature." He made a quizzical frown and met the pastor's kind gaze. "I don't anymore. It's as though I can see the hand of God in these circumstances and recognize it."

"A good first step." The pastor handed Ryan a folded sheet of paper. "Your assignment for the coming week."

Ryan opened it. "Prepare for Easter?" He eyed the pastor. "That's weeks away. You mean you want me to give up something for Lent, right? I can do that."

The pastor cuffed Ryan's arm gently. "We're way past scratching the surface here, Ryan. You want in? Well, make some atonement for all those years of putting yourself first. I want you to give of yourself. Give until it hurts and then give some more."

The old man's instruction tweaked a long-stowed memory. "Jesus, others, yourself. JOY."

"Just as true now as when you learned about it in junior high." The pastor nodded, pleased. He gave Ryan another jab. "Pity it took you so long to remember it."

Ryan couldn't deny the truth in that. He stood and nodded. "I won't argue that." He reread the instructions on the paper and nodded. "I'll work on it, Father."

"I know you will, son. Look forward, not back, and pray for the peace of mind only God can give."

Ryan hesitated. Thoughts of his mother flooded him, but this time they didn't stab quite so deep. Improvement? Maybe. "It's not as easy as it sounds."

The pastor splayed his hands. "What is?"

He walked Ryan to the door and put a hand to his shoulder. "You have the power to forgive your enemy, to make things right. Use that power. From that forgiveness come mercy and goodness."

"And they will follow me all the days of my life." Ryan offered the quote from the twenty-third psalm with ease.

The pastor smiled. "Exactly. That long-term memory of yours is quite a gift." His grin deepened. "I don't expect you've heard that verse in a while."

Ryan stretched out a hand. "Too true." He met the older man's smile with an honest one of his own. "Thank you, sir."

The pastor pumped his hand with vigor. "I'll see you Sunday."

Ryan's smile deepened to a grin. "Ten o'clock."

* * *

Kerry heard her phone ring, hoped it wouldn't die like it had been doing far too often lately, and grabbed it up. Jake's number flashed in the old-style display. She flipped it open quickly. "Hey, are you working in this?"

"I am, but I'm calling to make sure you're tucked in at home and not planning on going anywhere tonight. Right?"

He sounded protective, sweet, and a little bossy, and the put-together package meant he sincerely cared about her and her well-being. "Hannah and I are staying here. They've already shut schools again tomorrow."

"A smart preemptive strike," Jake noted. "Anything that keeps people safe during the worst of the storm is considered a total bonus on my end. An ice storm on top of a lake effect event is just courting danger. Tucked inside is the best possible scenario right now."

"Except Cassie is home with Jed," Kerry told him. "I can't deny I'm concerned. I dropped her off yesterday, and with no school today or tomorrow, who knows what she'll have to eat? I left granola bars and cereal, but I'm worried. How can a little kid handle being locked up in that awful house with him? This can't possibly be good for her mental and emotional health, and the place is cold under decent conditions. I can't imagine what it's like right now, and I'm sitting here with Hannah and the woodstove, with chicken soup on the stove."

"And feeling guilty about it."

"Yes. I should have brought her back here. I knew they were predicting a storm. But I also know he's getting upset with her more often lately."

"She said that?" Jake's voice went sharp.

"Yes. She's scared, Jake."

He muttered something gruff, then went silent for a moment. "We'll figure something out. We have to. I thought we might be able to work around Jed and have him just go along with it, but if he's involved with the meth circuit up in the hills, he's probably getting more and more nervous with people coming around. And that becomes Cassie's fault."

"How illegal would it be for me to keep her and let him keep getting the government assistance?" Kerry asked. "We both know that's the only reason he cares. Is that a horrible federal offense, to let him get paid for her care and let her live with me?"

"It sounds pretty fraudulent to me, honey. Wait, hang on." She heard noise in the background, and then Jake came back on the line. "They've just closed the entire southeast sector and declared a state of emergency."

"That's where Cassie and the Stantons live."

"Trees down. Power lines down. The freezing rain has caused an ice buildup on top of yesterday's snow, and it's bringing down branches and full trees. With the weight of yesterday's snow, I expect we're going to lose a fairly large number of flatter roofs. There's no way that shoddy construction can handle those combined forces of this magnitude. I've got to go, Kerry. I'll call you in a little while, OK?"

"Are the boys with your mother?"

"Safe and sound, and pretending they're explorers on Planet Hoth, the ice planet from *Star Wars*, last I knew. Probably smacking each other with the light sabers you got them for Christmas. I'll talk to you soon."

"OK."

She hung up the phone, plugged it into her charger, and moved to the front window.

Nothing moved outside, except the storm. The plows had banked the generous effects of yesterday's snow-dump into huge piles along the curbs and at the end of the road. Today's slightly higher temperature had brought freezing rain. Not only were the roads and sidewalks snow-covered, today's rainfall had created over a quarter inch of ice so far, with more to come.

"Did he say how things are in the hills?" Hannah brought the freshly-filled tea kettle from the kitchen and set it on the soapstone woodstove. "No sense wastin' good heat," she noted as she set it down. Then she crossed to Kerry. "You're worried, I know."

"Scared to death," Kerry admitted. "I kept second-guessing myself about dropping her off, and so many things ran through my mind. That maybe I was creating more of a problem than a help, that maybe I should back off to keep Jed calm."

"Oh, darlin'." Hannah settled herself in her favorite chair and patted the sofa alongside. "It is not a sweet thing like you that riles up the Jeds of this world; it's their very own emptiness goin' so deep inside. I look at Jed, and I see a man who could have done something with his life, and he chose not to. No one forced him, no one set barriers in his path. He just took it on himself to choose poorly."

"And Sara, his wife?" Hannah's frown deepened as Kerry sat down on the soft sofa. "A brilliant woman, so well educated." She sighed out loud and shook her head. "She should have gone places, but when drugs and liquor take control, everything you see, smell, or touch becomes tainted. So Jed doesn't look at Cassie and see the wonder of a child, the beautiful gift God gave him. He only sees the funds deposited in his account each month to support his downfall, because his brain has been muted for so long, he can't bear the thought of bein' normal. And that's the truth of the matter."

"And we're stuck doing nothing."

"That's where you're wrong." Hannah reached out and grabbed hold of Kerry's hand, firm and tight. "We pray. We take this trial to Jesus, where it belongs, and we don't sit and moan and whine about what we can't do, when God himself told us what to do: 'Where two or more are gathered in my name..."'

Hannah was right, of course. "If my people who are called by my name humble themselves..."

Kerry clung to Hannah's hand, and they prayed together. The tea grew cold, and the fire went low, but they held hands and prayed together, following Christ's words and his example. As the storm raged on around them, two women prayed for the safety of one small child in the midst of the tumult.

And still it rained, freezing on contact.

* * *

So cold.

Cassie stared at her breath as it puffed white inside the little house.

It wasn't supposed to do that. She knew it did that outside, but she wasn't supposed to be able to see her breath inside, was she?

No.

Her hands were chilled to the bone, but so were her feet. Her toes didn't want to move, and her head ached from trying to get warm.

Something was wrong. It had to be wrong, because the man was sleeping and didn't seem worried about the cold, and she didn't know how to make it stop being cold. The little heater in the corner of the front room wasn't warm.

She checked the plug and turned the heater off and then on.

Nothing.

Outside a big drift of snow had covered the front door, and when she tried to open it, it wouldn't budge.

What if she couldn't get the house warm?

What if the man never woke up?

Would she freeze solid like that little girl in the story, the one with the matches? Was that what would happen?

She hated that story. Addie had read it to her once, and she'd wanted to jump into the book and make someone be nice to the little girl. She wanted them to take her inside and invite her to Christmas dinner.

But no one did.

Cassie shifted her gaze as the darkness deepened. The TV wasn't working, and the heater wasn't working, and the man wouldn't wake up, and she couldn't get the door open.

She tried the back door, but the lock was too old and rusty. She couldn't push it enough to make it open up. And where would she go if she got outside?

She thought hard.

The Stantons.

It was a long, long walk up the hill, but that was the only neighbor nearby. Could she walk in the snow?

Maybe, once she got to the road, but the plows hadn't come back, so the snow would be deep. She'd seen the gleam of ice before everything started getting dark.

Was everything icy?

Could everything be icy?

She'd never seen that happen before, but as she stood inside, so cold and drained, she tried to plan how she could get outside.

There was one low window in the man's room. The front window broke a long time ago, and the man tacked a board over it. She couldn't remember a time when it wasn't broken. And most of the windows were too high for her, even with a chair, but if she could get out *that* window, the one by the man, she could walk away. Or maybe run away. Somehow, someway, she needed to get to someplace warmer, but how?

The man's box of matches sat on the counter. She'd tried lighting them a couple of times, but when Kerry told her not to, she'd stopped.

But if she couldn't see, how could she get the window open? And if the match was the only thing that gave light, didn't she have to use them?

She felt for the box with one hand, and when something furry brushed by her fingers, she fought back the scream. Maybe the rat was cold, too. Just like her. She couldn't even hardly hate him for seeking comfort, but she knew something the rat didn't.

There was no comfort in the little house.

She carried the matches to the man's room. It wasn't easy because there were things on the floor, the man's things. She tripped twice, and the second time she fell hard, right against the sharp edge of his bed. Her face took a wallop, but she didn't waste time feeling sorry for herself. Somehow she knew there wasn't time to waste.

She'd pulled her jacket on when it first started getting cold. She pulled snow pants on too, the ones Mrs. Stanton had given her a while ago. She couldn't find her mittens, but her boots were right where she left them. She pushed her feet into them, stood, and made her way around the bed to the window.

Crashing noises sounded outside. She peered out. There was no light to penetrate the blackness, so there was nothing to see. But she heard the noises, strange sounds she'd never heard before, in all her life.

The noise told her it wasn't safe to go outside, but it wasn't safe to freeze to death inside either, and so she pulled out one long stick match and swiped it against the shallow box.

Nothing.

She frowned in concentration, with no visual to guide her, locating the rough lighting strip with her fingers. She tried again and got a spark this time, but no flame. Still, that was closer, wasn't it?

She braced her feet hard against the floor, and struck the match again.

It flared bright, like a shining light in a river of darkness, but she knew it wouldn't last long. She held it up to the dirty window. The lock was high, too high for her, but there was a metal bar on the floor near the man's bed. She didn't peek over her shoulder at the man. She didn't want to wake him up, but she couldn't be cold one minute more, and if he told her to put the bar down, she'd have to do it. She was better off not knowing. She raised the bar and struck the window just as the match blew out.

Glass shattered all around her, but did it all break?

She couldn't tell, and she knew broken glass was dangerous. She reached up and hit the window again, but only a little glass broke that time.

Icy rain streamed in the broken window, rain so cold that she didn't even think rain could get that cold. She stepped back and withdrew another match. There weren't too many left, but she needed to see the window. To see if the hole was big enough.

It took three times again, and her hand grew damp from the rain, but just as she was about to crawl through anyway, the match flared.

Four big, long spikey pieces of glass poked toward the middle. She hit first one, then the others before the match got too close to her fingers. When the tip of her finger felt hot, she dropped the match quickly. Then she stuffed the matches into her pocket and zipped it with frozen, wet fingers.

Bracing her hands against the sill, she lifted one leg, then the other, pulling herself up and over the sharp, metal frame.

Glass poked her leg.

She ignored it.

But when a longer piece tore at her coat sleeve, she had to pull extra hard to free the slippery material. When it jerked loose, she fell to the ground below, slipping and sliding in a sea of ice and broken glass.

She couldn't stand. The ground was too hard and slippery, and when she tried to stand, she fell, and so she crawled.

Her hands froze. She couldn't feel her fingers, and maybe couldn't feel her palms, she wasn't quite sure, but she knew she'd never been so cold before, even on the very worst nights.

She crawled to the front of the house and turned toward the Stantons' farm. Envisioning the distance to the bend in the road, she had a scary notion that the Stantons' farm might be much further away than a little girl could crawl on cold, slippery ice. But if she didn't try, how would she know?

No cars came by to help her.

No lights shone in the distance, in any direction. That meant that she was alone in the darkness, just her, barehanded, with a dwindling box of matches.

Just like that poor, wretched little girl in the story.

chapter nineteen

Jake glared at the clock and the weather, then phoned his commanding officer. Yes, he knew there were people trapped in the cold all over, the logistics of the storm guaranteed that. But in this case, he knew of a small child, unsupervised, with no power. Command would have to let him go, and if they didn't?

Somehow or other, he'd get to Cassie on his own.

Tim Weller came up alongside him as the captain answered. Jake looked at his longtime friend, and when Tim gave him a thumb up, he knew Tim wouldn't let him go alone. "Captain, we have a situation."

"We've got at least a hundred situations, Jake, and it's crazy busy out there under the worst possible circumstances. What makes yours more important than anyone else's?"

Jake filled him in quickly. He understood the numbers; he knew the odds. The captain was a good man, but to assign a team to clear the road and get him out to County Center Road would be a massive undertaking, the kind that—

"I'm issuing the order for Phillipsburg Fire and Rescue to accompany. They've got a team of chainsaw operators on board. You leave in five."

Jake couldn't have heard him right. "You're serious."

"Deadly. That sector was shut down over thirty hours ago in the blizzard conditions, which means folks out there have no access to heat, and the ground temperature is dropping. I guarantee you that yours won't be the only rescue in that area, so let's make it priority one. But no cowboy heroics out there, from any of you. Come back alive."

That was the plan. "Thank you, Captain." Jake grabbed his gear and layered up. So did Tim. If the volunteer loggers couldn't get them all the way in, they'd walk the balance. It wouldn't be easy. Nothing about this night nor these conditions would ever be considered easy, but now that they had permission to go, they needed to make every single moment count because lives could be hanging in the balance. Including Cassie's.

* * *

Kerry couldn't wait any longer. She called Jake, needing assurances that Cassie would be all right. No matter how much or how hard she prayed, something told her Cassie *wasn't* all right, and she couldn't seem to corral her fears. "Jake, it's me."

He laughed softly. "The phone number was a clue."

"I'm scared."

"For Cassie."

She was relieved he understood. She'd never be scared for herself; she'd worked to kick fear to the curb a long time ago. But for Cassie, fear struck deep and held tight tonight. "We have to get to her."

"Tim and I are on our way."

"Really?" Relief swept through her, sheer, sweet relief. "Oh, Jake, thank you!"

"It's slow-going, Kerry. Real slow, we've got a team of firefighters and volunteers with chainsaws. They're removing debris ahead of us, but there's major treefall. They've cut power to the area, and I talked to Amanda. They have heat there from their woodstove, but there's no heat at Cassie's without power. I alerted the commander, and they made that sector a top priority for a rescue."

Kerry didn't want to ask the question, but had to. "How long have they been without power, Jake?"

"Over a day."

So long. While she sat cozy warm by Hannah's fire, Cassie had been freezing on County Center Road.

"You keep praying. Don't stop."

It seemed like so little when a child could be perishing under the harsh elements. "Can the Stantons get to her?"

"If Dave was home, they could, but he got snowed in at his mother's house outside of Wellsville. It's just Amanda and the kids, and she can't leave Addie and Brady alone."

"Of course not. I'll pray, Jake. But I wish I could do more."

"Just knowing you and God have my back will be fine, Kerry. Gotta go."

He clicked off quickly.

Kerry set the phone down more slowly.

She prayed.

Hannah had dozed off in the wide, comfy chair. She slept soundly, the warmth and flickering flames a comfort.

Kerry couldn't sleep if she tried, and she had no intention of trying. She prayed for Cassie's safety. She prayed for the storm to stop.

It didn't, nor was it supposed to.

And she prayed for Jake's safety and that of the other rescuers on a wretched mission to try and reach a child and others trapped in the cold.

She said the Our Father, a prayer of comfort and assurance, but when she got to the part that said "thy will be done," she stumbled.

She didn't want God's will if it meant losing Cassie. She couldn't believe God would want a small child freezing to death, abandoned by a troubled system, locked away from the people who loved her.

Do not worry about your life...

Christ's words to the people gathered around him, avidly listening.

"Look at the birds of the air; they neither sow nor reap nor gather into barns, and yet your heavenly Father feeds them. Are you not of more value than they?"

"Kerry?"

Hannah's voice cut through the aching silence. Kerry moved to her side, bent, and smiled. "It's late. Go back to sleep."

"And leave you to worry by yourself?" the old woman asked, and the tartness in her tone was just what Kerry needed to hear. "Now here's what we need to do."

"Do?" Kerry pointed outside, then frowned. "Our choices are limited, my friend."

"Not the inside ones," Hannah declared, fresh from her three-hour snooze. "There'll be folks needin' food, I expect."

Kerry nodded.

"Well, you've got a stove, and I've got a stove, and while the electric's not workin', the gas is. Let's pool our resources. There's not a thing wrong with prayin' and workin', and St. James would be proud to say so." She pulled the recliner into an upright position, tossed off the crocheted afghan, and hopped to her feet in a move many younger people would envy.

"Run upstairs and bring down anythin' you've got for a soup pot or a casserole, and I'll do the same. We'll cook like in days of old and sing our praise, and while weepin' may endure for the night"—she shot an antagonistic look to the steady freezing rain outside—"joy will be ours in the mornin'."

Kerry wasn't sure she was right, but she didn't argue, because being busy doing anything was far better than doing nothing. She tugged on her fleece hoodie and made her way upstairs, filled a few bags, and came back down. "I don't keep a lot on hand." She set the bags on the table. "But there are some good things here."

"Me either. That's the trial of livin' alone, but I have that little freezer on the back porch, and there's a nice ham in there, and frozen chicken breasts. We'll start there and cook up a storm, in the storm. No idle hands here. We are workin' to make a difference."

Hannah's words were a lifesaver. She was praying and doing, just like Jake. For Kerry, being able to put her hands to a task was a huge help.

And still she prayed for Cassie's safety.

* * *

Too much time, Jake thought as minutes, then hours ticked by.

A trip that would normally be a twenty-minute drive had taken them over two hours already, and they were stuck at a standstill while the crew attacked a massive black locust tree that had fallen across the road, snaring power lines and snapping three poles when it went.

Emergency flood lights helped the chainsaw crew, but the thickness of the tree fought them. Twice the chainsaw bars got hung up, and finally Jake pushed the matter with command. "Tim and I can make it there. We're less than a quarter mile out, and we're talking a possible life and death situation."

His commander hesitated, but then Tim upped the ante when he grabbed Jake's arm. "Fire."

He pointed, and Jake's heart stopped.

In the cold, bleak, icy darkness, the fresh fire flared like a beacon, but there was only one place that could be burning in their line of vision. Cassie Carruthers's roughshod shack. "Brad, we've got fire. It's got to be the Carrutherses' place. I'm grabbing two of these firefighters, and Tim and I are going in."

"Go."

They'd dressed in weather appropriate gear, but nothing prepared the men for the ice.

They went down instantly, almost in unison, and when they got back to their feet, they had to pick their way through the ice-coated snow and debris.

They were too slow. Jake knew it and pushed forward anyway while the cabin flames leapt high, sending back-lighting, billowing smoke in the air.

The small group moved as quickly as it could, and they fell several more times, but as they finally drew close, Jake's heart wasn't heavy in his chest. It was a boulder, crushing the breath right out of him because there was no way anyone was coming out of the engulfed shack alive.

His heart broke while anger grabbed him in a chokehold.

What if he'd headed south sooner, when Kerry first expressed concern? Could he have saved Cassie? Probably, and that was a truth he'd have to live with all of his days.

Grief hammered him, but he couldn't take time to grieve. He had to move forward and see if there was any chance, any chance at all...

When he knew there wasn't.

Tim grabbed his arm. "You can't go in there."

Jake shook him off and almost took a swipe at him. "Don't get in this, Tim. Stay here."

Tim grabbed hold again. He yanked him around and wouldn't let go. "You can't go in there, Jake. You've got two kids at home. You can't do this. There's no way in."

Frigid drizzle sluiced off their water-resistant gear. The steady rain sizzled into instant steam as it neared the flames, adding white puffs to the gray-black smoke mushrooming upward.

"We have to check." Jake pulled once more.

Tim tackled low and brought him down as the two firefighters agreed. "You can't go in there. That place is going to crumble at any moment," one said.

Tim kept hold of his arm, applying reason and pressure. "I can't let you do this, so blame this one on me."

On Tim?

This wasn't Tim's fault; it was his. His alone for following protocol and letting a little child—a child he'd come to love—suffer because he hadn't come soon enough.

His eyes grew wet. His throat closed shut. He wanted to scream and shout, but nothing came out, and the fire's roar would have drowned it out anyway. He wept silently, wanting a do over, but he'd learned the hard way that life rarely offered those.

Then something caught his eye, due south.

He blinked through the tears, then tried to swipe his face on his wet sleeve. No luck there. But then he saw it again, the tiniest glimmer of light where no light should be, like a match, flickering and fading in the cold, wet night.

Something was there, just up the road. Nothing else could give off the appearance of a light in the darkness. Could it?

He scrambled to his feet and charged that way, slipping and sliding, with Tim and the others skidding behind him. He shined his flashlight where he thought he'd seen the light and started calling her name. Tim used his light, too, fanning the thin winter forest, then the debris-strewn road.

And there she was, soaked and near-frozen, but when Jake's beam of light found her and she blinked in surprise, his broken heart started beating again. "Come here, darlin', come here. Jake's got you. I've got you. We're going to get you warmed up, honey, OK?"

She said nothing, but the look she gave him…

All his days, Jake knew he would never forget that look of trust and thanksgiving while the horrible little cabin burned to the ground behind him.

Tim's radio broke the quiet. "They've moved that blockage. Rescue One is on its way."

"I'm going with her, Tim."

Tim clapped him on the back, a big smile creasing his soaking wet face. "You sure are."

Rescue One rolled up the road, pausing while the volunteers removed additional debris. Watching, Jake cuddled Cassie close, crooning old tunes he'd hummed to his baby boys years ago. Once he and Cassie were loaded, the rescue wagon crept back to the nearby intersection in reverse.

But the wagon was warm and clean and dry, and as they unbundled Cassie's frozen, wet clothes from her little body, Jake stayed close, praying, because at least now they had a chance to save her, and not too long ago, he'd figured that chance was long gone.

* * *

Uncertainty dogged Cassie. She stared into the darkness, suddenly unsure.

Her face felt frozen. Not just cold, like on a windy winter day. More solid than that, as if her cheeks would never be warm again.

She crawled further, moving as far as she could, but her eyes grew heavy, and her hands ached one minute and went numb the next.

She stared up Adler's Hill, knowing she couldn't make it, but knowing she had to try. If Kerry were here, she'd cheer her on, just like she did with Dundee and with sledding and with everything they did together.

Think of warm things.

She'd tried that already, back in the house, and it almost worked for a little while, but then it didn't. Nothing worked.

But now she was free. She just needed to make it up the hill and down the road.

Maybe Mrs. Stanton would see her and come get her. If she had a phone, maybe she could have called them and asked for help, but there was no phone. The man's phone didn't work, and that was the only one they had.

She started to crawl again, and she counted the steps. One…two… three…but then the energy to make the next step seemed hard, so very hard. Still she pushed, and then she spotted a little nook in the snow along the side of the road. She took out a match and tried to light it.

Nothing happened, but she tried again and again, as if seeing the nook in the snow would make a difference. Finally the match glimmered, but so briefly, she barely saw anything.

She crawled into the nook. The nook wasn't much, but it protected her from the rain, at least. Her hood was soaked, and her jacket, too, and where the glass had torn her sleeve, the water ran right through, into her shirtsleeve.

She couldn't feel her feet or her hands, and it felt like her middle was shaking, all by itself, so she tucked herself into the nook for a short rest.

She yawned, then yawned again, and the shivering grew worse, and then something flashed in the distance.

A car.

No, not a car, a fire truck. And a police car!

A police car with Jake in it. It had to be. She stared hard at the flashing lights, then wondered if she was just dreaming, because the fire truck and the car stopped and didn't come any closer.

Would Jake stop and not come get her? Would it be too cold and wet and icy for him to try?

She wanted to holler and tell him she was here, but nothing came out of her mouth. And then she started shaking again.

She heard noises. Loud noises, not just the trees falling anymore, but from up the road, and then she saw that there were people working in the road, tiny shadows, moving.

Why would they work on the road at night?

It made no sense, and as the noise whined on in the distance, the cold overtook her once again.

And then something flashed bright and hot in her vision.

Fire.

Her house was on fire.

Her heart sped up, but so did the shivers, and none of it made any sense. A burning house, the noise in the road, tree branches crashing, and the lights, Jake's lights, she was sure of it— so far away and not coming closer.

She couldn't cry. She was too cold to cry and too cold to think, and even though she hated that story of the little girl, she pulled out that box of matches.

Two left.

She stared at her hand and tried to grip the match. It fell, disappearing into the ice-glazed snow beneath her.

One more. One more match, one more chance to light up the night. She breathed deep and bit down on her lower lip as she wriggled the match free. And then she gripped it tight between her thumb and her pointer. She couldn't feel the match, but she could see it, and using her eyes, she made sure those fingers stayed tight together.

It took two tries, but on the second time, the match lit, bright and flickering, dancing in the shelter of her little nook.

The rain and wind didn't douse it so quickly here, and when it came close to burning her, she had to throw it away, and how her heart hurt to see it sizzle and die in the ditch.

No more matches.

No more light, and it almost seemed like Jake's police car lights dimmed as the house fire grew brighter.

She leaned back, ready to sleep. Ready to dream of something else. Something new. Something different.

She started to lay back, then blinked.

Lights bobbed their way toward her. Four lights, moving and shaking across the thin forest edging the road.

She stared at those lights, fighting sleep.

Was she dreaming?

She thought she must be, but then she heard a voice…Jake's voice! Calling her, calling for her, and she tried to raise a hand, tried to call his name, but nothing worked.

And then she blinked when light hit her eyes. She heard him, his voice, his big, deep, policeman voice say her name, over and over again.

He picked her up so carefully, like she was special and wonderful and beautiful, just like his little boys. He cuddled her close to his chest, his face to hers, holding her gently and promising it would be all right. Everything would be all right.

Nothing made sense, and she wasn't sure he was right because her brain was confused…but she knew she'd never felt more loved and cherished and happy in her life.

She rested against him, snug in the arms of a kind protector.

chapter twenty

Jake stayed out of the way as the EMT used slow, cautious movements to remove Cassie's clothes. Jake wanted him to move faster. He wanted the sodden garments tossed aside in a hurry.

"Relax, Jake." Janet Lavendar settled a small mask over Cassie's face, and the fact that Cassie didn't struggle worried Jake. "Warm, moist air to start rewarming her. We have to move slowly to avoid cardiac problems, so you sit there and watch and pray, and we'll start warming this sweet little thing up." She began activating hot packs as her partner grabbed warm, clean blankets. "OK?"

Jake grunted.

He knew the drill. He'd had training, but he wanted speed. He needed to know she'd be all right because this was Cassie, and her little body was so cold he couldn't bear to think of it.

Then don't.

The memory offered a slap of reality.

Think of what you can do for her now. She's in good hands. Theirs and God's. Pray. Provide. Stake your claim and show the world how much this child means to you, how much Kerry means to you. You were brave and bold in the field. Now you must be brave and bold in your personal life.

Pray and provide.

Two words that seemed simple, but came hard. He'd trusted God once. He'd put his faith in him. He'd sung his praise at the quaint country church with Lorelei and Abe tucked alongside. It had been a beautiful existence, strong and wholesome and good. So good.

And then he lost his wife in one fateful moment, a stupid drunk, out on the road when he had no business to be, and suddenly Lori was gone.

The boys' faces swam before him. Abe, a solid, industrious little fellow, always questioning. And Ben, beloved by so many because of the tragedy surrounding his birth, but never by that one person who would hold him, talk to him, and call him her son.

He'd risked before, and lost. He wasn't sure he could do it again and not live afraid, but was that any way to live?

His conscience smacked him again, harder this time. *But think what you gained! A son, a child to offer into the future. Two boys, strong and hearty. A good job, a warm home, food on the table, shoes on their feet. And the chance to love again.*

Stake your claim. Now. He who hesitates is lost. Stop hanging back and do what needs to be done.

For unto us a child is born…

The beautiful image of the Holy Family came to him. Mary had risked all to bring forth the Christ child. Her body, her life, her reputation, her beloved. She'd stood tall and strong before the Lord and lent assent.

A teenage girl, accepting a momentous role, and then a young mother, knowing what time held in store and raising her boy as she promised in spite of it.

Raw courage. That's what he needed, a dose of Mary's raw courage.

Cassie moved just then. She writhed in pain as her temperature started to rise, and his heart clamped tight. He wanted to hold and protect her, like he did with the boys. He wanted to reach out and soothe that grimace from her face, erase all pain.

He couldn't do that, but he could pray. And provide. And when everything got settled with this precious child, he and Kerry needed to have a very serious talk, one that would begin on bended knee because from this point forward he was following his conscience absolutely, and that meant taking Kerry McHenry as his wife…and as mother to his children.

He didn't think about alternatives if she said no, because sitting there, watching professionals tend Cassie, he saw the truth: them, all together, one big, happy family. And that's how it was meant to be.

* * *

The flash of rescue lights drew Kerry and Hannah to the window as the rescue wagon headed west on Main. Her phone rang almost immediately with Jake's ringtone. "Tell me, Jake. What's going on? Did you find her?"

"We did. She's alive, Kerry, but she's hypothermic and not out of the woods. There's no hospital access. The roads are all blocked, and they won't have an ambulance route clear for hours, so they've set up a triage for storm victims in the church."

"I'll be right there." She grabbed her coat and scarf and turned to Hannah. "I'll come back to help you carry the food over to the firehouse or wherever they'd like to set it up. St. Mary's, maybe? Don't try moving stuff on your own. That ice is deadly, and I don't want you falling, OK?"

Hannah tapped her phone. "I'll get the phone tree involved. We'll grab some younger backs to cart things over. They can pick up Maddie's offerings, too."

"Perfect. I'll call." She hurried out the door, forgot her own advice, and fell before she'd gone fifteen feet. She stood back up, abandoned the sidewalk, and crossed to the road, following the salt-strewn tracks of the fire department vehicles. The salt wasn't fully melting the thick layer of ice, but it provided some traction.

She got halfway to the church, and there was Jake, coming toward her.

Dressed in his outdoor gear, he resembled a burly gray bear keeping to the salted tracks like her. And then she was in his arms, her face pressed against the cold, damp jacket, and she didn't care.

He hadn't waved off her concerns. He hadn't brushed them aside. He listened to her because he cared about her and respected her, and that meant so much.

He's pretty mad at God. Is that where you want to go? Is that the right way to go?

She wasn't sure about that, but she was certain of one thing. Jake Slattery made her feel good about herself. He lifted her up in word and deed.

She knew she couldn't marry a man who didn't believe in God, who spent his life angry at circumstances beyond his control, which meant Jake had to get a clue. Simple, really. "Can I see her?"

"Yes, but we have to let them do their job. No hugs or kisses or jostling her. Janet said her heart's fragile right now, so we have to be patient."

"And you do patient so well." She gripped his hand as they climbed the salted steps. "I don't know how to thank you, Jake. I—"

He put a finger to her lips, and in his gaze, she read the depth of his emotion, a yearning that matched hers. "I've got some things in mind, Kerry, but we'll discuss them later. I've got to get back out there, but before I go, I want to go pray our girl back to health. All right?"

Jake didn't pray.

Jake didn't offer up travail. He forged his own way. He'd made that clear, so when he used those sweet words, Kerry gripped his hand even tighter. "Let's."

He couldn't stay long, but he stayed long enough to pray with her, and as Kerry stayed by Cassie's side, the first responders brought in several more people who had been caught in the storm. It was long, cold, wet hours before Jake allowed himself a break. The villagers had set up food and drink in St. Mary's. Kerry hadn't taken time to go over, but when Jake showed up with two steaming cups of coffee, she smiled and reached out two hands. "Gimme."

"How's she doing?"

"Temp is rising slowly, but Janet said that's best. And she's beyond the pain part now, so that's good, because I cried like a baby right along with her." She sipped the coffee and leaned her head against Jake's arm. "What if you hadn't gone after her? Janet said the house was on fire."

"She had matches." Jake kept his voice soft so Cassie couldn't over-hear. "I don't know if that's what started the fire, but she had them in her pocket when I found her. I wouldn't have seen her in the dark and the rain, but then I saw this tiny flicker of light, waving near the ground. And it was her."

A tiny flicker of light… "Thank God she had them."

Jake nodded, but frowned. "It might have been the matches that caused the fire, and I'm not sure how well a little kid handles that."

"You think Jed was in there?"

He shrugged. "No way of knowing until things die down and we can send a team in, but the old car was there. We'll have to ask Cassie some questions when she's up to it."

"Interrogate a five-year-old?"

"I don't think I'd go straight to interrogate, Mama Bear, but we need to know how things went down. It's procedure."

"If Jed perished in that fire, then Cassie has no one."

"No one we're aware of," he said softly. "Social Services will have to take over and do a family search."

"They'll let her stay with me, won't they?"

Jake winced. "We'll call Aunt Susan when things are better. She'll have a better idea. She works with the county social workers regularly, but you might need certification, Kerry."

"To look after a child I've been looking after for months with the father's permission?"

"Don't shoot the messenger. Like I said, they'll know the drill. I don't. And maybe they'll make an exception. I wish I knew more."

The disappointment on his face was Kerry's wake-up call. He'd saved her life. He'd braved the storm to save others, too. He was a hero, and she was scolding him in his hour of need.

Trust in the Lord with your whole heart, your whole soul.

Hadn't God delivered Cassie this far? Yes.

She hugged Jake's arm, and the moment she did, she sensed his relief. "We'll take this step by step, just like we've been doing," she whispered up to him. "I tend to worry when I'm tired, so just ignore me because you've got to be exhausted, Jake." She snugged his arm tighter and gazed into his gray-green eyes. "Dear Jake."

She stressed the endearment, and when his eyes met hers, she smiled. He didn't wait, didn't hesitate.

He leaned right over and feathered the sweetest kiss to her mouth, then her cheek. "I love you, Kerry."

Her heart had been on tenterhooks for over a day, the rise and fall of emotions with the storm, the danger, with Cassie.

But right now she felt at peace, a beautiful, warm blanket of peace. She reached up and cupped his still-chilled, rugged cheek with one hand. "I love you, too."

"Yeah?" A slow grin moved the shadows from his face. "You sure about that?"

"I am."

He leaned down and kissed her again, slow and sweet, then sighed against her cheek. "Me, too."

* * *

It took days to clear roads, and still they had less than full access. Tree surgeons and electric crews came in from across the Northeast and Midwest to perform the tedious process of putting things back together, but even with the extra help, some people went without power for an extended period of time.

The Red Cross set up a shelter in the Phillipsburg school gym. Volunteers fought their way in from all over, but the number of volunteers stressed the already fragile conditions. In the end, the storm rivaled the ice storm of 1991 as one of the worst natural disasters to hit a populated region.

Jake worked night and day with the rest of the Beckett County deputies, the New York State Troopers, and some local police agencies.

Schools remained shut.

Emergency services were triaged on a critical need basis, and at the end of the first week, it seemed like nothing might ever be normal again.

Several old people living alone perished. Jed Carruthers's body was found in the ash and rubble on his messy lot on County Center Road.

Three meth labs were uncovered as police agencies combed the uplands in search and rescue missions.

And Kerry was given provisional custody of Cassie while the Department of Human Services began the paperwork to search for relatives and instigate Kerry's certification as a foster parent.

The thought that they might unearth a distant relative who could claim Cassie was unnerving, but as Cassie regained strength and composure, Kerry shoved worry aside. Cassie was safe and in her care for now. She needed to put the rest in God's hands and move forward.

As things began to calm down on day eight, Jake arrived at Kerry's for a scheduled appointment. A Beckett County detective was coming to interview Cassie about her father and the fire.

Cassie wasn't nervous.

Kerry was. She hated to have Cassie do a mental review of the horrible day, but Jake assured her it was better to know facts now than invent them later.

The downstairs bell rang midafternoon, followed by the sound of footsteps on the stairs. Kerry opened the door. A woman preceded Jake, well-dressed and self-assured. Maybe too self-assured.

But then Jake followed her into the room. He hugged Kerry, then dropped to his knees. "Got a hug, kid?"

"Yes!" Cassie didn't mind his uniform now. She raced into his arms and held on tight, the perfect reunion. Kerry held out a hand to the detective. "Kerry McHenry. And you're Detective Davis?"

"I am." The detective smiled as Jake stood, lifting Cassie into the air. "And this must be Cassandra."

"Yes." Cassie whispered the word, still clinging to Jake, but then she pointed to the detective's gold link necklace. "I like your jew-le-ry. It's very pretty."

Her mispronunciation made the detective smile. "Thank you, Cassandra."

"We usually use Cassie," Kerry told her as she hung her short coat over the back of a chair. "She likes that."

"Good to know." She turned back toward Cassie. "How are you feeling, honey?"

Cassie peeked up at Jake. He smiled down at her, and she cuddled closer. "I feel good."

Jake's smile deepened.

"You went through quite a time last week, I hear."

"But then Jake saved me." She waved a hand around the small but cozy apartment. "And now I'm warm all the time."

Her words seemed innocent enough to Kerry, but Mary jotted something in a small notebook. "Can we sit?" She directed the question to Jake.

"Sure can." He sat down, still holding Cassie. Kerry took a seat in the nearby chair, and Mary sat in the one opposite Jake, facing Cassie.

"Cassie, I work with Jake."

Cassie seemed to accept that easily. She nodded and patted Jake's cheek.

"And I wanted to come over here to see you because I'd like to find out what happened that day at your house. The day Jake saved you. Can you help me?"

Cassie frowned. "I don't know what happened." She redirected her attention to Jake. "Don't you know? I think you can tell her, OK?"

"I know what happened after I got there, but Rita needs to know what happened first. Before I found you. Do you remember what was happening in the house?"

Cassie's face went still.

She stared past Jake, then shot a look of entreaty toward Kerry. "I think I'm tired."

If it were up to Kerry, she'd stop the interview right then, but it wasn't. She reached out and patted Cassie's knee. "I get tired when I have to talk about things that make me nervous, too. But sometimes it's better to just get it over and done, darling."

Cassie stared at her.

She thrust out her bottom lip, thinking.

"Was the house cold, Cassie?" Mary asked.

Kerry wanted to yell, scream, or at least shout something right now. Of course the house was cold; it was a wretched, uninsulated, barely heated shack.

She closed her mouth and bit her tongue instead.

Cassie nodded.

"Like real cold?"

Cassie looked up at Jake. He gave her a reassuring squeeze. "It's OK to tell her. She's my friend."

She seemed to find comfort in his words and his embrace because she started to talk. "It was very cold. And it was dark, even during the day."

Mary looked pleased with her answer. "Did you try to warm up the house?"

Cassie nodded. "I turned the heater off and on, and it didn't blink. It wouldn't get warm."

No electricity, so of course, no heat. Rita made more notes on her pad. "Then what did you do?"

"Well, first I prayed."

The detective's pen paused. "You prayed?"

Cassie pointed to Kerry. "Kerry said God was always watching over me, even when we couldn't be together, so I told him what was wrong."

"What did you tell God, honey?"

"That the man wouldn't wake up, and it was cold. And I tried to go outside because maybe Mrs. Stanton would help me, but the doors wouldn't open."

Jake's grip on the little girl tightened. "You tried to get out the door?"

"So many times." She laid her head against his chest and sighed. "And then it got dark again."

Thirty hours without power. Emotion clogged Kerry's throat because she hadn't pushed Cassie to talk about that day. Hearing her voice, seeing her pinched face, made it all too real.

"What did you do?"

"I don't know 'zaclty." Cassie frowned as if remembering this part taxed her physically more than emotionally. "I remember the matches and the rat."

Mary's pen stopped again. She took a breath and worked to regain her composure. "There was a rat?"

Cassie nodded as if that was to be expected. "He was on the counter when I looked for the matches." She sent a worried look toward Kerry. "I know I promised not to touch them, but I didn't know how else to see anything. I just wanted to get warm."

"So you started a fire?"

Cassie quickly shook her head no. "Fire is dangerous."

Mary made another note.

"But I couldn't see to get out the window," Cassie explained in a low, grave voice. "And the man kept sleeping, and that was the only window I could reach, so I lit a match to see how I could get out. Then I broke his window with a metal stick. But it didn't break all the way," she explained, "so I had to light another match and break some more. But it was raining hard, and the matches kept going out. But then one didn't go out. And then I climbed out, but I fell and slipped on ice and glass and more ice." She sighed and thought about sticking her thumb in her mouth, then decided against it. "And then it just got colder."

"Do you remember walking away?"

Cassie frowned. "I remember I couldn't walk." She drew her brows together, tighter. Her lips pinched shut as she struggled with the right words, and then she twined her hands like she did whenever she grew nervous or afraid. "I don't know, really. I remember seeing police lights and thinking Jake was coming, and then he didn't, and then he did."

"I'm sorry it took so long, honey." Jake pressed a kiss to her head. "I'll be faster next time you need a rescue, OK?"

His promise eased Cassie's angst. "OK." She yawned, and Kerry stood, crossed the room, and reached for her. "Come here, darlin'. I think you need a little rest even though I know you're big and don't need a nap every day. Just so we're clear on that."

Cassie let her lift her with no protest, and when Kerry laid her down in her bed, she popped her thumb into her mouth and closed her eyes almost instantly.

Kerry leaned the door shut and returned to the living room. "I'm sorry if you need more, but she looked spent. We can finish another time, can't we?"

"I've got what we need," Mary said. She stood and faced Kerry. "We were pretty sure the fire started near or on Jed's bed. We had to make sure that Cassie didn't deliberately burn down the house with her father in it."

"Deliberately?" Kerry stared at her, then Jake. "Who in their right mind would imagine a five-year-old would do such a thing?"

"They're just covering all the bases, honey. Doing their jobs," Jake told her.

"Cassie's cognitive level puts her at an eight- to nine-year-old functioning level in certain areas," Mary added. "Kids that age have been known to commit crimes. Clearly that was not the case here, but we had to check. I hope you understand."

Kerry didn't understand, and said so. "What if her answers hadn't been clear? What if her memory loss from the cold started before she got outside, seeking the safety and warmth our stupid legal rules denied her?"

"Miss McHenry, I—"

Jake laid a gentle hand on her arm. "Kerry, it's protocol. Nothing more."

"It's a lot more, Jake." She faced him, and maybe it was the stress of the last ten days, or reliving Cassie's ordeal through five-year-old eyes, but suddenly she wanted, no make that *needed* to protect Cassie from anything that might threaten her. "It's about standing up for what's right, for seeing the worth of a child, for protecting and guarding from day one. What kind of society questions an innocent child because they had the intelligence to try and get out of a life-threatening situation? A situation that went on for far too long as it was because of society's rules?"

Mary crossed the room and quietly retrieved her coat. "I'm done here, and I see no reason to go further. Miss McHenry, I'm sorry I upset you, but like Jake said, we're just doing our job. I'll see myself out." She went out the door, and the sound of her stylish boots against the wooden stairs marked the silence she left behind.

Kerry wanted to hit something. Or maybe somebody, and Jake was close.

She turned and walked away instead, but there wasn't far to go in a small apartment with a little kid sleeping in the only extra room.

"I'm sorry, Kerry."

He shouldn't have to be sorry. She knew that, and she was angry anyway. He moved closer but still gave her space. Smart man.

"I knew Mary had to ascertain the timeline, but it was standard procedure. It had to be done once they investigated the fire and established Jed's proximity to what they thought was the point of origin."

"Did you doubt, Jake?" She'd been facing away from him, but now she turned. "Did you for one moment think that precious child might have killed her father?"

"Of course not."

"Are you sure?"

"I've always been sure; the thought never crossed my mind, but Kerry, police work is different." He splayed his hands. "We can't make decisions based on emotions if evidence suggests otherwise. Mary had to do her job, and she did it. It's over. Done."

Kerry wasn't sure where the swarm of negative emotion rose from. Her childhood? Old anger, old issues? Or the fact that society was perfectly willing to leave a small child in wretched conditions, but charge full steam ahead when it suited them?

The disparity cut deep.

Yes, Cassie was safe now. She was warm and dry and cared for at long last, but until the travesty of a deadly storm, rules had kept her trapped in a shameful existence, and that wasn't Cassie's fault.

That was society's choice.

"Kerry." Jake settled his hands on her shoulders, and his strength became hers. "The last thing I want to do right now is fight with you about anything."

She didn't want to fight, either, and she wanted to stop borrowing trouble. This wasn't Jake's fault. None of it was Jake's fault, so why was she attacking the hero? She turned and lifted her gaze to his. "I'm sorry. Listening to her touched too many old buttons, brought back too many memories, and I lost my cool. I'll send Mary a note of apology."

"There's no need. She's dealt with crazy women before."

His teasing made her smile, but there *was* a need, and she said so. "I'll send it because I acted out of character, and respect for another person's job is important."

"So scolding people and fighting for the rights of children is out of character for you?" He raised one thick, rugged, skeptical brow, and she laughed.

"Possibly more in character than it should be."

"Mm-hmm." He lifted his hands to cradle her face, then drew her in. His kiss uplifted her. The pressure of his lips on hers made her want to climb tall mountains or possibly linger in his embrace forever. "I like kissing you, Kerry."

She smiled against his lips, glad her heart wasn't the only one racing. "I can tell."

"I'd like to go on this way, actually."

She couldn't deny a similar emotion.

"Which means…" He pulled back, reached into his pocket, and dropped down on one knee. He held out a blue velvet ring box and snapped open the lid. "Kerry McHenry, will you do me the honor of becoming my wife and the mother to my boys? Sharing our pew in the church, and welcoming any little Slatterys that might come our way?"

He gazed up at her, his light eyes filled with love and hope. His face, his smile, his strength, his devotion…

Her heart swelled. This dear man, this hero, was on bended knee, asking for her hand. She felt amazingly good and totally undeserving, but she put one pale hand to his caramel-toned cheek and smiled. "I would be most honored to share your pew, Jake. Yes, I'll marry you. The sooner, the better."

He slipped the ring onto her finger, stood, and kissed her again, and then again for good measure, and when he finally stopped kissing her, he scrolled on his phone to a calendar page and handed it over with a smile. "Feel free to pick that quick date, darlin', because I'm feeling exactly the same—although if you want or need a big wedding with all the trappings, that's fine, too, Kerry. Whatever you want."

She smiled, tapped the phone shut, and handed it back. "I don't need too many trappings, but I do need some time to sit down with Jenn and Claire and plan this. Maybe we could drive up there this weekend? Or they could come down here," she supposed. "But knowing Claire, she'll want to have a little engagement party."

He didn't wince or whine, so she gave him extra points. "My mother might do the same, so we'll be going into this eyes wide open." He raised her hand that now wore his ring and kissed it. "I love you, Kerry."

Her heart soared. "Me, too."

"Well, then." He winked and grabbed his coat. "I've got to get back to work, then pick up the boys. Can we celebrate with them tonight?"

"Gino's for pizza and wings equates three happy kids."

"That's perfect. We'll come by for you ladies around 6:15, OK?"

"It's perfect, Jake."

And it was.

chapter twenty-one

"We get to plan a weddin'!" Hannah threw her hands into the air before she wrapped Kerry in a hug that afternoon. "I could not be more pleased by all of this. First and foremost, I am praisin' God for the safety of that sweet child playin' yonder, blessed be his holy name! And thankin' him mightily for bringin' you to my door, lookin' for a room, and me havin' one right then. And for Jake Slattery's devotion to helpin' others that brought him into your classroom last fall. I just see the hand of God at work here, bringin' his people together, mm-hmm!"

"So you don't mind helping?" Kerry asked, but she knew the answer. Hannah would be glad to help. She'd bake some terrible cookies and help make really good food, and everything would be beautiful because it was done with love.

"It will be joy, plain and simple! And if your aunt and sister don't mind me bein' a part of all this, I can just see how beautiful the bride will be and that dashing groom. And three children." She folded her arms across her thin middle and just grinned. "God's mercy and blessin's abound, that's for certain!"

They did.

The following week *U.S. Teacher* offered Kerry a monthly column for their ten-month subscription magazine at twelve hundred dollars per month. She jumped at the chance and was pretty sure she'd won the lottery.

The ice melted. So did the snow, although more slowly. Cassie seemed tired and a little vague, but who wouldn't be after her ordeal? The local doctor gave her a clean bill of health, and Kerry moved ahead with her foster care certification.

The county declared several first responders as heroes, including Jake and Tim. They were to be recognized at a ceremony at the Hall of Justice, with a light reception following. All of Jake's family would be there, which was reason enough to be nervous, but when time grew short and Kerry decided to blow-dry Cassie's hair, the outcome turned nerves into a possible total meltdown. Hers, not Cassie's. She called downstairs quickly. "Hannah. Get up here. I need help."

Hannah took one look at Cassie's frizzed-out head of hair and had to walk away, chin down, to control her reaction. When Kerry came up alongside her, the old woman whispered, "My land, child, what have you gone and done?"

Kerry scolded her with a look, but Hannah took no notice. "What did you wash her hair with? Kitchen cleanser?"

"Not funny, Hannah."

"I'll say." She sent a pretend look of fear over her shoulder and tsked softly. "And what a day for this to happen, mmm, mmm." She shook her head. "Not a thing we can do about it now, look at the time."

"You're kidding. There must be something. Anything," Kerry half-hissed the words, and she was pretty sure she was begging because she couldn't possibly take sweet little Cassie to Jake's big moment looking like a frenetic energy science lesson.

"How did you do this?"

"We were in a hurry, so I blew it dry."

"Oh, Lord have mercy, child. You have gone and done it now."

"Done what?" Kerry whispered as Cassie returned to the room with her coat and hat. "It's not that bad, Hannah. Is it?"

"Folks have been hanged for less, that's all I'm sayin'. You are bridgin' a gap between two communities, and that gap is governed by good hair."

"Stop." She'd felt bad before. Now she felt worse, and Hannah couldn't be right. One bad hair day couldn't really make a difference, could it?

"Suit yourself," Hannah told her and patted her gray curls to make her point. "If white folk are determined to have multiracial children, then they best figure out how to work hair in the proper manner. And whatever you did there, honey," she hiked her eyebrows and slid a sideways glance toward Cassie. "Do not ever do it again. That you must promise me."

Oh, man. Why didn't she just leave the child's hair wet? It would have dried after a while, but she'd worried about the cold and Cassie's exposure. Well, this kind of exposure was a whole other thing. "Will she be embarrassed?"

Hannah's frank expression said "who wouldn't be," but she softened it by saying, "Not if we pretend it's all right, but it's not all right, so you make the promise, and I'll pretend for the day, and then we'll take a ride this weekend to see Mavis and Sharon down in Olean. I would have thought with all the information we've got at our fingertips on computers, that someone would have offered advice, includin' myself. We won't say another word about it."

They didn't have to.

Jake's mother and sister took one look at Cassie's hair when they walked into the small auditorium at the Hall of Justice, and their mouths dropped open.

Jake's sister winced, then tried to cover it up to spare their feelings.

His mother rolled her eyes as if she'd suspected Kerry's ineptitude all along, and when Jake and the boys came her way, even he gave Cassie a funny look. He hid it quickly, but not quickly enough for Kerry to miss it.

Least said, soonest mended.

It was a wise saying, and if they could just get through this day, this one single day, she'd make it a point to learn everything there was to learn about curly hair.

Including not blow-drying it into a huge mound of frizz. She put her chin in the air and decided to take one for the team as Jake approached.

He didn't tease her. He ignored the situation entirely and kissed her, then Cassie, but when Abe caught sight of Cassie's hair, he laughed out loud and pointed. "I think that's the biggest hair ever!"

Cassie looked confused, then hurt. Until that moment, she had no clue her hair was an issue.

Oh, it was an issue, all right.

In the minutes before the ceremony commenced, Susan McCabe texted Kerry three great websites for hair and two online ads for hair lotion and coconut oil.

And in case the situation couldn't get worse, it did. When Jake picked Cassie up for a requested photo-op, her wild hair hid his face.

It was a debacle, a hair debacle, and while Kerry tried to get it out of Jake's face, poor Cassie was the center of a beauty controversy she didn't need, want, or deserve.

Kerry wanted to hide. She wanted to take Cassie someplace quiet, eat their cookies, and run.

She couldn't; she had to stand there as if everything was all right because the major things were all right. Cassie was safe, she had a home with Kerry, and Kerry and Jake were getting married, and Abe and Ben would have a mother again.

Jake's mother didn't look thrilled by any of it. His father…

Kerry would remember to bless God all her days because of Big Abe's kindness. He didn't just come up and extend a polite hand.

He hugged her in front of everyone, then clapped his arm around her shoulders and introduced her to every single member of Jake's family before the ceremony began, ending with Jake's mother.

She extended her hand as if holding court. "At last we meet."

"Time and Mother Nature have thwarted us, haven't they?" Kerry took her hand and held it. "It is an absolute pleasure to meet the woman who raised such a fine man. Thank you for that."

"It was our pleasure. And to have two beautiful grandsons?" She directed a fond look to the boys, then raised her gaze back to Kerry. "If God never gave me anything else, those two precious boys would be enough."

Kerry wasn't sure if that was a slight or a loving observation. As the ceremony was called to order, Jake, Tim, and Cassie went up the three stairs.

Cassie looked terrible.

Far worse than she'd ever looked at Jed's place. Not her clothes, those were fine, but that mop of frizzed out hair made her look like a wild child, raised by wolves.

Kerry wanted to cry.

She couldn't and wouldn't, but boy, she wanted to. How could she have totally messed up such an important day?

Abe and Ben looked perfect, their short haircuts and preppie clothes fitting for the occasion, and that set Cassie apart even more. ·

Hannah grabbed her arm. "It's one day; nothing to get all steamed up about."

"One very important day with a lot of pictures," Kerry hissed back. "How did I manage to mess up like this on today of all days?"

"Trying to do your best," Hannah whispered back. "Now look there, it's all fine as long as Jake keeps his cheek pressed against the side of her head. No one will even notice, I'm sure."

Because they already had, Kerry knew, but there was nothing to be done now.

"Jacob has told me you're a writer. Is that so?" Jake's father hung fairly close to her side in a sweet show of moral support.

"Yes. I've just secured a monthly column in *U.S. Teacher* magazine."

"And you teach at Daystar."

"Yes."

"And Cassandra is enrolled there?" Jake's mother had turned their way and caught the end of the conversation. "Do you anticipate that Abe and Ben will attend there also? Because it might be in their best interests to remain in a more diversified setting."

Kerry was pretty sure her heart stopped. What could she say to this pale-skinned woman who seemed determined to make things rough for her? "We've got a lot to discuss, of course, education being just one of the topics. And hair," she admitted with a rueful look at the stage.

"Communication is a big component of a successful marriage," Jake's mother added, and the tightness in her tone suggested Kerry should pay heed. "Of course *Jake* knows that. It's an example we've tried to set from the beginning."

"The other being that we should mind our own business and let our adult children live their lives, much as we have." His father sent Jake's mother a look of warning. "Jake and Kerry will have enough on their hands handling three kids under age six."

"You expect to keep Cassie?" Aria leaned closer and didn't seem nearly as upset by Kerry or by Cassie's hair as her mother. "If it's approved?"

"We hope to adopt her, yes. Of course they're doing the legal family search right now, but if she's available, then yes. We want her to be ours."

"Well, I will love being her auntie, Kerry." She smiled up at the stage, then at Kerry, "Because I haven't seen my brother this happy in a long, long time, and I'm absolutely thrilled for him, and you. And those children."

Her kindness eased the moment. "Thank you. And having said that, if you were willing to give me pointers about dry, curly hair, I'd take them to heart."

Aria laughed. "I'll do that. I expect hurrying got you into this mess."

Kerry didn't deny it. "Yes, ma'am."

"And that is the first lesson of multicultural beauty," Aria told her. "We never hurry the hair."

Wise words. Kerry winced as she watched Jake and three beautiful children cross that stage. "I see that."

* * *

Kerry was engaged.

Ryan was tempted to skip his weekly pre-confirmation meeting with Father Cummings because he'd rather pummel something than philosophize about old words and new heartaches.

He hesitated as he approached the defining expressway exits. Right took him home to his bayside condo and college basketball.

Left steered him toward the lake and the old stone church.

He turned left and wasn't sure why he did, but it felt like a test, and Ryan always aced tests. He pulled into the small parking lot abutting the rectory, climbed the steps, and knocked on the door.

Father Cummings never kept him waiting, and with the brisk night air, Ryan was glad of it. "Hi, Father."

"Ryan."

He pulled off his coat, hooked it on the rack inside the kitchen door, and turned.

"Rough week, I heard."

His father had forewarned the priest. Ryan scrubbed his hand through his hair, then ground his back teeth together. "Agreed."

"And still you came."

He followed the aging priest into the small, warm sitting room. "Almost didn't." He took a seat in his customary chair and set his hands on his lap, restless.

"But you did, and that makes all the difference."

Ryan was pretty sure it made no difference, but he wasn't about to argue with an old man.

"Do you ever build with Legos, Ryan?"

"Now?"

The priest nodded.

"No. But yeah, sure, when I was a kid. I loved them. My dad still has a huge box at the house."

The priest nodded, happy. "Sure he does! And when you build with Legos, and I mean the old way, before there were wide platforms to anchor everything, you had to use lots of those little bricks, right? Back and forth, locking them in, doubling them up, until you had a base strong enough to hold a castle or a spaceship? Correct?"

"Y-e-s." Ryan elongated the word as Father Cummings lifted the coffee carafe. "Otherwise the whole thing fell apart."

"Exactly my point!" No hesitation on the priest's part as he poured Ryan a tall cup of fresh, hot coffee. "Each brick adds strength to the structure, just like each choice we make builds our personal platform."

Ryan set his mug on the small table next to his chair. "Personal platform? Like political issues?"

"Like good and evil."

Now he had Ryan's attention.

"No one begins life by being just plain good or intrinsically evil. We build our platforms with all of the little choices we make, each and every day. The slights, the smiles, the shortcuts, or the long haul. Each choice we make," he explained as he returned to his corner of the worn, comfortable sofa, "good or bad, adds strength to our platform, and makes it easier to continue in that direction."

"Avoid the slippery slope."

"That's it." Father Cummings slapped the arm of his chair and about a thousand dust bits danced in the beam of the shaded lamp. "Coming here tonight builds your commitment to go outside of yourself and stop being a jerk."

"Gee. Thanks. I think."

"You're welcome." The old man looked overjoyed by Ryan's choice and his proclamation. "Now I know we'll be ready come Easter."

His confidence helped, because when Dan had delivered the news of Kerry's engagement, Ryan had been tempted to dump the whole idea of confirmation, cancel his appointment with the kind priest, and go on his merry way.

But you didn't.

The warm voice sounded good. Felt good.

If my people who are called by my name humble themselves, pray…

Old words again. Ancient words, still wise. But so was Ben Franklin, and he wasn't pushing religion.

Me, either.

The gentle nudge wasn't so gentle this time.

Faith, yes. The religion part I leave up to you.

"So what is your plan?"

Father Cummings's question drew Ryan a little forward in his seat. "Head to Phillipsburg and tell her she's wrong."

The priest winced.

"That was my first reaction. But then I realized that if I truly care, I want what's best for her."

"Magnanimous. But is it doable?"

"Anything is doable; we just talked about that. It all comes down to choices. I acted like a jerk for way too long, and she made a choice."

"And you can come to peace with that?"

Ryan regarded the older man and frowned. "I can own my part in it. But the regret isn't easy to swallow."

"Often our greatest tests come when we're most inclined to fail."

"That's not very nice of God," Ryan told him, but the priest quickly shook his head.

"They're not of God, my friend. Those tests and temptations are much like Christ faced in the wilderness; they come straight from the evil one, making his presence known. When we are vulnerable, his works are most likely to appeal. He knows this."

"You talk as if the devil exists as a person, a being. Isn't it just the temptation to do evil, and we humanize it?"

The priest pressed forward and laid his hand on Ryan's. "Never underestimate the power of evil, or how it presents itself. It might not be a comic book rendition, but it exists and watches for the weak and unholy to do its bidding. When you e-mail a prescription to the pharmacy, do you see it go through the air?"

Ryan shook his head.

"And yet it does. Evil may take any shape or remain formless, but never believe it isn't present and hunting. You've defeated him once."

Ryan made a skeptical face. "I know I messed up, but are we going straight to evil?"

Father Cummings held his gaze until Ryan squirmed, recalling his past in far too vivid detail. "All right, I get your point."

"He hates defeat and will watch for a chance to trip you up. Don't let him get it."

"I won't, Father." Ryan finished his coffee and stood. "I've been putting in time at the Villa."

Father stood too. "I expect some of those kids are kicking your butt in hoops."

"They are. And we lost two sixteen-year-olds last week to the Ghetto Dogs."

The priest cringed. "I presided at Manny's funeral with Father Marino. Do you know which gang fathered the Ghetto Dogs?"

Ryan shook his head.

"Los Satanas. If you ever doubt the presence of evil, the temptation of the dark one, come and stand with me at these funerals as we bury so many young Latino and black men. It is like watching our future change before us." He reached out and grasped Ryan's hands. "Let us pray. Our Father…"

Ryan recited the trusted words, but this time he didn't just say them. He knew them, and when they got to the words "*deliver us from evil*," he recognized what the priest had been saying.

Evil wasn't a term.

It was an essence, and he never wanted to be in its clutches again.

* * *

With her glasses perched toward the end of her nose, Claire O'Donnell tapped information into her electronic tablet the following week, then peered up at Kerry. "We should be having an engagement party."

"And yet we can't, because how awkward would that be?" Kerry made a face at her. "Aunt Claire, I honestly can't even imagine Ryan and Jake meeting, so pushing that agenda sends me into a tailspin. Let's just skip it, OK?"

"I gave one for your sister."

"And it was wonderful, but no." Kerry agreed as she made notes on her laptop. "We're all going to have to adjust to being a cozy, related-by-marriage family as it is. Let's not rush things."

"All right. But if we were throwing a sweet, welcome-to-the-family engagement party, I'd give you this." Claire slid a thin envelope her way. "Because we love you and Dan and I want you to relax and enjoy your wedding."

Kerry opened the card, read the check, and shook her head. "I can't accept this, Auntie. It's too much."

"It's not. If it wasn't awkward, we would have simply done the reception at the restaurant, but that would be weird, and we thought you and Jake might prefer a place down here."

"He's got a sizable family here," Jenn added. "It makes sense."

It did, and while a part of Kerry loved the idea of a wedding, she'd discovered she hated planning one. "It does, and I thank you, Auntie. This will actually remove any worries I've been having about crazy costs. Every time I think I've made a move to keep costs down, something happens to drive them back up."

"That's a weddin' for you, darlin'," offered Hannah from her chair. "It's just how it is, 'specially these days, but Shelly Anne over at the bakery was sayin' a bunch of ways to save money, and I wrote them all down for you, every last one, but she did tell me not to spare the hair lotion."

Claire winced on Kerry's behalf, but Kerry laughed. "I will never live that down, and I want to tell you that dry, curly hair has a mind of its own." She glanced up at the clock and stood. "Gotta leave, ladies. Bridal appointment in thirty, and it's a twenty-minute drive."

"You think Jake and Will are all right with the kids at Jake's place?"

Kerry grabbed her lightweight jacket and headed for the door. "Let's assume they are, because if they're not?" she winked at her sister. "We're better off not knowing."

Dress?

Done.

Veil?

Ditto.

Cake?

Ordered.

Church?

Reserved and so was the cozy Depot restaurant nestled against rarely used rail lines. They'd chosen the menu and ordered linens and simple spring flowers, the boys had new suits suitable for Easter and a wedding, and they'd found a perfect and reasonably priced flower girl gown for Cassie online.

"Who knew planning a wedding was this exhausting, woman?" Jake breathed the words against Kerry's hair, and she laughed the next day.

"I thought I was a detail-oriented person until this came along, and I quickly discovered I don't care about details. I just want to marry the absolutely amazing man I've fallen head over heels in love with."

"You are buttering me up so I'll man the grill."

"Since God sent us a beautiful day for March, I think it's only right. Look at those kids, Jake." She leaned back against him as the three kids chased a handful of others around the town playground. "Aren't we blessed?"

He nuzzled her cheek and took his sweet time doing it. In his arms, in his presence, she felt safe and beloved. But then there was the matter of the upcoming Easter dinner. "Are you sure I can't bring anything to your mother's for Easter? A cake? Dessert? A nice ham, gently roasted?"

"Not a thing. Just you and Cassie."

"She probably doesn't trust me to make a decent cake. Or warm a ham. Or—"

"Stop. Yes, she overreacted to the hair thing. Who knew it was a thing with women? Not me, and I lived with the woman for over twenty years."

"Because she knew how to do it properly." She fought a sigh because the thought of not getting along with Jake's mother had never occurred to her. "She's worried about the boys."

His arms tightened protectively. "There's no need."

"She thinks there is."

"She's wrong." Jake turned her in his arms. "Kerry, there's no denying that life can be different for children of color. People of color. It's not exactly a Pollyanna world they live in."

"I see the statistics, Jake. I'm fairly literate."

He lifted one shoulder. "It's not about the numbers; they're atrocious. It's about the immersion into society. My mother's been in a mixed relationship for decades."

"Oh, she made that clear at our first meeting."

A tiny muscle in his lower jaw tweaked. "I know. Aria filled me in, and I tried to lay Mom's fears to rest, but she thinks my uniform offers me a biased view."

"So you're not good enough to raise your boys either?" Kerry swiped her forehead. "Phew. I feel better."

"A uniform brings power. She sees that as a division of sorts. The boys won't have that, and because they're darker skinned than I am, she thinks I'm not as aware of what might await them as they grow up."

"You're their father."

"Except that most people meeting me assume I'm Latino, so in that case, she's correct. Abe and Ben are definitely black children, so by my marrying a white woman now, she sees them as becoming an oddity."

Back in Rochester and the surrounding area, international adoptions were the norm, and lots of families looked like a miniature United Nations meeting. It had never occurred to her that could be problematic. "She can't look beyond color?"

Jake started to answer, but Kerry put a hand up to stop him. "I have several friends who've done cross-racial and international adoptions. It's the norm for lots of people. There are mixed families everywhere, Jake."

"You're talking a city with a university-based economy drawing thousands of international students a year. It's not as common down here."

He was right. In the rural setting of the Southern Tier, there weren't as many people of color, but should that make a difference? Or more importantly, would it? "Should we move?"

The thought didn't make him happy. "I've thought of it. But my family's here. Our jobs are here. And there's no one in Phillipsburg who's ever given me or the boys a hard time. Mom's concern is that teenage black boys have a stigma all their own, and that a white stepmother might not be able to step up to the plate as needed. Not because of capability, but simple lack of knowledge."

She thought Kerry might be insensitive to the boys' problems?

Jake watched her, as if concerned about her reaction, and he was right to be, but she refused to go ballistic. Drama cured nothing. Actions spoke louder than words. "Here's the deal, Jake Slattery."

He looked more worried now but also a little amused.

"Me and Jenn?" She hooked a thumb north, toward upstate. "We're survivors. We joined hands over twenty years ago and kept each other sane and safe in circumstances that looked a whole lot like Cassie's life with Jed. We looked out for one another, we clung to faith and the future, and we climbed out of a rathole existence to become two young professionals who left the past behind. I don't just bring a pretty white girl to the table of this marriage."

She poked him in the chest, and he pretended to wince. "I bring an overcomer, a woman who didn't just see the dark side, she lived it. So if there is anyone who tries to mess with our boys or Cassie, they will have to mess with me first. And I'm going to promise you, Jake Slattery"—she wasn't big by any means, but facing him and declaring this, she felt big—"going through me is not an easy task."

"You're not offended?"

She snorted. "I'm terribly offended, but I'm also aware that your mother is right. Disparity can rule the day if we allow it. So we don't let it happen. End of story. Are you hungry? Because I'm starving, and those kids are going to hit the wall and demand food soon."

He grinned down at her. "The fierce mother bear, protecting her cubs. You've got me convinced, darlin'."

"And that's all I need," she told him firmly. "Everyone else will come around eventually, but as long as you believe in me—"

"Not a doubt in my mind."

"Then we're good to go."

"I'll go light the grill and see if Hannah's potatoes are ready."

"We'll be along soon." He kissed her good-bye, crossed Main Street, and walked back toward her place.

They'd sat in church together that morning. They'd prayed and worshipped and laughed as a family. It was perfect, a dream come true, and she wasn't about to let anything mess that up.

chapter twenty-two

Four fresh, small bruises marked Cassie's honey-toned skin as Kerry helped her out of the bath that night. "Honey, did you fall on the playground today?" Playground bumps would account for the two on her legs, but the one on her back and the one on her hip made no sense.

Cassie shook her head. "I jumped on the playground, and I chased Abe, and he's so fast!" She paused, then added, "I slipped down the ladder maybe, once. But I didn't cry, and I climbed back up real quick."

"That must be it." Kerry toweled her off, got her ready for bed, said prayers with her, and tucked her in. "There you go, sweet cheeks. I'll see you in the morning, OK?"

"OK!"

Excited. Happy. Joyous.

Such a difference in a beloved child, it made Kerry happy to see it, to be part of it. They'd been blessed to know her, then to find her and rescue her in the storm. And now home here with Kerry, and soon with Jake and the boys.

She didn't want the county to find family for Cassie. Yes, that was selfish, but she loved Cassie, and Cassie loved her, so what good would come from giving her to strangers? Was she wrong to want that? It didn't feel wrong, and yet, it did.

Trust in the Lord with all your heart…

She loved the proverb, but the whole trust thing was easier said than done. She liked engineering her own outcome. It suited. She'd learned to lean on her own understanding a long time ago, and she'd done all right.

He will make straight your paths…

Her current path was facing forward, straight as an arrow. For the first time in years, she felt grounded and secure. It was a feeling she loved and intended to keep by her side. God's blessings supporting human choices.

Perfect.

* * *

Cassie slumped down at her desk on purpose. Maybe if she stayed low, Anthony wouldn't notice her and make fun of her.

He walked by on her right, so she edged toward the left.

Maybe he'd be nice today. Maybe—

"Teacher's pet, teacher's pet, ugly, ugly teacher's pet."

Her eyes stung.

Her throat wound up tight.

Usually she could ignore him, and Kerry and Mrs. Dumrese and Miss Morehouse made him mostly be good, but he liked being naughty when they were busy.

Chin tucked, she focused on the tracing pad in front of her, a gift from Jake. Her desk jerked—

Anthony again, kicking the narrow leg—

And it made her tracing pencil tear a jagged line into the thin, transparent paper.

Hot tears stun her eyes. She blinked them away, but two fell onto the paper below, sprawling across the pretty princess picture she'd just traced. It was too much. Just too much!

She stood up quickly and shouted at him. "I hate you, Anthony! You're so mean, and you're not nice, and I don't think anybody on this earth will ever, ever like you because you're meaner than Darth Vader and every single one of the storm troopers put together!"

"Cassie." Kerry had been working at the sorting table with Izzie, Micah, and Noah. She stood and moved toward Cassie while Mrs. Dumrese approached from the opposite direction. "What happened?"

"He ruins everything!" Cassie gasped the words, pointing toward Anthony, and when he smirked, she only got madder. "He says mean things, he makes mean faces, and he always waits until grown-ups aren't looking, and he ruined my best princess paper on purpose."

"I didn't cry on it and smear it," the tough little boy scolded back. "That was your fault, you big baby."

"I'm not—"

"Stop it, both of you. Mrs. Dumrese, will you escort Anthony down to the principal's office, please?"

"Yes, Miss McHenry."

"And she gets to stay here?" Anthony braced his legs, unmoving, and pointed to Cassie. "After saying mean things? Nobody else gets to be mean and get away with it!" Anthony shouted as Rita led him away. "This isn't fair! It's not fair! It's only because you like her best!"

Kerry turned to Cassie. She squatted low and kept her voice soft. "Is that how we're supposed to treat other people, Cassie?"

Cassie stuck her lower lip out, stubborn.

"Are we allowed to yell in class?"

She stared at Kerry, and when she saw the disappointment in her eyes, Cassie wanted to cry. Not just a couple of tears, but real ones, a lot of real ones.

She didn't, though.

The man had told her people would be mean, and that they would make fun of her.

He was right. Anthony liked being mean. The man liked being mean.

She didn't understand any of it. How could someone be happy and mean at the same time?

She looked down at her desk, not wanting to face Kerry and see the sad look on her face. Maybe she would send her away. Maybe she would find another place for her and drop her off and say, "Here is the little girl who stayed with me for a while. I thought she'd be nice all the time. She wasn't. Good-bye."

Her heart felt heavy in her chest, so heavy.

Her head hurt.

And her skin felt choppy, like it wasn't happy anymore.

Kerry bent low. "Can you pull yourself together, or would you like some quiet time?"

Cassie knew what quiet time meant. A time out. A punishment.

She'd never had to be punished in school for anything, so the thought of making Kerry put her in time out stung deep. "I'll be good."

"All right. Class?" Kerry stood and turned her attention to the rest of the class. "Sparrows have five more minutes of free time, the cardinals will move from sorting to free time, and the robins will meet me in the reading corner while the sparrows join Mrs. Dumrese for the spring art project table. Consider this your five-minute warning."

Cassie breathed relief, eyes down.

She wouldn't have to be with Anthony when he returned. She was a sparrow; he was a cardinal. Ava and Minnie were sparrows, and they didn't make fun of her anymore. Ava even let her hold her doll once, and Minnie gave her five fruity dinosaurs out of her snack bag.

But still, Anthony's words pinched deep.

She'd looked in the mirror that morning, and she didn't look ugly. She was sure she didn't. But she felt ugly, and her skin pinched, and right now the thing she'd like to do most is lie down and take a nice, long nap.

* * *

"I can't go to the wedding," Ryan explained to Father Cummings the following week. "It's tricky enough to maintain a low profile, and my stepmother didn't throw her an engagement party, and I know that was because of me, but there's no way I can show up at this wedding and pretend I'm happy when I'm not."

"Of course not," the older man agreed, but he agreed too quickly which meant he'd make a point, and he didn't wait too long to do it. "The thought of coming face to face with Kerry and admitting defeat would be too much to expect of anyone. No, stay home, pretend you're working, and it will pass like any other day. Wise choice." He passed Ryan a hammer as the two of them double-teamed a broken wall divider at the Villa. Two teens had gotten into a tussle the week before, and the divider took the worst of it.

"Of course there's always the other option," Father Cummings supposed.

"I was pretty sure there would be."

"Which is," the priest went on as if Ryan hadn't spoken, "to man up, face the music, and move forward. Did Christ shirk from his accusers?"

He didn't. The question wasn't worth answering.

"Did he hide out in that upstairs room or go to the garden, knowing what awaited him?"

"Well, he was God," Ryan reminded him.

"And you're not, but I can't exactly equate a wedding with a cruci-fixion, so it's not as apples versus oranges as you'd like to make out."

"You think I should go."

"You nailed it!" He clapped Ryan on the back as if proud that he figured that out. "We gain nothing by hanging back when facing forward is the better choice, but then, it's totally up to you. I think, actually…"

Ryan could hardly wait to hear what the priest thought, because he was pretty sure he was going to hate it instantly. And then do it with great reluctance, only to realize it was the right thing after all.

"You should do something nice for her. Break the stalemate. Let her know her choice is all right with you."

"In other words, lie."

Father Cummings waved that off. "We're talking degrees of separa-tion. She knows you cared, and you both know the timing was wrong. So you let her know that you want her happy. That's not a lie, is it?"

It wasn't, but it wasn't exactly how he'd seen the whole thing going down, either. He was supposed to get fixed, get religion, then get the girl.

"God's will and his timing. We trust, we learn, we move forward."

He heard the priest's directive, but did the celibate old man really think it was that easy?

Father Cummings put a hand on his arm, a hand that was still sprightly after all these years but bore the weight of time. "Being the bigger person, setting her free, easing the tension. All this is in your hands." He noted Ryan's hands with a smile. "That's a whole different kind of power, my son."

He took the words with him when he went home that night. Vic and Mandy were meeting with a printer for invitations, spring bulbs were blooming around the condominium complex, and the evening sun was tipping west, slanting broken beams of light through rose-toned clouds.

He'd think about it.

He pushed his hand through his hair and sighed.

He'd do it. Not because he wanted to, but because the priest was right. He needed to.

There were two half-empty bottles in their small bar. One of them called to him, inviting him to drown his sorrows for the night. He stared at the bottle, then at the descending sun. And when the sun was cut just about in half by the horizon, he walked back inside and dumped the bottle down the sink.

He didn't need quick shots anymore or a six-pack of long necks.

He stared at the sink, then the bottle, then tossed the bottle into the recycling bin.

Father hadn't suggested he stop drinking, but Ryan knew the truth. True strength didn't need booze to soften life's edges. It needed faith. And the only way to fly solo was to man up and do it.

But he still didn't want to go to the stupid wedding.

chapter twenty-three

Anne motioned Kerry into her office a few days later. When she invited her to have a seat, Kerry knew something was up. "This can't be good." She sat down and faced Anne. "What's going on?"

"Anthony's mother has gone to the school board."

"Because he was disciplined for being mean to another student? That will get her nowhere. Our school board expects children to behave in school. That's part of what drew me here."

Anne locked eyes with her and sighed. "She's requesting, no, let's make that *demanding*, that Cassie be taken out of the school because Daystar isn't equipped to deal with emotionally disturbed special needs children who burn down houses."

"No." Kerry couldn't have heard right. First, no normal, decent person would do this, would they? And second, Cassie had done no such thing. She'd dropped a match during wretched, scary conditions. "Anne, that's not what happened. Yes, she dropped the match, but—"

Anne held up her hands. "Save it for the board, Kerry. I don't need convincing, but it's been taken out of my hands by Angela Perrotto's official request. She went directly to the board, and they're putting this on their calendar for next week's scheduled meeting."

"They would actually consider this?"

"They are required to listen," Anne told her. "She'd demanded an emergency meeting, and they refused to do that. But whether or not they choose to act isn't up to me. It's up to them. You said that the sheriff's office had a detective interview Cassie, right?"

"Yes."

"Talk to the detective. See if she'd approach the board next week on Cassie's behalf. I'd also ask Susan McCabe to address the board. She instigated Cassie's enrollment last year. And if you could document Anthony's antagonistic behavior to show a pattern of antisocial development, that could give a clearer picture of what's been going on."

Kerry shook her head quickly. "I can't do that to a six-year-old. I can't throw him under the bus at a formal meeting as if he's a wanted criminal when he's actually just a spoiled brat."

"I understand your reluctance," Anne replied. "But Angela is married to the owner of an influential business that pumps money into the county tax fund and employs over a hundred people. Money talks, Kerry, even when it shouldn't. And if they raise a fuss and pull Anthony out of school, other parents may follow."

"So you think I should remove Cassie to calm things down?"

"No, of course not, but I think you need to come to that meeting ready to present the facts. The school board isn't on-site. They only hear what is offered at meetings and our weekly update. They deserve to weigh Anthony's behavior into their decision."

Kerry couldn't do it. She didn't need to think about it or give it consideration. There was no way she could go before a board of professionals and destroy a little kid's self-image. "If you present the list of times he's visited your office, that's a choice I can live with because they should be able to draw conclusions from that. The rest we leave in God's hands."

Anne didn't look convinced, but she stood. "Next Thursday, seven o'clock in room seven."

"I'll be here." Kerry stood, too, but the thought that a Christian school parent would do this stung deep. "But I sure wish I didn't have to be."

"Me, too."

* * *

"She what?" Jake couldn't have heard right. Kerry shushed him with a finger to her lips. He moved closer so the kids couldn't hear, but the boys were destroying an alien planet with sponge bombs. Their loud bombing runs were enough to cover even a very loud voice, and Cassie was curled up with her dolls at the far end of the room. "Angela's demanding they let Cassie go?"

"Yes, while impugning her name and accusing her of arson and possibly murder."

"She said that?"

"She doesn't have to, Jake. It's the implication that Cassie willfully burned the house with her father in it."

He couldn't believe it. How could a parent do that kind of thing? "I'll talk to Mary."

"I already did." Kerry added water to the potatoes and put them on to boil. "She's coming to the meeting to refute Angela's allegations."

"You called her?" He couldn't deny a sense of pride that Kerry hadn't waited for him.

"Instantly, and when I told her what was happening, she promised to address the board in her official capacity, but here's the thing, Jake." She lowered the flame beneath the potatoes and turned. "It's not just proof that decides things like this. For a small private school, it's the intimation of wrongdoing. For some folks, a breath of a scandal is enough to send them running for cover and moving their kids to another school."

"Guilt by association." He didn't want to think that. Not of their town or of the school that had been doing so well, bringing all kinds of kids together in a warm, ecumenical setting. "Would it help if we register the boys there? Ben won't go for another eighteen months, but I'd be OK switching Abe over. That shows our support for the school."

"Except that parents should pick a school for the benefit of the child, not the benefit of the school," she reminded him.

He shrugged. "We're talking timing, honey. We were going to discuss the pros and cons once the wedding plans were set. Angela's ultimatum is pushing the agenda, but that shouldn't make a difference. I like the school." He bent and kissed her cheek, softly and slowly. "And I really like the staff." He kissed her other cheek the same way. "Which means I'd be fine with the boys going there, as long as Cassie's there. I want them all in the same school anyway, because that just makes sense."

"What about your mother? She didn't seem happy about the idea of Abe being shifted to Daystar."

"He's five. I expect he'll adjust." Her expression said she was more worried than amused, so he tugged her away from the stove and into his arms. "Kerry, my mother has her opinions on a lot of things, but I raise my boys my way. She knows that and respects it. That doesn't mean we always agree, but she loves those boys."

"Yes."

"So we register Abe for school, and we can send Ben for preschool, which means all three kids in Daystar. And we go to the meeting together, a united front. I'll ask Mom to watch the kids."

"But then she'll know that there are problems already."

"Oh, honey." He pulled out his phone and raised it up. "My mother has lived a long time. She's probably got that part figured out." He called his mother, and she agreed to watch the kids, but when he hung up the phone, he touched Kerry's arm. "How hard did you work Cassie today?"

She followed the direction of his gaze. "She's sound asleep."

"Zonked."

"She did that the other day, too. Hannah said she's probably having a growth spurt, that kids get tired out when that happens."

"Except she seems a little off, Kerry." He'd noticed it the past week, that Cassie's normally eager-to-please nature hadn't been all that eager. "Have you noticed that?"

She shifted her gaze from Cassie to him. "She's been tired, like she's fighting a cold, but doesn't have a cold. Do you think something's wrong?"

He couldn't say yes, but the change niggled him. "Listen, I'm not one of those parents that runs their kid in for every little thing. If I was, I'd be living at the doctor's office with those two hooligans, but yes. Because remember what you said about those bruises last weekend?"

She nodded.

"There was one on her cheek when she came home from school."

Kerry crossed the room and stooped by Cassie's side, and there at the top of her cheek beneath her eye was a fresh bruise. "Jake, that wasn't there when we left school today. Where did it come from?"

He shook his head. "I have no idea."

She crossed to the boys and signaled a time-out. The boys paused their in-flight weapons. "Guys, did either of you bump Cassie when you were playing before?"

Abe shook his head. "She just wanted to do girl stuff, so we *bignored* her."

"Ignored," Kerry corrected him. "So nothing at all? No bonks or bumps?"

"No because her dowwies wanted to go to sweep," Ben explained in a most serious voice. "So we pwomised not to wake them up."

"Thanks, guys." She stood and faced Jake, and he read the concern in her eyes because it reflected his. "I'll call first thing in the morning."

chapter twenty-four

Acute Lymphoblastic Leukemia.

Cassie had cancer.

Kerry heard the doctor, but couldn't believe it. She gripped Jake's hand and held on tight. "Are you sure? Couldn't there be some mistake?"

He shook his head. "The tests are conclusive. It's a form of leukemia that responds well to treatment in over 85 percent of the cases, but we'll need to send her to the Children's Hospital up in Rochester. They've got some of the best pediatric oncologists in the country on staff there, and she'll be in good hands."

Good hands.

Kerry's gut rose up into her throat.

How could this happen? Why did this happen? Hadn't Cassie already gone through' enough?

She turned to Jake, big, strong Jake Slattery, and when she saw him swipe moisture from his eyes, she almost lost it, but then he bent forward. "How soon can we get her up there, doctor? Because I don't want my baby girl fighting this any longer than she absolutely has to."

"We'll set everything up from here, and my front desk will call you with details. It's a ninety-minute drive each way..."

Kerry knew that drive well.

"And she'll most likely be hospitalized during a good share of the treatment, but they have multiple hospitality houses on site, with one built into the Children's Hospital to accommodate out-of-area parents. Rochester Pediatric Oncology will take over her case from here. And I promise you, they're as good as anyone available on the East Coast."

Rochester Pediatric Oncology.

Ryan.

Her hands shook, and a slight tremor hit her sideways, because she'd avoided seeing Ryan for months. But now—now, all bets were off.

Ryan O'Donnell had it in his power to save Cassie's life, and despite all the crazy romantic drama they'd been through, Kerry couldn't imagine Cassie in better hands. She stood and held out her hand to the doctor, wishing this was all a bad dream, knowing it wasn't. "I know Dr. O'Donnell personally. He's actually part of my family."

Jake raised his eyebrows as he realized what she meant. He grimaced slightly, but put a strong, gentle hand on her shoulder. "Let's get her up there as quickly as we can, doctor. All right?"

"I hear you, Jake. And they have a no-wait policy, so you'll most likely want to cancel anything you had scheduled for the next day or two. And then," he paused and shrugged, "for the next six months."

They exited the office quietly. Too quietly.

And when they got to Jake's car, Kerry pulled out her phone and texted Ryan immediately. *"Cassie's been diagnosed w/ ALL, coming to your practice. Please help us save her, Ryan. Please."*

Her phone rang almost instantly. She took the call and a deep breath at the same time. "Ryan."

"Kerry." His voice, deep and strong, sounded reassuring.

"We need your help, Ryan."

"And you've got it. I'm so sorry you have to deal with this, but we'll get her through it, Kerry. I promise."

She winced, because 85 percent meant that 15 percent weren't helped. "Don't make promises you can't keep. The pediatrician told us the stats, and that means 15 percent of kids…" She couldn't say it. If she said it, the potential for loss became too real.

"I *don't* make promises I can't keep. At least not anymore," he added, and the lightness of his tone helped unexpectedly. "But we've got an over 95 percent cure rate working with other peds oncology centers, and it's rare we encounter a garden variety ALL that doesn't respond well to one of the weapons at my disposal. I'll call the office and have her put with me. Can you get her up here ASAP?"

"We can. We'll make arrangements as soon as we hear, and Ryan?"

"Yes?"

"Thank you."

He took a deep breath, a sound she remembered well. Too well. "You're welcome, Kerry."

* * *

By the time they got back to Kerry's apartment, everything had been arranged. They'd leave for Rochester first thing in the morning, and Jake's sister would take the boys.

Cancer.

Jake wanted to punch something. Maybe someone. But there was no one to hit, so he thrust his hands into his jacket pockets and took a quick walk to settle his brain.

When he got to the church, he purposely kicked dirt at the concrete corner.

He didn't care that it was childish. He didn't care that someone might see him having a hissy fit on Church Street. He cared that a belief in a loving God seemed in constant conflict with reality.

Why Cassie? Why now, after all she'd been through? What was the point of a little kid getting cancer and having to fight through months of debilitating treatment?

Why not him? He was big, strong, and tough. He could handle anything. He wanted to beat his chest like Tarzan and challenge God to test *him*—not a tenderhearted child.

Hannah came up alongside him. "Kerry's lookin' for you."

He nodded and swiped a hand to his face.

"She is lookin' for you because she knows this is a kick in the head."

"You can say that again. I just need a minute, Hannah."

"You take that minute, because truth to tell, Jake Slattery, that's all you are goin' to get when it comes to this. I've been down this road, and it is not easy, but there is a difference today."

He thrust one brow up.

"Today children can live," she whispered, and her grip on his arm grew tight. "Today they have treatments, and parents bring their sweet babies home. It wasn't always that way, and I know the truth of that personal, so while this is a tough row to hoe, young man, there is hope, and that hope is what gets us through!"

She was right. The landscape for childhood leukemia had changed dramatically in the last thirty years.

"And once you've had your minute, then you put on your happy face any time you are around that little girl, you hear me?"

He heard, all right, and so did half the town because Hannah wasn't whispering anymore.

"She is too smart by half, and she will know what's goin' on, so you be there with a big, strong arm and a lap for holdin' on, while you tell stories and play silly games and dress dolls."

"Hold on, woman, no one said anything about dressing up dolls in the diagnosis." He made an outrageous face to show he was teasing.

She smiled and hugged his arm. "You be strong, Jake. That is your task now, and I know that might seem unfair, but you're the leader of this new family. And your break-downs need to be in private for a while. If you can manage it."

He could manage it. He had no choice, and she was right. "I'll be fine."

"Hmm." She glared at the church, and the splat of dirt skirting the corner. "Maybe you will and maybe you won't, but bein' mad at God will get you nothin' but a headache. God doesn't want cancer. God isn't sittin' up there on some throne handing out diseases to little girls, but I'll tell you what I do think, Jake Slattery."

Jake was 100 percent sure he couldn't stop her if he tried, so why try?

"There's a reason for why things happen when they do. You came into Kerry's life at the right time and the right place. Cassie's, too. She wouldn't be alive today if it wasn't for you, and even that old boyfriend of Kerry's has his place in all this. I've been on the planet long enough to see timin' work wonders if we humans know enough to take it in stride. And you've had your share of practice, Jake."

He didn't want to think of losing Lori, but the minute he'd heard the life-threatening diagnosis, his mind had gone straight to that loss and kind of frozen there.

"The Lord giveth. And the Lord taketh away. Blessed be the name of the Lord," she quoted softly, but she hugged his arm as she said it. "But the Lord has also opened a big window for our precious child, and if there's anything I can do to help, I'll be right here doin' it."

There were times he thought being in a small town and a close-knit community was stifling.

Right now he'd welcome every bit of help he could get. "And we'll appreciate all of it, Hannah."

On the walk back to Kerry's, he called his commander and filled him in. And when he got to Hannah's little duplex, he squeezed her hand lightly, grateful for the saucy old woman's advice.

He'd turned a corner when he met Kerry, and that new direction brought him to an unexpected crossroads today, an intersection of unclear choices and unmarked roads.

He climbed the steps, put a smile on his face, and walked in because Hannah was right. No matter what happened, he was the leader of this new family, and he'd take that job with pride.

* * *

"Cassie Carruthers, age five, just diagnosed with Acute Lymphoblastic Leukemia."

Ryan shared the slim folder with Sam D'Amico and Reilly Shaughnessy the next morning. They examined the numbers, and Sam's mouth thinned. "Typical for this stage. You said they're bringing her in this morning?"

"Probably arriving about now." Ryan pressed his hands flat on the table top and stood, knowing he had to reveal this next part. "I have a connection to this child."

"Connection?" Reilly looked confused. "Explain."

"I had a relationship…"

She arched a brow, and Ryan backtracked. "Not that kind of a relationship, but yes, a relationship with her foster mother. Who is also my stepmother's niece."

"Convoluted."

It was, so he nodded.

"So this kid is family to you?"

"Not officially, but yes, in a way."

She started to say something, but Sam raised a hand. "Kerry is her foster mother?"

"Yes." Of course Sam would remember Kerry because he'd been pushing Ryan to marry her six months ago. "Kerry and her fiancé are planning to adopt this child if all goes well, so we've got a ward of the county with a family relationship to me."

"I'll take over the case." Reilly put out her hand, and Ryan knew what he should do. He should step back and let Reilly go forward as lead, because she wouldn't have any messy emotions clouding her judgment.

Ryan didn't take second fiddle readily. He didn't hand over the reins or control, ever, so Reilly's outstretched hand wasn't only annoying…it was a test of his humility.

If my people who are called by my name humble themselves…

Ryan sucked a breath and handed over the folder, envisioning a new little plastic brick in his strengthening platform. "Take lead."

She nodded and moved toward the door. "Let's do this."

Ryan started to follow her, but Sam put a hand on his arm. He turned. "You did good, son."

He hadn't wanted to hand that folder over. He'd thought all night about how he could take on this case, cure Cassie, and be the hero. Right now he desperately wanted to be the hero, and that was reason enough to step back. "Thanks, Sam."

Sam clapped him on the back, clearly pleased. "You're welcome."

Ryan stepped out of the small meeting room and spotted Kerry. She stood profile to him as she answered questions at the front desk. He changed his angle slightly and spotted Cassie in the arms of a man.

His heart squeezed. An adrenaline shot made his fingers buzz.

Cassie was laughing up at the guy, and her laughter was reflected in the man's joy. And then he gathered her close, his chin resting on her head, his eyes half-closed.

Praying.

Ryan was pretty sure the guy was sitting right there in the waiting room, knowing the child had cancer, and praying.

How could he hate him?

"Ryan."

Kerry had spotted him. She crossed the soft, carpeted floor and reached out to grab his hands. She didn't shy away or hold back. She met his gaze like she always had, straight and true. What a fool he'd been to run scared. Facing her, he saw that clearly. Why had his vision been so fogged last year?

She squeezed his hands lightly and said, "Thank you so much for getting us right in. We know she's going to be in good hands here."

Jake stood up, still holding Cassie. He set her down. She turned and spotted Ryan, and her eyes went wide. "Doctor Ryan, you're here!" She raced across the kid-friendly waiting room and threw herself into his arms. "I'm so glad to see you. Look how big I am!"

His heart didn't squeeze this time. It melted, like warm butter on hotcakes, because despite the diagnosis, Cassie's face and voice teemed with life. New life. "You look great, kid."

"Do you like my hair?" She showed off pretty, multicolor barrettes with a winning smile. "And I've got new shoes and dresses, and I get to stay with Kerry *all the time!*" She stressed the time frame deliberately. "And we're going to have a wedding, and I'm going to be the flower girl and have brothers who are very, very loud children."

"Wow." Ryan grinned at her, because he couldn't help celebrate the change in her. The joy. It exuded from her, and the difference from the quiet, introverted girl of last fall was amazing.

He picked her up and stood, then stuck out a hand to Jake. "I'm Ryan O'Donnell, Jake."

Jake took his hand in a solid grip. "Good to meet you. And like Kerry said, we're grateful to have you on hand."

He looked sincere, but a little questioning, too.

Would Ryan be that nice if the roles were reversed? Probably not six months ago, but now?

Maybe. And remembering his father's kindness to his errant mother, he still wasn't sure it was the smart thing to do, but maybe smart and right weren't always synonymous. He motioned them toward a door. "Dr. Shaughnessy is taking lead on this. Let's go meet her."

"Not you?"

Kerry's voice, concerned, and he almost caved. He paused and faced them both. "With our history, it made sense. I'll be involved, but Reilly can be effective and impartial. And when it comes to this cute kid?" He smiled into Cassie's green eyes. "I can't pretend there isn't a personal investment."

"Because we're family." Kerry kept her gaze and tone direct as she made her point. Their past was over. Done. She'd moved on.

But seeing her sparked a wave of old emotion, and a smack upside the head.

Reilly stepped through the door. "Miss McHenry? I'm Dr. Shaughnessy, Ryan's colleague. And Sam says you've met before?"

Kerry shook Sam's hand. "I'd like to say it's nice to see you again, but it's not, and I hope you take my reticence the way it's intended. It is, however, an absolute blessing to have our girl in good hands."

Sam held her hand, then exchanged looks with Ryan and Reilly. "Ryan, can you take Cassie to see the fish?"

"Glad to." He moved down the hall, knowing what was coming. Sam was about to explain medical custodial procedure to Jake and Kerry, and Ryan was pretty sure she wasn't going to be one bit happy about it.

Which made him glad to take Cassie and stay out of the room.

chapter twenty-five

"We can't make any decisions regarding her care?" Kerry stared at Sam and reached for Jake's hand so she wouldn't throw something. Not at Sam, he was a good man.

But that didn't mean she wasn't still inclined to fight with someone, and Sam was handy. "How can that be right? I know we're in the middle of a hot mess of crazy, but I've been her caretaker off and on for over six months, and my foster care application is being approved as we speak."

"And we've already informed the county of our intent to adopt Cassie as soon as it's legally possible," Jake added. "Doesn't that come with some kind of parental responsibility?"

"Not until the adoption is complete." Sam folded his hands and pressed forward. "This is a convoluted case in some ways, but in others it's crystal clear. The state is Cassie's legal guardian, which means their assigned people are in charge. Her expenses are covered by Medicaid. Your county social worker will work with our social worker and the medical staff here. For each step of care, we'll need permissions from the Beckett County Director of Social Services to proceed."

"Can't they just offer blanket provision to save time?"

"I wish it was that easy, but no. We need to ask step by step. This isn't usually a problem, but occasionally the timing is slower than we'd like. Not all agencies get back to us quickly."

"I'll be in Beckett County. I can help facilitate that if I'm informed," Jake told him. "I'll hand deliver things, if necessary, doctor."

"And it might be. Give me your cell number, Jake. That way we can let you know when we need something ASAP. But let me assure you that if Cassie's in crisis, we proceed as needed to do anything to save her. The permissions don't affect that."

Anything to save her…

Those words struck Kerry hard, because looking at Cassie right now, nothing appeared all that wrong. And yet it was wrong. Grievously wrong.

"Our goal is to maintain an open relationship with the social workers. Kerry, it says here that you're going to stay with Cassie, is that correct?"

"I took a leave from my teaching position."

"And we postponed our wedding until Cassie's healthy enough to do the honors as our flower girl," Jake added. "Her health comes first. Kerry and I will iron out everything else later. Listen, doctor." Jake gripped Kerry's hand tighter. "We just want our little girl to get through this as easily as possible and come home to us." His voice trembled, not from anger. From fear. "We know that cancer treatments are not easy. She's five." Jake pulled in a deep breath. "And she's already gone through so much. We want what's best for her, no matter what."

"We'll do whatever we can to ensure that," Sam promised. "Dr. O'Donnell's father has also offered to guarantee any over-expenditures on Cassie's behalf if that's a help. He sent me a note last evening, Kerry, to make sure that you're comfortable while you're here."

Jake rebuffed that offer instantly. "We don't need his money."

"Jake." Kerry turned his way. "Dan loves me. He's been more like a father to me these past few years than I've ever had, and Aunt Claire has been there for us since we were little. He's only trying to help."

"We can take care of our own." Jake's expression was resolute. "I can take care of my fiancé and my kids. That's my job. Not his."

It wasn't the thought of Dan helping that was tweaking Jake. It was the idea that Ryan's father might be helping. Kerry let it slide for the moment. She understood Dan's magnanimous desire to help, but the last thing she wanted to do was fight with Jake over anything.

Sam hit a button to call Ryan and Cassie back in. "Let's get started on the real reason we're here. Cassie's treatment."

Kerry kept her hand in Jake's, but their questionable legal status unnerved her. Would strangers take Cassie's health seriously? Should she push for some sort of legal status to give her authority? And if she hired a lawyer to do that, would that anger officials in the system? Would they then consider removing Cassie from her care?

Fear rose, and not just fear of cancer. That was bad enough.

Fear of the same bureaucracy that let Cassie linger in squalid conditions for years. She was being asked to put faith in a flawed system. That was bad enough in the abstract, but it was absolutely impossible when it came to Cassie.

They got Cassie admitted, and one of the volunteers showed them the hospitality house built into the hospital. Each child's room also had a bed for parents.

It was a beautiful and comfortable setting thanks to the largesse of a community benefactor who wanted the best for area kids.

Now it was Kerry's job to make sure Cassie got just that.

* * *

The pediatric social worker faced Kerry and Jake and tapped a beautifully sculpted nail onto Cassie's folder. "The first rule is: Stop concerning yourselves over what cannot be changed. Cassie might be in the hands of Beckett County, but they've granted you temporary custody, which means yes, you can stay with her. Both of you, if you'd like."

"I've got the boys back home," Jake began.

The social worker jumped right back in. "Divide and conquer, welcome to parenting when crises walk in the door." She set the folder down. "I am here to help. Our staff is here to cut red tape, to make sure everyone's on the same page, and yes, to ease the psychological symptoms of life-threatening illness on the whole family." She showed them the lounges and the play areas and explained visiting privileges, but when they got to financial concerns, she brushed that off.

"Cassie is covered under Medicaid. Her medical coverage is as good or better than many private insurers would allow."

"Are you sure? The doctors said…"

"Honey, they are doctors." The tall, dark-skinned woman said it as if they might possibly be an alien species. "We can't expect them to know everything. Billing and insurances and permissions are a whole different thing, so we'll let Ryan and Sam and Reilly do the curing, while we quietly settle the details." She faced them directly and pointed to a plaque on her wall. "This right here, this is our motto on Four North. *'I have known over the years that when one's mind is made up, this diminishes fear. Knowing what must be done does away with fear.'* Rosa Parks. One of my heroes."

"A brave woman."

"Yes, ma'am." Stella sounded quite sure of herself. "And a great example of how one small act can be felt around the world."

"So we vow to win and fear nothing." Jake sounded so strong, so sure, while Kerry was pretty sure that right now she feared everything.

No nonsense, Stella faced Jake. "Don't get ahead of yourself, here, deputy. You *will fear* a great many things on this journey. Poor test results, bad reactions, hair loss, the change in appearance, the lack of affect, the loss of memory and cognitive reasoning that can accompany chemotherapy. And being so far away while your loved ones go through this alone is going to put you to the test, a test you might fail."

When Jake's copper-toned skin paled, she nodded. "But when it's all done, most children return to normal, and this becomes a bad memory, if she remembers it at all."

"Can the boys come visit?"

She shook her head. "She's going to be in a sensitive state with a diminished immune system, so no. Not for a while. They can call or chat on the computer, but the doctors will put strict limitations on visitors. For you," she faced Kerry, "because you're staying, this will become a home away from home." She shifted back to Jake. "And for you, the harder part might be that you're ninety minutes away, leading your life, feeling guilty that she's here, and that you're not with Cassie for this journey. When there are other children involved, that's the reality. For the next six months, you are embracing a new normal. Let's get to it."

* * *

Jake drove a completely empty car back to Phillipsburg, and the vacant seats yawned cavernous around him.

He wanted to thrash something.

It was all so wrong. Kerry, putting on a brave front. Cassie, fighting a life-threatening disease. And Kerry's old boyfriend, right there, on hand all the time, ready to help.

A cold chill shimmied its way up his back.

He shouldn't be leaving them. It made his big heart ache to think of the long road Cassie was about to endure. He and Kerry should be facing this side by side.

But they couldn't. Abe and Ben needed a father, same as always. And at least Cassie had Kerry now. He couldn't imagine how things would be if this had happened a year before, with no one but Jed in her sweet, little life.

Hannah told him to be strong. What she didn't say was how.

He spotted a sign for Walmart and veered off the highway. Kerry had asked him to take a picture of her and Cassie before he left, so he'd have something to hold close to his heart.

He'd wanted to cry.

He hadn't.

He'd taken the picture, hugged and kissed them both, and walked through the automatic locking doors, gone down the kid-friendly elevator, and marched out to the parking garage.

And then he'd cried, but not for long because there were things to do.

He walked into the store and had the picture printed. He ordered a half dozen, colorful reminders of why the next six months were so important.

He clipped one to his visor and sighed.

Hannah's reminders hit him again. He needed to be tough. Normally that wasn't a problem, but the sight of Cassie in Ryan's arms unnerved him. He pushed the image out of his mind, but it wouldn't stay gone. He stared at the photo he'd snapped right before he left: Kerry and Cassie, heads together, blowing him kisses.

Ryan was there, and Jake wasn't. When Cassie needed help, Ryan would give it. If Kerry needed advice or comfort, would she call Dr. Shaughnessy? Or turn to Ryan?

This wasn't a time to doubt, but to trust, only he'd seen the mix of affection and regret on Ryan's face when he looked at Kerry.

A text came through from his mother as he started the car. *"Boys have eaten, saved you some stew and fresh bread. We shall be strong together. One in the Spirit. For my God is a righteous God!"*

Was God a righteous being? Did he hear anything? Did he exist? And was Jake man enough to put his sweet girl in God's hands?

Driving home in that empty car on gray, rain-slicked streets, he wasn't one bit sure, but would give it his best shot. That meant while Kerry stood guard in Rochester, he'd do the same in Beckett County. He checked an address directory via his phone and pulled up to the Perrotto's house just outside of town. He strode to the door and knocked.

Phil Perrotto answered and looked surprised. "Can I help you?"

"Jake Slattery, Mr. Perrotto." Jake extended his hand as Phil's wife came through from their gracious and spotlessly clean living room. "I stopped by to talk to the two of you, if that's all right. I'd have called first, but I'm just getting back from the hospital and didn't have your number."

"What do we need to discuss?" Phil looked from his wife to Jake and folded his arms.

Jake noted the defensive move and kept his voice and face easygoing. "Your request to the Daystar School Board to expel a kindergartner, Cassie Carruthers."

Phil didn't look surprised by Jake's words. He looked absolutely dumbfounded. "I don't know what you're talking about."

"I see that." Jake redirected his attention to Mrs. Perrotto. "I expect your wife does, sir."

"Angela?" He stepped back so he could see her and Jake. "Do you know what he means?"

"Phillip, I explained all this to you."

"No." Her husband looked distinctly uncomfortable. "You didn't."

"I told you about that child, the one who burned down her home with her father in it. There is no place in a Christian school for a child with a mental disturbance like that. Daystar doesn't have the means nor the staff to handle children so far off the spectrum."

Tiny hairs rose along Jake's neck. A good portion of his skin rose up, but he kept Hannah's advice front and center. "The Beckett County Sheriff's office has no reason to believe the fire was anything other than an accident caused by a child on the verge of freezing to death. It was investigated fully because any time there is a combination of events, it's our duty to determine cause."

"Your duty?" Phil Perrotto looked at him more closely. "Are you a deputy?"

"I am. And I hope to adopt the child in question and keep her in Daystar, so I will admit my vested interest in your wife's petition. I would like her to drop it and stop all attempts to make trouble for Cassie."

"You have your nerve." Angela moved forward quickly. "Coming here, out of the blue to stir up trouble. You might be a deputy, but you don't run the town, you don't run the school, and you sure don't run me, Mr. Slattery! We take care of our own!"

The same words he'd thrown onto the table a few hours ago, and they sounded just as stubborn and bullheaded now.

He held up the picture in his hand. He showed it to her, then re-angled it for Phil to see. "This is Cassie."

"With the teacher!" Angela looked and sounded triumphant. "Anthony says she's the teacher's pet. I'm pretty sure this proves it."

"Ange, she's a little kid." Phil looked at the picture, then his wife. "She's Anthony's age, for heaven's sake."

"That doesn't mean she's not a—"

Jake didn't let her finish. "Cassie is fighting cancer right now. She's been diagnosed with leukemia. Kerry— Miss McHenry—," he amended, "will be taking a leave to stay with her throughout her treatments. And when Cassie gets back next fall, we'll go ahead with our postponed wedding, and I want our little girl to be able to walk into first grade with her head held high."

"Cancer?" Phil's gaze sharpened. "Angela, you brought a petition to the board against a five-year-old with cancer?"

She looked shocked and embarrassed. "Phil, I—"

"Mrs. Perrotto."

She turned Jake's way and didn't look one bit pleased to do it.

"Cassie's got a big fight ahead of her."

She nodded, chagrined.

"And I know it's awkward when two kids don't get along. I have two boys of my own, but can I ask you a favor?"

He'd put her in a difficult place to refuse. Her jaw moved, and she lifted one shoulder. "I'm listening."

"Will you all pray for my girl?" He said it softly. Very softly. "She's had a rough road from the time she was born and hasn't known many hands of kindness along the way."

It was the last thing she expected him to say. She looked surprised and then almost sympathetic. Her voice went quiet. "You want us to pray for her?"

"If you would. Right now she could use all the prayers and good wishes we can get, and I've seen you folks coming into St. Mary's on Sundays."

"Most weeks," Phil replied. "It should probably be more, come to think of it."

"Father Joe's keeping a candle burning to remind folks to pray for Cassie, so when you're there, or here, I'd just be grateful to know we're on the same page. To see Cassie get healthy and come home to the first folks who've ever shown her the least bit of love."

"We'll do it." Phil reached out and clasped Jake's hand. "The whole family, and I want to thank you for stopping by to tell us quietly. I can't imagine how this would look if folks showed up at the board meeting on Thursday, trying to expel a little kid fighting cancer."

"Thank you." Jake gave him a firm handshake. "Kerry will rest easier knowing it's a nonissue." He started to leave, but Angela reached out. She put a hand on his arm, and he turned back. "Yes?"

She hesitated until it almost grew uncomfortable, and then she sighed. "I apologize. I overreacted because Anthony was so upset one day, and I'm embarrassed that I did that. It won't happen again."

For the past few days there hadn't been much light shining in Jake's world.

This apology, small as it was, meant something. It meant he could and would do what needed to be done on the home front while Kerry helped Cassie fight a different war in hospital rooms.

Together, but separate.

"Thank you, Mrs. Perrotto." He met her gaze, then her husband's. "I appreciate it." He walked back to the car and saw the picture hanging from the visor. He pressed a kiss to his finger and gently touched the matte-finished print. "One thing done, darlin'. Day by day."

He drove to his mother's and spent time with two beautiful boys, too young to fully understand what was happening.

He was OK with that. He'd be OK with tucking the whole thing away someday, old photos in a dust-coated album. But right now, he had a job to do and he meant to do it well.

chapter twenty-six

Kerry thought she'd be strong. It was just hair, after all, and it wasn't unexpected, but when clumps of Cassie's hair began falling out, she had to cower in the restroom to hide her tears.

Be still, and know that I am God...

She wanted that peace, but right now she'd almost rather kickbox her way into exhaustion. But she couldn't. She splashed cold water on her face, opened the door, and saw Ryan playing Uno with Cass. He glanced up, took one look at her face and winced, but went on with the game. "Reverse!"

Cassie laughed, oblivious to the fresh hair dotting her pillow. "Reverse and draw four!"

"Unfair, Cassandra."

She grinned, held up her last card, and said, "Uno!"

He studied her, then his cards, and bless her heart, Jake had taught her well because she stayed stone-faced the whole time. When Ryan finally played a green three, she slipped her wild card onto the top of the pile and dimpled. "I won."

"Saving the wild card, great strategy., Who taught you that one?"

"Jake!" She laughed and yawned. "He taught me and Abe to not make faces and how to fool people so they don't know what we're going to do. He's a good teacher for kids," she added matter-of-factly. She handed Kerry the cards and yawned again.

"Rest time."

"Again?"

"When your body feels tired, you should rest. Doctor's orders. And when you feel like playing, you should play," Ryan told her. He leaned down and kissed her cheek. "I have it on good authority that Aunt

Claire is going to meet Kerry with some possible treats for you. And for the entire floor staff. And possibly a coffee from Finger Lakes Roasters."

"Is Jake coming?" Cassie frowned up at Kerry as she lowered the hospital bed slightly. "I thought he was coming to see me. I miss him so much."

"Abe and Ben are sick, and because your body is busy fist-fighting the cancer cells, you can't be around people who are sick right now," Kerry reminded her. "Once the boys are better, Jake will come see you, darling."

"I want him to come now." Her chin trembled. Her eyes filled. "I don't care if he's sick. I just want to see Jake. I miss him. And Miss Hannah. I want to see all my friends so much."

All her friends. She'd barely had a chance to make a couple before this latest stumbling block hit.

Kerry's heart ached. Her throat went thick. She breathed deep and leaned in close. "Well, Miss Fussy Pants, here's the 4-1-1."

"The what?" A tiny *w* formed between Cassie's brows, but she smiled at being called a fussy pants.

"The info. The scoop. It's code."

"Oh!" Her smile deepened as if that explained everything. "I love codes! It's like a little mystery when it's in code, Ryan!"

"Cool." He smiled at Kerry across the bed. "So what's the scoop, Mom?"

"After your nap, we're going to talk with them on the computer."

"Like we'll *see* them?"

"Yes, ma'am. You lay down and rest while I go see Aunt Claire, and later on we'll call Jake and the boys, OK?"

"OK." She snuggled down a little more, then peered up at Kerry. "Can you tell me about the wedding again?" Cassie frowned, confused again because the ongoing chemo was messing with her memory. "Did we do it?"

"No." Kerry bent close again to repeat the same thing she'd said several times. "We're going to wait until you're feeling better, and then we'll get married. How on earth is a girl to have the perfect wedding without her number one best flower girl in attendance?"

Cassie giggled, then sighed. Her normally golden skin appeared pale and dry. "I'm tired, Kerry."

Kerry feathered her cheek with butterfly kisses. "I know, baby. The medicines make you tired because they're helping the good cells fight the bad cells."

"What if I get too tired to fight?" Cassie laid back against the pink and white striped pillow and studied Kerry. "What if I just get too tired?"

Kerry couldn't speak.

Her throat choked shut and her hands went numb, and she couldn't form words to save her soul.

"When you get that tired, that's when the doctors kick in," Ryan assured her. "Remember I told you that you'd get tired a lot while we were fixing things inside?"

At first she shook her head, then nodded. "I might remember that."

"It's normal, Cassie." He crossed his heart like a little kid. "Cross my heart."

"For real?"

"For absolutely real."

She frowned a little, but then her eyes drifted shut.

They slipped out the door. Ryan took one look at Kerry and pulled her in for a hug. "Sorry. That gets tough when they throw questions like that at you."

"I was about to lose it."

"I know." He kept his arm around her shoulders as they moved toward the first set of double doors. "Totally understandable. I was choking up myself."

She leaned her head against his shoulder for just a moment. "Thank you for jumping in, Rye. I don't know what I would have said or done, and I don't want to scare her."

"The one thing I've found in my years with kids and cancer is that they know it's serious, even if we say nothing." He squeezed her shoulder gently. "They feel the struggle inside their bodies, they sense the fight, and they seem to know it's not an easy win. Cassie's smart. We're not fooling her by pretending, so we'll just stay honest."

"Well, isn't that the hard part?" They walked through the first double doors, and there was Claire waiting. But not just Claire. Ava Slattery stood by her side, and there wasn't any problem reading her reaction when Kerry walked through those automatic doors with Ryan's arm around her shoulders.

If Kerry had won any ground with Ryan's mother, she lost it in that moment.

Claire's eyes went wide.

So did Ava's.

And Kerry wanted to drop into a puddle on the floor, or at least have a do over.

Nope.

"Hey, honey." Claire jumped into the void and hugged her. "You look tired."

"She is." Ryan had let go of her shoulder, but he sent a look of sympathy her way. "But she's doing great. It's a tough treatment, and it's hard to watch someone you love go through it. We're hoping for a great blood report next week, but the waiting is real hard on parents."

"How's Cassie holding up?"

Tears smarted Kerry's eyes. She dashed them away. "She's doing well. She's tired, and she's losing her hair, and she's wondering if she's strong enough to do this. Ryan just got through assuring her she is." She turned toward Jake's mother. "Ava, this is Aunt Claire's stepson, Ryan O'Donnell. One of Cassie's doctors."

Ava's slow gaze moved from Kerry to Ryan and back. "I'm aware of the relationship in all manner of speaking. Jake felt bad that he couldn't get in here with the boys sick. I hadn't been near any of them, and he wanted you to have this." She handed over a large box. "The pink box inside is for Cassie."

"The new crayons and markers. She'll be so excited to get them."

Ava didn't acknowledge that, and she didn't look one bit pleased.

Ryan moved toward the exit door. "I'm heading out. Enjoy your visit, ladies, and Kerry, if you need anything, just call me or Reilly. Even if it's just to talk."

"I believe she has a fiancé who fits that bill, doctor."

Kerry had to hand it to her, Ava was a prime example of a strong mother, and the look she aimed at Ryan wasn't just a caution. It was more like a warning shot.

"Medical things," he assured her, but Kerry knew Ryan, and she suspected a part of him enjoyed sparring with Jake's mother. "Strictly medical, ma'am." His words were fine, but then he added a wink.

Ava stiffened.

Claire stifled a groan.

And Ryan strode out the door.

Silence left a void until Claire motioned to a chair. "Here, sit down, honey."

"I'd actually love a walk," Kerry told her. "I don't get out much, and a walk in that sunshine would be marvelous."

"Then we'll walk. I brought you a coffee from downstairs."

"Ryan hinted you would, and I can't say I wasn't excited. And Jake sent me a gift card for the coffee bar, because he knows I won't spend that kind of money on myself."

"Why should you when others seem quite willing to do it for you?"

Ouch.

Ava's tone hurt more than her words, but could Kerry blame her? She took the box from Jake back onto Four North, then returned, determined to clear the air, but Ava was gone. "She left?"

"With nary a word." Claire took Kerry's arm and tucked it through hers. "She's upset, Kerry."

"But there was nothing to be upset about," Kerry protested. "Ryan was just offering comfort because the cumulative effects are wearing on Cassie. Is that so bad?"

Claire paused. "That may have been all it was to you, dear. But to anyone seeing Ryan's face, it was more. Much more."

A mix of emotions flooded Kerry, but she didn't dare say anything here in the pediatric corridor. She waited until they walked into the clean, fresh spring air and turned. "I can't do this, Aunt Claire."

"Of course you can," Claire argued. "You are already doing it, honey."

"Not the Cassie part." Kerry pressed the heel of her hand to her forehead to thwart the growing ache. "The Ryan and Ava and Jake thing. It's like my brain just needs to focus on Cassie right now. Then the rest of the drama presses in, and I feel like my head's going to explode. I never feel like this." She stopped and faced her aunt. "I don't do overwhelmed or overwrought. I don't allow myself the luxury of drama, but I'm doing both right now, and I think I might be going crazy."

"Oh, honey." Claire hugged her close and held her.

She wept. They sank onto a hard, uncomfortable metal bench, and Kerry cried.

"There, there, darling." Claire held tight and rocked her gently. "You have a good cry, and then we'll get you a fresh, hot coffee, and then we'll have a little talk about blocking people out when they insist on stealing your joy."

Joy?

Kerry pulled back and stared down at her hands. The beautiful diamond from Jake caught the midday sun and twinkled like Venus on a late spring horizon. "I have no joy right now." She stared off toward the busy road tunneling people this way and that. "Cassie's sick, she says she's getting tired of fighting, and her hair is all falling out. And I have to sit there all alone and pretend it's all right, and it's not all right. It's stupid and horrible, and I can't be with Jake, and I know Ryan still has feelings for me, I'm not stupid…" She put her head in her hands and sat like that for long, drawn-out seconds.

"So I pretend. For the last six weeks, all I've done is pretend. I pretend I'm strong, I pretend it's all going to be OK, and I pretend that Ryan's just being a nice doctor, invested in his patient. And then, today, this happens." She waved back toward the hospital. "Ava won't hesitate to tell Jake, he'll be hurt, and he's already going through enough because he can't be here to support us like he thinks he should."

She lifted her head and sat, hands clenched. "I pray. I talk to God, and I beg and I plead and I pray, but it feels so empty right now. Just empty." She tipped her gaze up to Claire, sitting quietly at her side. "I haven't felt empty like this in a long, long time, Auntie."

"I know." Claire didn't touch her or hug her. She simply nodded.

Folks walked by. Some gave them a look of interest, others ignored them completely, but as Kerry faced Claire, an elderly woman began to pass them, aiming for the bus stop. She glanced their way, walked by, then came back. She bent low in front of Kerry, looked her right in the eye, and whispered, "I'm so very sorry for your pain. I will pray for you."

That.

Just that.

And then she straightened and continued on down the walk.

A complete stranger who didn't ignore her struggle. Who took five seconds to make it her own.

"The first to help you up are the ones who know what it's like to fall down," Claire quoted softly.

"The fruits of the spirit." Kerry sat more upright.

"Love, joy, peace, kindness…," Claire paraphrased the verse. "The kindness of strangers, honey. The hospital staff, the whole town of Phillipsburg, Father Cummings."

"He's been here twice this week, just to let me know he's praying for us."

"Cassie is on so many social media prayer lists she's become a household word. Take heart. Take hope."

Good words. Wise words. She stood and reached for Claire's hand. "Let's take that walk, OK?"

"Let's."

chapter twenty-seven

Ryan holding Kerry.

Ryan, comforting the woman Jake loved, when Jake couldn't be there.

Ryan, taking center stage.

Anger didn't just nudge heartache aside, it shoved its way into Jake until he couldn't see straight.

No one moved in on Jake Slattery's woman. No one messed with Jake's heart, his family, his love. That is—if she was still his love?

"Daddy, when are we going to talk to Cassie? You promised!"

"Is she coming here?" Ben asked, the image of three-year-old innocence. "We can play wif my wescue dogs! We can wescue everybody!"

Jake struggled for internal control.

He found none.

He'd spent the last six weeks feeling like an outsider looking in, while Kerry and Cassie fought the great battle alone. But now he knew—for a fact—that she wasn't alone.

But he was.

He'd settled the boys into the car and walked out on his mother. His mother, the woman who'd stood by his side, helped with the boys, and who'd believed in him all along.

A man shall leave his mother…

The words from Paul's timeless letters to the people of Corinth knifed Jake's soul. He believed in the bond of one man to one woman, but if the woman wasn't so inclined, did that make him stupid?

"Cassie can't come here." Abe answered his brother's question when Jake didn't. "She's in the hospital, and they're trying to make her better because she's so sick, remember?"

A text came through Jake's phone just then. *"Cassie's hair is falling out. It's everywhere. She's getting tired. Really tired. Please call. Please pray."*

She's scared.

His heart pinched as he read between the lines.

His beloved was scared, and he was ninety minutes away with two other beloveds who had just fought the norovirus into submission, which meant he couldn't go near Kerry or Cassie.

A quick rap sounded on his door, and Hannah let herself in to take part in the scheduled computer call. "It's almost time, I do believe! I love that we can hook up with our girls and see them face-to-face! I brought cookies."

Jake loved her giving heart, but he knew the truth about Hannah's cookies.

"And a carrot cake I want you all to sample," she continued as she set a plate and a small bag on the table. "I'm plannin' on runnin' a carrot cake table at the big benefit for Cassie."

"Benefit?" That caught Jake's attention. "What benefit?"

"Your mama didn't tell you?" No, his mother had been too busy filling him in on what she saw in Rochester.

"The entire town is gettin' together to hold a fund-raisin' benefit to help out."

"To help out what?"

She gripped his arms. "Whatever you might need, come what may. Are you all right, Jacob?"

He wasn't, but he pretended to be. "Sure. Yes. Of course."

She peered up at him. Disbelief deepened her features. "Hmph."

She did a quick, Hannah-like spin and crossed to the the silverware drawer. She withdrew a knife and cut three slices, then settled them on small plates. "Boys, you can taste this now or wait until after we talk to your sister, but I want to know sincerely if you love it or just kind of like it." She waggled her head as if unsure. "When it comes to carrot cake, that makes a world of difference."

Jake didn't want cake, but if he didn't try some, Hannah would be even more likely to suspect something was wrong. "Explain to me about this benefit."

"Well." She watched as the boys each took their first bite, and when they both grinned, so did she. "We want to make sure that whatever happens, you have a little stash to see things through. What if you need to take time off?"

He had two weeks of vacation coming, part of which had been planned for a honeymoon, but he'd witnessed what other deputies had to deal with when it came to life-threatening illness and family. Two weeks wasn't a whole lot of leeway.

"And Kerry's losing three months of salary bein' at the hospital night and day. That's a hard hit on a young family."

"But, Hannah…"

"Now, there are no buts allowed, Jake, and that's all I'm going to say to that." She faced him squarely with her "Hannah-runs-the-universe" expression, and everyone in town knew you didn't mess with that face.

"This isn't about you or some manly pride or some self-imposed sacrifice, while that's all well and good. This is about a town seein' a need and workin' together to fill it. This is what it's all about, Jake." She laid one thin, brown hand against his arm. "God's people, comin' together, workin' toward a common goal. Now them Amish folk up the road, they do it for a barn, and everyone sings their praise. Well, Jake Slattery, how much more important is a child?" Wise brown eyes met his.

Put like that, what could he say?

"This is so deeeeeelicious, Miss Hannah!" Abe's loud approval broke the moment.

"I wuv it so much, I might wanna marry it!" Ben giggled through the words as he stuffed another forkful into his mouth.

"Well, you enjoy it boys, and then we'll have your dad put through the call on the computer." She rubbed her hands together in excitement, and when they opened a connection with Kerry and Cassie a little later, Hannah took lead, and that was good, because Jake wasn't sure what to say. How to start. Just seeing Kerry pop into view put a scramble on his emotions, so he focused on Cassie and had to bite down hard.

Hannah waded in, joyous as ever, as if the past week hadn't left a grim shadow on a precious child's face. "Cassie, look at you, right up there in one of the most famous and wonderful hospitals made just for children! Law, child, it's good to see them sparklin' green eyes again. Miss Hannah has missed you so much!"

"I love you, Miss Hannah." It didn't sound like Cassie. The voice was weakened and flat, as if she struggled to talk, and when she looked toward the camera, she squinted hard. He wanted to be right there to ease her struggle. To help. To hold.

"I love you, too," Hannah exclaimed. "And just look at these two brothers of yours, they're 'bout dyin' to say hello!"

"Hi, Cassie!" Abe went first, grinning his widest.

Cassie's return smile was a faint imitation of the real thing. "Hi, Abe." She paused, breathed deep, and her eyelids fluttered. And then she gazed hard at the tiny camera lens again. "How's school?"

"It's almost summer vacation!" All boy, Abe half-shouted the words. "And then it will be summer, and then you will come home, and then we're going to school together, you and me and Miss Kerry!"

She blinked three times, as if processing the words, and Abe's excitement was too much. Her fingers played with the blanket's edge, restless. "I miss school."

"I miss you!" declared Abe. "I'm going to let you play with *all* my dinosaurs *and* my cheetahs *and* my snow leopards when you get back, OK? Like anytime you want, OK?"

"K."

"Cassie wooks funny."

Jake wasn't sure if he should clap a hand over Ben's cute but honest mouth or let it ride, but Kerry jumped in to save the day like she did so often. "The medications that are helping Cassie get better make her tired. She falls asleep a lot right now."

"And my hair is falling out." Cassie reached up and pulled a tuft of hair loose, and Jake was pretty sure he'd burst into tears on the spot.

"Does it hurt?" Abe stared at the clutch of hair, dumbstruck. Hannah had to move, out of the camera's range to regain her composure.

"No. I'll just look funny."

"Not funny." Jake drew a deep breath, trying to hide his struggles. "Beautiful, darlin'. Just beautiful."

Kerry grinned and put a gentle hand to Cassie's cheek. "Well, if she has no hair, at least I can't ruin it, right, Cassie?"

It took long seconds for Cassie to shift her gaze to Kerry, and then she tried to smile. "Maybe you can practice while I get better."

"I will." Kerry smiled down at her, then turned back toward the laptop camera. "Jake, you'll be pleased to know that she's a model patient. The doctors and nurses love her to pieces, and they're pretty sure she's got the prettiest green eyes they've ever seen."

The compliment made Cassie's dimples flash, and then she yawned.

Jake looked back over at Cassie, concerned. "Should you be resting, honey?"

"She's got to stay awake for her next meds, and then she can take a nice, long nap. And by the way, that Uno game you sent last week is a huge success. Cassie has played it with two of her doctors, two nurses, me, and three other kids. With mixed results. I'm here to say that while she doesn't like losing, she's done so with fairly good grace. And she can't wait to try the new crayons and markers you sent in with your mother today. Nothing like new crayons to bolster a girl's spirits."

"I'm glad, Kerry." He looked right at her. Not at Cassie, not the room. Her. Just her.

She looked back at him. Their gazes held, and he read more than he wanted to in her face. Fear. Determination. Then fear again.

She was struggling.

So was he.

But he was surrounded by family and friends, while Kerry was tucked away in a contained environment. "The doctor said if I don't get sick, I can drive in on Wednesday night."

She reached out as if to touch him, and he'd give anything to take that pretty hand in his and hold it forever. "Please do. We miss you, Jake. So much."

He held her gaze and read the silent message in her eyes.

She loved him.

Just him.

There was only so much she could say in front of four other people, but he knew that look. "I love you, Kerry. You girls mean everything to us. We are a"—he put an arm around the boys and Hannah—"somewhat interesting and slightly mixed-up American family, darlin'."

She sighed, but it wasn't a sad sigh. It was a happy sigh, as if his simple words made things better.

Trust.

The Sunday sermon had been about trust, trust in God, trust in Christ, trusting yourself to know what was right.

There is no love without trust.

He squared his shoulders. "Did you find the coffee card I sent you?"

She picked it up off a windowsill filled with stuffed animals and toys. "A lifeline, Jake. Thank you."

"You're welcome. And on Wednesday, I'll buy you a cup in person, OK?"

"Yes."

They closed the call when Cassie needed to use the bathroom, and Jake had another wake-up call.

Tending Cassie right now was like having a newborn baby, only one that weighed forty pounds and was fighting death.

Kerry looked weary, but he saw something else, too. She looked courageous and honest and true, the very qualities that drew him to her eight months before.

"Now here is something for you, Jacob."

Hannah reached into her unwieldy purse and withdrew a small, colorful card. "A St. Joseph prayer card."

She pointed to the artist's rendition on the front of the wallet-sized card. "Now our church doesn't talk 'bout saints and such, and I can be OK one way or the other, but this man." She regarded the image of Jesus's earthly father with respect. "Jacob, when you are fatherin' a child not your own, this is the saint to turn to. He took on a woman with child, a child not his own, and he pledged his life, his love, his fidelity. Whenever I see a father flounderin', or a husband wonderin', I think of Saint Joseph and all he did. And that's the way I see you and Cassie and Kerry. You're her strong, patient rock of a man, the one who doesn't fade or fall when the goin' gets tough. A famous writer once said us common folks are from the race that knows Joseph, and that's the kind of man you are, Jacob. Now, if you'd like, I can come over here on Wednesday and mind the boys. I expect Aria will be busy at her place with her kids. Unless your mother's free?"

Jake wasn't about to ask Ava to step in with the boys. Not right yet. They needed to even their playing field, or at least set up out-of-bounds lines.

She wasn't thrilled that Kerry was his choice.

But he was.

And while he loved his mother, she was a woman with children and grandchildren. Why didn't she see the difficulty in Kerry's task? Because she didn't like her?

It didn't make sense, but then it didn't have to. His God-inspired mandate was to look after his family, and that's what Jake intended to do, but Wednesday seemed like a long time away.

chapter twenty-eight

Father Cummings waved from the side porch of the old rectory when Ryan pulled into the adjacent lot on Monday. He climbed out of the car and crossed the grass holding two cups. "Vanilla for you, chocolate-banana-strawberry for me."

"An Abbott's milkshake!" Father Cummings accepted the cup and took a long pull on the wide straw. "Well, if that doesn't just hit the spot on a nice, spring night. Thank you, Ryan."

"It's all right." Ryan settled into the left-hand rocker while the aging priest did the same on the right. "Thank you for taking the time to stop up at the hospital to see Kerry and Cassie. It meant a lot to them, Father."

"I saw that right off. Oh, that young woman, she is a fine thing, isn't she? Beautiful and kind and good."

Ryan nodded. "All of the above. Yes."

"So it took me no time at all to understand the attraction," Father continued.

"Right?" Ryan raised his milkshake cup as if toasting someone. "She's amazing."

"Oh, she is." Father took another long sip of his treat and set it down. "Of course it must be hard, working in the professional building next door and not popping in to see her all the time," the priest surmised.

Ryan narrowed his gaze.

"Maintaining your distance when you don't need to be on the floor."

"Father, I—"

"That is what you've been doing, right?"

Ryan gripped the cup a little tighter. "I care about Cassie. And Kerry. I'm family."

The good priest choked a little bit on his milkshake, and when he set it on the little round table, he tipped his rocker closer to Ryan. "Are your choices honorable?"

"Yes. Absolutely."

But the priest shook his head, and something began to tie a cinch knot in Ryan's gut. "Not your *intentions*, Ryan. I understand that you've changed. What I'm asking about are your choices. Is pursuing an engaged woman who is caught up in traumatic circumstances an honorable thing to do?"

The cup bent under the pressure of Ryan's hand. He set it down and stood. "She's not married."

The priest said nothing.

"No vows have been spoken. Isn't that how religious people measure things? By vows?"

Father Cummings studied him. "Similar to the vows you made on Easter at your confirmation? Or do we keep those vows as a matter of convenience?"

Convenience?

Nothing about trying to be a better person was convenient. Far from it. But it felt better, and more righteous than the man he was before. So why—

"Do you reject Satan?"

Ryan shot the older man an annoyed look. "I believe I answered that in front of a church full of people, Father. Yes. I do."

"And all his works?"

Palms sweating, Ryan glared at him.

"And all his empty promises?"

"Stop. This is ridiculous. Being attracted to a wonderful woman isn't from the devil, and there's no way you can convince me otherwise, Father, but nice try."

"Then how about this? Thou shalt not covet thy neighbor's wife."

His voice, so soft.

His eyes, gone sad as he studied Ryan. And his hands, as if folded in prayer.

"She's not married."

The priest sat silent, praying.

"This sucks." Ryan stood to go and knocked over his milkshake in his hurry.

And then he swore, ripe and ready, under his breath, and still Father Cummings uttered no sound. He sat, eyes down, hands folded, lips moving.

Ryan bent to retrieve the cup. Some had leaked through the top, and a neighbor's cat dashed onto the porch, quite ready to help clean up the mess.

He turned and started for the porch steps, determined. The priest was wrong. He was dead wrong, because if he was right, why would Cassie and Kerry be put right there, on his ward, under his nose?

"He hates defeat and will watch for a chance to trip you up. Don't let him get it."

The priest's words last winter.

His gut twisted again. His arms felt suddenly heavy and burdensome. Don't let him get it.

He turned back toward Father Cummings. The old man hadn't stopped praying the whole time, and watching him, Ryan knew why.

The spirit of temptation had overtaken him. Not the good fruits of the spirit that rained upon God's people, but the temptation to have what he wanted, regardless.

He stood rooted, torn but not torn, because he knew what he had to do. He hated it, and it was the last thing on earth he wanted to do, but that only made the need more pressing. "You got time for a guy's confession, Father? It won't take all that long, because you've already figured out the sin."

The priest raised his head. He looked right into Ryan's eyes, and Ryan was pretty sure the old guy would like to weep, but were they tears of joy for his wake-up call?

Or spent tears earned by fighting the sneaky and powerful presence of evil?

"I'll gladly hear it, son."

Ryan sank back into the chair.

Close. He'd been so close to slipping right back into those same old ways, making everything all about him. And he'd convinced himself that there was absolutely nothing wrong with it. He bowed his head and gripped the sides of the rocker. "Bless me, Father, for I have sinned, and it hasn't even been all that long since my last confession."

The priest's lips curved in an understanding smile, and he listened quietly as Ryan spoke.

And when he offered Ryan a penance, Ryan understood exactly what he needed to do. And after Jake Slattery's mother saw him with his arm around Kerry on Sunday, he hoped it wasn't too late.

* * *

Jake wanted to race through the hospital halls on Wednesday afternoon.

He couldn't, but the urge to hold Kerry and Cassie, to be there for them, to stand sentinel when he could, pushed him to walk fast.

"Jake?"

No.

It wasn't Kerry's voice calling his name. It was Ryan's, and Jake had to grapple emotions before he turned. Yes, Ryan was part of Cassie's care team...

But he had a thing for Jake's girl, and Jake was pretty sure a solid pop in the jaw might straighten out the doctor's priorities. He was 100 percent certain that he'd be happy to do it, just to see.

He turned slowly, a maneuver cops did well. He braced his feet and stood, arms crossed, and that wasn't easy to do with flowers and a box of treats.

But Jake managed it.

Ryan drew up to his side and motioned to a room close by. "Can we talk?"

"Do we need to, doctor?"

Ryan flushed.

Good.

And then he proceeded to the door and pushed it open. "After you."

Boiling point.

The term used to be a chemistry lesson separating elements on the periodic table. Now it was Jake about to lose it and go ape on a polished young doctor who would soon be part of his family.

The awkward element spiked.

"Is this about Cassie?"

"No."

Jake started to leave.

Ryan caught his arm and almost got punched right then, but that move might ruin Kerry's flowers. "Let go."

Ryan did, and Jake was pretty sure it was the three-inch height advantage and thirty-pound weight differential. In any case, he let go. "What?"

"I need to apologize."

Jake thrust a brow up and waited, but forgiveness wasn't ranking high on his priority list right now.

"I love Kerry."

"Tell me something I don't know."

Ryan winced. "I was afraid of that, but listen, I didn't bring you in here to mess with you. I asked you in here because I want your forgiveness. I was using the past weeks to make myself look indispensable in Kerry's eyes. And Cassie's eyes."

"That's despicable."

Ryan scrubbed his hand through his hair and agreed. "So a friend said, which made me realize I was being a first class selfish jerk, and I'd promised myself I wouldn't be like that anymore. My penance—"

"Penance?" Did Jake hear right?

"Catholic tradition, when the priest thinks you're a moron he gives you a penance."

Jake's shoulders relaxed a little. "I like this priest, and I haven't even met him yet."

"Yes, well, he reminded me that I need your forgiveness. And he was right."

"You're kidding."

"I'm not."

Jake tightened his gaze. "You are actually standing here, man-to-man, and asking me to forgive you for coming on to my fiancée while she was stuck in the hospital caring for a child with cancer."

Ryan winced. "Yes? And by the way, the way you said it makes it sound way worse than even the priest's rendition."

"This isn't a laughing matter."

Ryan faced him straight and locked eyes with him. "Do you think giving up a wonderful woman like Kerry is ever a laughing matter?"

Jake knew it wasn't.

"Listen, I was a jerk. Kerry called me out on it, and I had to work real hard not to be a jerk. And then the minute I saw her, I slipped back into jerk-mode. But I know better now. And it won't happen again."

"We're going to be related."

Ryan nodded. "I probably hate that about as much as you do."

"Except I don't hate it."

Ryan studied him a little more carefully. "This is where you pretend to be nice to me, and I end up dead, isn't it?"

"No. This is where we join forces to make this as easy as we can on Kerry and Cassie. Because neither one of them deserves any less than our best." He stuck out his hand, and Ryan clasped it. "Deal?"

Ryan locked eyes with him and took the offered hand. "Deal."

* * *

Kerry glanced up at the wall clock in the play area and stood. Jake would be here soon.

Anticipation mixed with trepidation.

They'd talked a couple of times a day since Sunday. He hadn't said a word about Ryan, or his mother. She wasn't sure if that was good or bad, but she knew one thing: No matter what, Jake Slattery needed to know he was her one, true love. That nothing— and no one— had the power to change that.

The door to the play area swung open quietly.

Jake.

She crossed the room and didn't wait for him to set down the pretty spring-toned flowers or the box of chocolates. She just waded in and grabbed hold, and didn't let go.

"Hey." He whispered the word against her hair, then her ear. "Hey, darlin'." His breath and his cheek and his lips touched her face, her head, her ear. "Miss me?"

She pulled back and fake-punched his arm. "More than should be humanly possible."

Cassie had been playing with another patient on the far side of the room. She turned and spotted Jake. "Jake!" He released Kerry with a wink and crossed the room. He checked to make sure he wasn't messing up an IV or a port or any other hospital paraphernalia and then folded Cassie into a gentle embrace. "How's my best girl?"

She blinked up at him and smiled, and if he was shocked by the change in her, he didn't show it. "My hair's gone."

He shrugged. "Beauty comes from within, darlin', and hair grows back. You will always be my little beauty, no matter how long it is, how short, or what dreadful things your new mama might do to it."

Cassie giggled. It was the first giggle Kerry had heard in days, and when Dr. Shaughnessy and Stella came into the room, they heard it, too. "I hate to interrupt your game, but we need a few minutes of your time, Miss Cassie."

The numbers.

They'd done the testing to check the numbers, to see if this first dose of chemo had accomplished its goal to drive the cancer numbers down to remission levels. If it did, the course of action proceeded as planned. If not—

Kerry slipped her hand into Jake's and waited, knowing they'd handle whatever happened, together.

"I'll play with Shauna." A volunteer took Cassie's place at the table. The small group moved to the far side of the big playroom and sat on the living room-styled sofas.

"First, the numbers." Dr. Shaughnessy gave them a double thumbs-up. "You aced it, kid. Exactly what we were looking for. Ryan, Sam, and I are thrilled because this means your white cells are responsive to the treatment. This is very good news and means we're on track as originally planned."

Relief flooded Kerry. She gripped Jake's hand. "I'm so glad, doctor."

"Me, too." Jake bent and kissed Cassie's forehead. "You're doing great, darlin'. Just great. Even if you don't feel all that great right now."

"Really?" Cassie looked up at him, then Kerry. "Is it really better?"

Dr. Shaughnessy covered Cassie's hand with hers. "For real, cross my heart, I never kid about stuff like this. You feel bad and tired because of the medicines, but the medicines are making all the itty bitty bad cells in your body go away. And then your body has to make new cells, and that takes time and energy, so you're very, very tired while this goes on. But then it gets better, honey."

"Can I go home?"

The doctor shook her head. "Not for a while, but don't be disappointed. We need you to stay here, to keep getting treated and to keep you away from germs for a while more. But I'm happy to say that these numbers make me very, very happy, Cassie." She faced Cassie but glanced up to Kerry and Jake, too. "Reason to celebrate, Mom and Dad, and I know you've both been waiting to hear those words."

"I sure have." Jake put his arm around Kerry and hugged her close. "We both have."

"Now for other news." Stella opened a manila folder and withdrew a single sheet of paper. "Donna Bunting from Beckett County sent me this today. They'd been doing a search for relatives, as you know."

Kerry's heart gripped. She nodded. "Yes."

"They have found a cousin on the maternal side."

"Where?"

"In Florida, but there are no concerns because this cousin has signed off any rights, and furthermore showed the county that there were no other living relatives on that side, and the county had already determined lack of status on the paternal side, which means…" She raised both brows and smiled wide. "Your application for adoption can now go through the typical approvals. There are no roadblocks."

"You're serious?" Kerry didn't take this news sitting. She jumped up, hugged Stella, then Reilly Shaughnessy, then Jake. And then she knelt by Cassie's side.

Oh, that face.

That beautiful, wonderful, trusting face that had known so much hardship and deprivation. It didn't matter than she had no hair, that her cheeks were puffed from the meds, and that her eyes looked tired.

The only thing that mattered was her, Cassie Carruthers, and the new chances awaiting her. And them! She bent close. "Cassie, do you know what Miss Stella just said?"

Cassie shook her head, bewildered.

"She said that Jake and I can adopt you. That you can be our little girl and live with us forever, and your name would change to Cassandra Lee Slattery. Is that OK with you?"

Tears formed in Cassie's eyes. The meds had a drying effect, so even when Cassie wanted to cry, it was usually without tears.

But she looked from Kerry to Jake, and a tear slipped down her left cheek. Then her right. Her chin quivered, and Jake got right down onto the floor next to her. "Are you OK, honey? Are you all right? What can I get you?"

Her chin quivered more, and she reached her arms out to hug him.

He hugged her back and raised a look of concern to Kerry.

What could she say? She had no idea what was going on, but then Cassie leaned back. She took a tissue from the wheelchair's pocket and swiped her face, then sighed. She looked at Kerry, then Jake, then back to Kerry. "All my whole life, even when I was so little, I just wanted to be someone's little girl."

Kerry's throat went tight. Her own chin trembled. Her eyes smarted, and Jake didn't look one bit better.

"When you saved me," she stared up at Jake, then reached up and touched his face, "I just wanted you to hold onto me forever. And now you can."

He cried.

Big, brawny, bold Jake Slattery knelt on the floor beside this precious child with tears streaming down his cheeks.

Kerry was no better, and the other two adults reached for tissues, too.

And then he held Cassie, held her close, whispering words of love, while his other hand cupped Kerry's cheek. And when they finally stood and decided that ice cream would make a great day even better, Jake put his arms around Kerry and drew her close. He kissed her, not too long and not too slow, because there were other things to pay attention to right now, but when he drew back, he cradled her face in his hands. "Thank you." He swept Cassie a sweet look, then brought his eyes back to Kerry. "You didn't just bring me love, Kerry. You brought me hope. And faith. You brought me back to the kind of life I thought I'd lost, but I didn't lose it. I just misplaced it for a while. And I would love to spend the next fifty years or so showing you how happy that makes me."

She reached up and kissed him, a kiss that held a promise and a pledge. "I can't think of anything I'd like better, Jake."

"Well, good." He grinned and moved behind Cassie's chair. "How about that ice cream, ladies?"

Kerry picked up the flowers and the candy. The door opened automatically, sliding wide to accommodate wheel chairs and gurneys, a reality on Four North. "That sounds absolutely perfect."

epilogue

Ryan parked his car on a tiny Phillipsburg side road and walked the two blocks to the church under a canopy of gold and tangerine leaves.

A cool breeze in the shadows hinted coming change, but the sun waxed warm from its southern angle.

A hymn rang out above him as he strode up the broad stone steps of the quaint, country church.

He paused.

Old words came back to him. Sweet words. True words about freedom and simplicity and appreciation.

The carillon danced through the notes of "Simple Gifts" as people passed him, filing into the church.

Bouquets of flowers decorated the handrails. Bright-toned pumpkins and gourds lined the outer edges of the steps in harvest-tones of golds, greens, oranges, and reds.

And as he stepped into the church entry, potted mums sat among more displays, bringing the beauty of a country harvest inside, totally Kerry.

"Ryan!"

He laughed and dropped to one knee as Cassie dashed toward him in a very pretty, very full, and amazingly sparkly dress. "Look at you! So beautiful and so stinkin' healthy, brat!"

Cassie threw her arms around him and held on tight. "I feel good now!"

His heart melted, or maybe it grew. It didn't matter. It felt good, whatever it was doing. "I'm so glad. And you're a flower girl today, just like Mom promised."

"Do you like my dress?" She slipped from his embrace, stepped back, and twirled. "It was the very prettiest, most sparkly one we could find, and I love sparkles so much!"

"She does love sparkles."

Kerry...

He looked up, and there she was, stunningly beautiful and righteously simple. But mostly beautiful. "Aren't you supposed to be hiding?"

"I am." She pointed to the small clock. "You're making us late, but I think the reverend and Jake will understand. Doesn't she look amazing, Ryan?"

"She does. You don't look too bad yourself," he joked. "You clean up nice."

She smiled and looked so happy that he was almost afraid his heart was going to ache again.

And then it didn't.

It just felt good.

"Kid, kiss Ryan. You can pester him later, and maybe he'll even dance with you—"

"Will you?" Cassie turned excited eyes his way and twirled again. "I can dance so pretty now!"

"I'd be honored, Munchkin. Go get in line. I'm holding things up." He started to turn, then turned back. "And Kerry?"

"Yes?"

Claire was bustling from behind, adjusting Jenn's shawl and Cassie's basket of flowers.

"My very best wishes for both of you."

She knew he meant it. He read it in her gaze, in her smile. "Same to you."

He walked in and slipped into a pew with his father as the dancing notes of the carillon came to an end.

His father pointed upward. "Did you hear that?"

It was a silly question because the entire town heard it, that was the purpose, after all, but Ryan simply nodded. "Beautiful."

"Lord of the Dance," Dan murmured. "One of my favorite hymns, seeing the times of Christ's life through each verse. Are you OK?"

He meant with the wedding, with Kerry and Jake, with everything, and when Ryan nodded, Dan looked satisfied.

Simple Gifts.

Lord of the Dance.

Such different versions of the same tune. Like life, he realized.

One series of notes. Different vantage points. One living God, longing for goodness, allowing free choice.

Soft, trickling notes of a flute had people turning their heads in the full church.

Cassie stepped forward in her most sparkly dress, flanked by Jake's sons. Abe tugged at his collar as if already hating suits and ties. Ben reached out for Cassie's hand and held on tight.

They walked forward, and when they got close enough to spot Jake up front, they hurried their steps, excited, and grabbed him in big hugs. He bent and hugged them back, ignoring protocol. By the time he stood back up, Jenn was halfway down the aisle, and Kerry had stepped into view, with Claire escorting her.

Everyone stood.

Kerry's eyes sought Jake's.

His gaze found hers. They smiled at the same moment, bound in love.

Perfect.

A sigh rose inside Ryan.

He choked it back.

Father Cummings had slipped him a prayer card the day before, a beautiful autumnal spray on one side, a valley vista in deep, autumn tones. And when he flipped it over, Ecclesiastes 3 was printed on the reverse. "For everything there is a season, and a time for every matter under the heaven..."

A time for every purpose.

He saw that now. He tried to live it, and when he thought he might mess up, he remembered the old priest's wisdom. "Don't let him fool you with his deception."

Ryan faced the altar. He listened to the reverend's welcoming greeting and watched Kerry— his first real love— marry someone else, and it was all right.

Evil might *tempt* him again. Ryan wasn't stupid; he saw his weaknesses more fully now.

But it would never be allowed to fool him again.

* * *

Cassie let her gaze wander the sweet room.

Her room.

Pink, white, and green stripes marched up the walls halfway and then pretty flowers in the same colors wandered around the walls on thin paper.

She had bookshelves.

She had toy shelves.

She had a basket for laundry and a basket for toys and a rug so soft that when she stood on it, her toes sank deep in, warm and cozy.

She liked that idea of sinking toes so much she almost laughed.

Her pretty dress was hanging from the closet door, all glittery and good except for where she spilled some punch, but no one minded. No one got mad. No one sent her away for being naughty.

She got kissed.

She got hugged.

She danced with everyone, and when Jake picked her up in his big, strong arms and they all danced together, everyone clapped and cheered. That felt nice and good and weird all at once, and she'd ducked her head, but when she lifted it up and smiled…

Everyone cheered again!

She decided people were a little strange, but she liked dancing a lot.

She yawned again as Aunt Claire came into the room. "How are we doing? Did you brush your teeth, honey?"

She nodded. She hadn't brushed them real well, but enough, she thought. Enough for tonight.

"Let's tuck you in." Aunt Claire snuggled her down beneath the covers. "You and the boys had a big day."

Cassie nodded. She yawned once more, tired out from so much time, so much food, so much fun. "It was my best day ever. Can you tell God that if I fall asleep too quick?" A wave of sleepiness overtook her.

The clean, sweet pillow felt good. So good. A little nightlight shined from the outlet, just enough to break the darkness.

And this room was warm. Not too hot, not too cold, it was just right all the time.

Auntie leaned in and kissed her cheek. She smelled like wedding cake and flowers, special and good. "Dear God, Cassie wants you to know she had a wonderful day and she thanks you."

"So much," added Cassie. "She thanks you *so* much." Her eyes drifted shut. She felt Auntie's kiss once more, one last sweet kiss before she tiptoed out the door.

She didn't worry about the night so much now.

It wasn't really scary anymore.

And she wasn't hardly ever cold, except when she went outside without a jacket.

She had shoes and boots and a warm bed and a mom and a dad and brothers and food.

She might be dreaming. Each day she woke up now and wondered if it was real, or maybe a dream?

But it wasn't a dream, she realized as sleep overcame her.

It was a dream come true.

And that made all the difference.